BECCA JUERGENS

book one

IN ANGELIC
ARMS

a struggle between light and dark

In Angelic Arms by Becca Juergens

Cover and Interior Design: Rebecca Images and Design
Publisher: Becca Juergens
www.beccajauthor.com
ISBN-13: 978-0692973660

First Edition Printed in United States of America

10 9 8 7 6 5 4 3 2 1

Papap, I wish you could have read this novel.
Your tales first started my love for stories.
Your legacy lives on in these pages and our hearts.
We love and miss you.

"Woe to those who call evil good and good evil, who put
darkness for light and light for darkness, who put bitter for
sweet and sweet for bitter."
Isaiah 5:20

"I waited patiently till dawn, but like a lion he broke all my
bones, day and night you made an end of me."
Isaiah 38:13

IN ANGELIC ARMS
book one

BECCA JUERGENS

CHAPTER 1 ONE

The Bridge

I had to get away from the darkness—the dark thoughts, the evil fears—there had to be something more. So, I ran.

It had been months since I laced up my trusted Nike's, but it was all I could think to do—run. I pushed against the uneven ground trying to eliminate the pain that had begun to burrow under my ribs. I breathed deeply. The crisp air only added to my discomfort. I didn't care. Regardless of the pain, I had to get away; as if a two-horned monster were chasing me, I just ran.

Why I thought running away would change anything, why I thought putting miles between myself and that house would matter—it wouldn't. There wasn't anything I could do to escape *that* monster.

The kind woman that used to tuck me in at night, the humming angel singing in the kitchen, the doting wife submitting to her husband's every whim was gone and replaced by a monster. In her absence, my memories of her puréed together, intertwining pleasantries and twisting them into a jumbled mess of destitution and despair.

I couldn't "remember the good times", they only caused pain. I couldn't "think of her in a better place", it only reminded me she wasn't here. I couldn't think of her at all without thinking of the nothingness that replaced her. The emptiness grew quickly after her death. It was subtle at first: a coffee-stained mug with "World's Greatest Mom" written in a creative script sitting in the sink, or a cotton scarf draped over the back of her floral chair. I should have recognized its beastly powers then and eliminated it while I still could, but I didn't. I left the scarf and the mug, trying to keep her memory intact. Instead, her absence grew into an unbearable monster. My desperation for her essence to remain was its fuel and my undoing.

Panting, I stopped, grabbing my knees and gasping for air. *Where am I? How far did I go?* My head spun, demanding oxygen along with my tired lungs.

After a few seconds, my chopped breaths became easier, deeper, and fuller.

"Where am I?" I murmured, wiping the sweat from my brow. There was an open field, dirt road, and old rickety bridge—nothing looked familiar.

My feet carried me to the middle of the bridge, where I could see a river flowing for what seemed like miles. For a second, I forgot about the monster. I forgot about what I was running from and simply watched the sun crest over the horizon. It was the first time since her death that my mother didn't instantly come to mind. Inhaling deeply, I was able to just *breathe*.

I gazed out at the winding river and saw the earth slowly swallow the sun, glutinously lapping up every bit of light before consuming it completely. Only pink remnants scattering the sky would eventually remain, attempting to survive, but soon, they too would dissolve, not able to match the insatiable appetite of this world and the cloak of darkness to follow.

A chill moved down my shoulders to the small of my back, flipping my stomach with an uneasy feeling. I pulled my jacket tightly around my neck and flipped the black hood over my bleached locks in attempts to encase the heat my body produced.

My ears perked and body stiffened to a sound rumbling just out of sight. *Is it my monster?* Had it materialized somehow, birthed from the recesses of my mind into a real-life, breathing beast? I knew it sounded insane, but in a way, I wanted it to be true. Then, I wouldn't be crazy. The feeling of something looming over me the last few months, watching me as I moved about that house, isolated and alone, taunting me with its evil thoughts, wouldn't have been my imagination or early signs of my impending psychosis, it would have been real.

I searched the trees lining the desolate road but saw no indication of a creature growling under the cloak of twilight. The sound continued in the distance.

My fingers encircled the bridge railing tightly as I looked back toward the rushing river, away from the hypnotic noise hurtling at me. I didn't want to look out at the tree-lined road any longer and see nothing.

The sound increased, rattling my ear drums with its veracity. Simultaneously, I felt a slight movement beneath my soles.

"It isn't real." I shook my head, begging my mind to believe the simple words that were barely audible. Tremors from below made my knees buckle.

My mind commanded me to move, but I remained still, frozen in uncertainty. I was losing the little hold I had on this world. Was this my psychotic break? I put my hands over my head. *Make it stop! Make it stop*! As quickly as I thought the words, the noise blared with a final scream of violent intent. Monster or no monster, whatever it was made contact. It had found its source—me.

CHAPTER 2 TWO

The Night Before the Bridge

As the streetlights rose and the evening sky emerged from behind the billowing clouds, I sat lazily on the oversized sofa; its floral pattern muted in the dimly lit room. A glow from the flat screen TV illuminated the walls decorated with family pictures and memories of a past I tried to forget.

I lounged lifelessly on the couch. A grumbling emerged from the depths of my empty stomach, moving me slowly to the kitchen. I searched for any evidence of sustenance, only to find an empty fridge, amongst an even emptier home. It was six o'clock at night, and there were no cheerful hums bustling in the kitchen with pots of water boiling or oven timers dinging. The kitchen was quiet, and the house was even quieter.

It was hard for my thoughts not to go to my mother; they always seemed to, even in the most unassuming moments—from the mundane tasks of doing laundry and washing dishes to an empty fridge and lonely kitchen.

I slammed the fridge door refusing to let the sadness of her death creep into yet another aspect of my life. With my aggression, an envelope fell to the floor. It read *Kara* in my father's impeccable penmanship, a trait I definitely did not share. Opening the envelope revealed a handful of twenty-dollar bills and a post-it-note that read, *for food*. A simple gesture lost in my father's lack of empathy for his daughter's basic needs: food was the last thing I truly needed. I needed a parent. I needed my dad, not two words written on bright yellow sticky paper.

I crumpled the note into a ball and tossed it to the floor. I quickly realized how out of it George really was. There was no way pizza would cost two hundred dollars. But, then again, maybe this was his way of telling me he might be gone a few extra days from the typical overnight business venture. I shoved one of the bills into my jean pocket and the rest in a hand painted Mason jar that read, *My Play Money,* in my mom's creative script. Yet another reminder she was gone.

Shutting the jar quickly, I pushed the thoughts of her away before the agony of privation could begin to find solid ground.

I dialed for the nearest pizza place, ordered my usual bread-sticks and Coke, and slumped back onto the sofa. Within thirty min-utes the doorbell rang, mocking me with its happy chime.

With my dinner and binge watching complete, I flipped off the TV and headed upstairs for my normal routine of crashing to bed just after eight. My father's bedroom door was ajar, allowing the light from the hallway to fill the sacred space. I hadn't dared enter since she died—fear of falling deeper, of hurting more, kept me back.

I instantly saw the boxes stacked against the wall and open bins scattered around the room. My mind hesitated, taking a minute to process what my heart knew upon first sight: my father had begun to pack away my mother's things. He was removing her from the bedside table, clearing out her closet, throwing away her old notes, and donating her literature. My heart broke as I saw the remainder of who she was packed away so callously.

My hands flew to my face, covering my mouth in disbelief as I entered the room.

My mother's purple sweater lay on the top of one of the open boxes. Instinctively, I picked it up, and I breathed it in deeply, hoping the scent of her still remained. To my ultimate despair, it was gone. There was nothing. No sweet floral aroma, no presence of her at all, only the smell of musty wool remained. Picking up another shirt and then another, only to find the same absent smell broke my heart in ways I didn't know was still possible. *How can I fall deeper? How cab I miss her more?* Yet, here I was, desperate for her scent on an old piece of cotton.

Defeated, I sat on the bed. My face fell heavily into my hands. *How can he do this? How can he just throw everything away?*

I swallowed the lump forming in my throat and scanned the alien space. Beside the bed, I saw a bin filled with books and magazines. A small book on top was easy to recognize as one of her Christian devotionals.

Every weekday before school my mom would call me into her room. We would sit together as she read the *Verse of Day* and thoughts that went with it. I never valued those moments, complaining for her to finish, so I wouldn't be late for school. Now, I longed for just one more second with her. To go back, slow down, and enjoy the time we had together before it was ripped away.

I put the devotional back into the bin and noticed another familiar book with brown binding and worn edges under undisclosed paperbacks. Pulling the book from its hiding place, I saw the golden letters etched in the lower right-hand side of its shabby leather cover.

"Lilian Rose Colten," I said quietly into the hollow room, tracing her name as I read.

Tears welled in my eyes and then fell slowly down my face at the sound of her name on my lips. I had been strong, holding back the emotions for so long, not letting myself even cry. But now, the levee had broken. I could feel it. Speaking her name and being amongst all her most personal items made it impossible to hold it in any longer. Tears turned to sobs.

Through blurred eyes, my fingers found the words *Holy Bible* centered in oversized print. My mom cherished her Bible, taking it almost everywhere she went. She called it her *lifeline*. I used to roll my eyes at the thought of a book being someone's life. Now it brought more anger than the indifference it once did. This book she held to so tightly, did absolutely nothing for her in the end. In the end, she still died.

No longer able to hold back the intensity that welled within me, I threw her Bible on the ground in a fit of rage. The tears streamed down my face faster and more erratic than before.

I wiped my cheeks with my sleeve and tried to calm my irregular breathing, but my mind was unable to remove the sound of my voice speaking her name. After a few moments, I moved toward the book, now tumbled over in the center of the room. Strewn papers littered the floor. I could see my mother's messy handwritten notes on the back of Sunday programs and pamphlets. Placing them nicely back in her Bible, I noticed a bent page and a folded piece of notebook paper tucked neatly between Proverbs and Psalms. My hands quivered as I pulled the paper from its hiding place. The evidence sent me crumbling to the wood floors below.

On my hands and knees, over scattered Biblical stories, I held a lost note that read: *For Kara.*

CHAPTER 3 THREE

The Bridge

I instantly knew I was not hallucinating. This was real. Monster or not, something had slammed into me. Within an instant, my feet came off the ground and I could feel myself falling toward a world spinning and twisting around me.

The powerful sound surpassed to something even more terrifying, a multitude of cracking bones and dislocating joints. My bones. My joints. The sounds magnified and radiated in my spinning head.

I knew pain would follow—it had to. Nothing that sounded like that came without pain, but the pain didn't come as I expected. Instead, I felt nothing—possibly more terrifying. I was simply a jumbled body tumbling toward the unknown.

For a second, time stopped, maybe to help my head catch up to what was happening, or to protect me somehow, shielding me from feeling an intense agony I knew was hidden under a frozen cloud of stillness.

Then, the cold water below slammed into me, reinvigorating time along with my comatose limbs. With this, pain followed, angrily awaking from its slumber. My once dormant body now ignited with the fury of a thousand stings.

My feeble struggles to keep my head above the surface were useless. Quickly, the thick water began to move and twist maliciously. I could feel it. It was alive. No longer had two simple hydrogen molecules molded with oxygen. Now, it was something more, something evil. My monster was back!

The sounds of churning laughter filled my ears. There was something delighting in my anguish, in my struggle to survive. An unknown darkness coated the murky water, a tar-like substance forming around my battered body. This unknown darkness seemed to swallow me, relishing in the meal it ingested, pulling me into its inner bowels.

I could feel the thick, black water filling my lungs slowly. Gasping for breath, I made a final attempt to keep my head above the water before slipping under completely. The surface began to slip away as if cinder blocks were pulling me toward its depths; the river bottom quickly becoming evident. A kindling of burning embers began to ignite in my lungs under the lack of oxygen.

Then, reality hit me. I was drowning.

I was dying.

CHAPTER 4 FOUR

The Night Before the Bridge

With trembling hands, I lifted the note to my face, breathing it in deeply. Amongst recycled paper, I smelled the sweet aroma of floral fragrance wrapped with subtle traces of vanilla—a smell I had yearned for only moments before.

Crumbled on the floor in its intoxicating memories, I clenched the letter against my chest, crying uncontrollably. The tears streamed down my face even more than they had when she died.

We were alone in the small hospital room. Multiple machines monitored my mother, all with blinking lights and alarms that would ring from the silence, sending my heart into jolts of despair. Her cancer had progressed beyond treatments and making her comfortable was the doctor's only objective. Death was inevitable.

I knew she was in pain. I knew that she needed to let go in order to end her suffering. But, I couldn't let her go. Day in and day out, I sat next to her, holding her hand, begging her to hang on just one more minute, one more day. I couldn't bear to think of my life without my mother. So, she did. My mom held on another two weeks after the doctors said she wouldn't make it through the night. Her strength amazed everyone.

When the day came that she couldn't hang on any longer, couldn't fight anymore, she held my hand tightly until her grip gave out. The monitors all rang with excitement as the nurses ran in to try to revive her failed body.

Within minutes, it was official.

"Her fight is over," the head nurse said holding my shoulders gently.

My feet became weak and gave out from underneath me. The gravity of life pushed down on me, no longer allowing me to stand in a world that my mother did not exist in. I was alone for the first time ever, and the tears poured out of me violently. She was gone—forever.

Holding the note in my hands, a piece of her so close to my trembling body, brought back all those memories from when I had first lost her: the loneliness I instantly felt as I was orphaned by the one true parent in my life, the hopelessness that I would never see her again, and the emptiness as a part of me died with her.

Those were the thoughts I fought desperately to keep at bay, pushing them away as the days rolled on without her. Now, they were streaming in fast and hard, violently pushing me to my father's bedroom floor in a crumbled heap—gravity once again pressing its mighty hand against my fragile body.

Moisture from my tears pooled under my aching face. I felt the cool of the night sweeping into the room through the open window. I didn't move. I couldn't.

Beep. Beep.

The sound startled me, sending my body jumping into the air and heart racing from the unknown noise.

Beep. Beep.

The noise chirped again from inside of my back pocket.

I pulled my phone from its hiding place and saw the glow of a text message coming from an unknown sender.

With wet cheeks, I pushed against the hard floor and found rest against the bed behind me. My phone alerted a message sent from my father's work number I had neglected to program into my contacts.

"Just landed in Detroit. I love you, Kara," the text read.

"I love you?" I read aloud quietly as I sat alone in the empty house.

I love you. My father's words rang inside of my mind. The words were simple, yet, powerful. It was a phrase I had not heard since my mother died a year ago. Either out of fear or discontentment, love was not a word that George uttered.

I shoved the phone back into my pocket and assumed the text to be a glitch at most. My mother's note went in the top drawer of my desk, next to her Bible which I had saved from the donation boxes.

I sat alone at the small desk unable to shake my father's words from my mind.

I love you.

Tears began to fall down my already salty cheeks. The floodgates ripped open, and there was nothing I could do to hold back the tsunami of pain.

Different visions of my mother saying the same phrase my father had just written repeated relentlessly in my damaged mind:

"I love you, Kara, have a great day at school," she said, kissing my youthful face.

"I love you, Hun. Don't be upset," I stomped to my room.

"I love you. Always," my head lay across her withering lap.

There was no longer comfort in her loving words, they only brought intense pain and loneliness. Tucked in a fetal position, I rocked gently as image after image of loving moments we shared pounded against my fragile mind.

CHAPTER 5

The Bridge

A black cold encircled me. I couldn't move and didn't want to. I knew it would only cause intense pain. So I remained still, dying slowly.

How did I get here? How did death find me? I am too young, too innocent, too insignificant for life to end this way. I was supposed to die old, a gray-haired woman reading *Pride and Prejudice* for the hundredth time, my cat curled at my feet. I would have been content then, happy to slip away to nothingness. But, not now. Not before I was even able to live. I didn't even have a chance to cliff jump in Acapulco or scuba dive with great whites in South Africa. I didn't have time for anything.

Why am I here? Why darkness and not a white light? I am a good person. My mother had died, and I didn't lose it—that much. So why this? I guess questioning it doesn't change anything. This was the end. My end.

I felt the water rush into my weakened lungs, filling them completely with their icy sting. Within seconds, the murky water began to slip away and I began to lose myself.

I hadn't thought much of death. *I should have.* I had thought a lot about leaving this Earth, leaving the pain, running away from it all, ending it even. But actual death, the process of it, wasn't something I had thought about.

If this was death, which I was most certain it was; it wasn't cold or scary. It was the opposite, warm and comforting. Death was a heated blanket embracing me, pulling me into its ameliorating touch. Thoughts of my mother's warmth filled my mind.

On the first snowfall of the year, my mom would make hot chocolate on the stove; the smell would fill the entire house. She would wrap a quilted blanket around the two of us, and we would sit in front of the fireplace with our warm drinks. I could feel her with me now, teasing me about the cute boy in my Biology class I had a small crush on. I could almost hear her sweet voice, smell the scent of her vanilla lotion, and feel the touch of her hand on mine. Thoughts of her filled my whole being as I allowed myself to drift toward the warmth she possessed.

If this is death, let it come, I thought.

Then, it faded. All of it -the crackling warmth of the fire, my mother's comforting embrace- it disappeared as quickly as it had come.

My body moved with the slight current, dragging my exposed legs against the jagged rocks on the bottom of the river. No longer was I in the comfort of my living room under the protecting arms of my mother. The warmth was just a mirage, a sick joke, played out masterfully to think that I might actually get to be with my mother in death.

I felt the icy water encase me with more intensity than ever before. It was agonizing, painfully intense chills stabbing at my crippled body.

A darkness stirred in the water, and an unknown, malicious laughter filled my ears and mind. A sickening feeling rose in my gut as bile burned the back of my throat. I knew something was coming—something even worse than death.

Out of the black water, shadows began to fill the space between the surface and my cracking shell. The river bottom was a shield to my back. The pain, still evident, began to numb next to the intense fear that rose within me.

Dark, hawk-like hands emerged from the thick waters. Painful, sharp icy knives stabbed at me, lacerating my legs. I couldn't see a face, only an animalistic form emerging from the depths, revealing the source of the attack on my legs. The creature reached toward me again, it's long barbs pressing into my supple skin. I expected pain, intense feverish pain. Instead, the injection brought upon feelings and emotions magnified beyond reason. Feelings of emptiness, loneliness, hatred, anger, fear… All the negative emotions I had ever experienced overtook me. Standing out from the rest, loneliness rattled me to my core. It was the opposite of love—a complete inactivity of any ardor what-so-ever. My greatest fear was being alone, completely and utterly alone. And that is what I was, alone, without any form of love. I knew this feeling would go on forever; a never-ending torment of isolation—Hell.

Seconds later, I felt another hand grab my leg, and another on my shoulder. Sharp hooks dug into my right heel while an anchor locked into my upper quadriceps.

Screaming in pain only allowed more of the frozen water to fill my already full lungs. They burned in tortuous anguish as more animalistic claws reached out of the darkness, pulling me in all directions, and ripping me apart.

Maleficent hands grabbed me, yanking on my unprotected extremities. I felt every inch of pain imaginable.

Just when I thought the stinging agony, paralyzing fear, and complete destitution couldn't get any worse, death truly began, and the realization of an eternity of these feelings filled my mind.

A darker shadow emerged from behind the horrific creatures digging into my flesh. The already thick, ebony water became even darker, cloaked in an evil that was beyond measure. As it neared, I lifted my mind toward the only thing that could ward off this much depravity. Not able to move my head from the creatures hold, I lifted my eyes upward and begged for reprieve.

Through the abyss, I saw it; a bit of charcoal off in the distance, a hint of the darkness relinquishing.

Quickly the muted object became a faint light. The unknown blue and white hue quickly increased, parting the blackness and moving swiftly toward me.

I was transfixed. *What is this light?*

Panic began to move within me. I desperately wanted to yell to the light to run and flee from the darkness all around me; sure it would consume the light too.

But, it didn't.

The light grew in intensity and radiated to the bottom of the water where they held me captive. To my surprise, the darkness cowered from the light as it neared my broken body. The sharp, talon-like grips relinquished from my arms and legs, sending the creatures wailing in defeat.

Pulled from death and lifted from the shadows of darkness, I left the dark creatures to the icy waters below. As I emerged from the water, intensely bright rays filled my eyes, blinding me. Suddenly, I no longer felt the water, only the frigid air against my skin, attacking me with each blustery whip. My body began to shiver uncontrollably in hypothermic reaction. Violently, water left my lungs as two massive hands pushed on my chest. Choking and gasping for air, I struggled for breath. My shaking body transitioned to more elaborate tremors; my chattering teeth inhibited me from taking the deep breaths my lungs desperately needed.

Through the chill, warmth emerged from pressure on my right arm. I couldn't see the source of the comforting heat, instantly alleviating the numbing chill in my limbs. The light obstructed my view of the mysterious heat source I now felt moving up my arm and over my chest. It was a fire bringing restorative heat to my entire glacial body.

Just past the warmth, I could feel the pressure of fingers gripping my arm. A face came into focus, and eyes became clear behind the bright light emanating from a man's face.

Unable to focus, I strained to see the source of the light, the source of my mysterious savior. His face was pearlescent with sharp sapphire eyes and red lips that parted and moved with no sound coming from them.

"Do not be afraid," strong words, not my own, beamed in my head.

I tried to understand what was happening around me, but my head was spinning uncontrollably. All I knew was that he was absolutely stunning, a beauty beyond anything I had ever seen, angelic even.

The grip on my arm surrendered its magnetic hold and with

its release, pain rushed in allowing me to feel the cold air on my wet skin. A deafening noise rang in my ears, and I closed my eyes tightly as another surge of pain thrashed through my body.

I felt the rocks underneath me, a sharp and stabbing distress on my legs, back, and head. Opening my eyes with great difficulty, I strained to see the face in front of me again, filled with such beauty and peace.

But, he was gone. The light was gone. I was alone.

Overtaken with pain, I faded away to nothingness.

CHAPTER 6 SIX

The Night Before the Bridge

The night was long, battering me with the intense pressure to find release from the agony of my mother's death. It hurtled me toward an all-consuming monster that held no escape. A seemingly innocent phrase, *I love you*, had sent me falling deeper than I ever thought was even possible.

I didn't even feel the cold enter the room. I simply lay there, amongst the cryptic note my mother had left me. It wasn't until morning that I felt the icy sting of the open window against my chilled cheeks.

It was hard to sleep; tears were the only thing that seemed to come in systematic waves of intense emotions.

The end—I let it build in my fragile mind.

My mother's death.

My death.

The end.

My end.

It was a thought I would have never entertained before. *How could I?* I had a life ahead of me then. Now, there was nothing to live for—nothing or no one for me.

But, ending it, killing myself? How could I do that? Mentally and physically, the questions rang through my mind. *How?*

Flashes of my mother intertwined with the fantasy of death—my death.

I couldn't think straight, and nothing seemed clear. My life was a blur, meaningless without my mother. I had no one now, not my mother or my father, not my friends. Even her belongings would soon disappear.

The morning light entered my room as my mind continued to battle with thoughts of leaving this troubled world.

What am I thinking? I couldn't kill myself.

The sun's warmth filled my room, releasing my sore face from the sting of the evening's cold embrace. The heaviness within my mind seemed to fade into the shadows cast from sunlight filling my room. As much as I desperately craved an escape from the pain within me, I knew I couldn't leave this world. I wasn't strong enough. I was weak and scared. Disappearing to nothing, fading away to an unknown end wasn't something I wanted.

Growing up in a church might have deluded my mind to think like this, but, then again, maybe it was something more. The *fire and brimstone* preachings were probably just a pastor's exasperated attempts to put a few extra dollars in the offering plate. But, then again, what if it wasn't? *What if it was true? What if everything my mother had tried to teach me about life and death, Heaven and Hell—what if it is real?*

It was a gamble I wasn't ready to take. Even if I didn't believe there was a Heaven or Hell, I wasn't ready to find out for sure.

The morning and afternoon meandered from motionless actions of mundane life. I flipped through early afternoon television, allowing me to mindlessly escape the troubling thoughts from the night before.

A little after two in the afternoon, I decided to try to sleep but was unable. Every time I closed my eyes, I thought of death. My death. My mother's death. Death was everywhere, all around me, calling out to me. It was an evil monster, begging me to join him in the darkness.

I had to get out of that house. Everything about it pulled me to a dark place I knew deep within I didn't want to give into. Not allowing any further thought, I threw on a pair of sweats, a black jacket, and my old sneakers. I was out of the house within minutes. I had no intention of running, no intention of doing anything but getting out of *that* house. I had to get away from the sinister monster that grew inside. Little did I know, the monster was inside of me all along.

CHAPTER 7

After the Bridge

My eyes opened slowly as if weights were holding them in place. I saw a man, blurred and distant in a chair on the right side of me, his head was down and face rested on his exposed arms. It was my father. I tried to reach for him but was unable to move. Panic began to set in when I saw the cables inhibiting my movement.

Where am I? What happened?

It took all my energy to move my fingers. Touching his hand slightly was all it took for his head to dart into the air, eyes wide with bewilderment.

"Kara?" George's voice was low and raspy.

His tired brown eyes looked years older than his sturdy build. His salt and pepper hair only added to his aging face that looked at me with deep worry and an intense care I hadn't seen in what felt like a lifetime.

Unable to speak, only whimpers escaped my chapped lips, barely audible above the steady beeps from the monitors behind my head.

"It's okay," George said quietly, holding my hand in his, "It's going to be okay," He repeated over and over again.

George's vulnerability sang in the quiet room, allowing me to see past the wall he had encased around his heart. Even if he wasn't the present father I longed for him to be, he still loved me. His absence over the past year wasn't a reflection of his apathetic feelings; it was his way of coping with the loss of his wife. I could see that now, in his loving touch and caring eyes.

I faded in and out of consciousness until the sun peeked through the thick blinds covering the window adjacent to my bed. My father was no longer sitting next to me but snored, rather noisily, in a reclining chair in the corner of the room.

A shot of pain ignited down my right leg as I scooted myself to the back of the bed, adjusting to fully sit upright. My back ached and head pounded with my limited movement. Instinctively, my jaw clenched and teeth bared to prevent a painful cry from escaping my mouth. Body stiff, I tried not to move, allowing the pain time to lessen with my newly reclined position.

Looking around the room, I noticed its sparseness: an empty bed only a few feet from me, a TV placed high on the wall next to where my father rested, and a white board on the far wall with the doctor's instructions written messily. Still confused, I searched my surroundings for any additional information as to what had happened to me and why I was in this sterile hospital room.

Why am I in here? What happened? The thoughts continued without answers.

The last thing I remembered was finding my mother's note amongst the discarded remnants of her past: a letter written to her only daughter—a note she probably had wished would bring hope and light during a difficult time. Instead, dark thoughts had filled my mind, throwing me into a cavernous void leading me to question my own existence in a loveless world without my mother.

Is that what happened? Did I try to kill myself? No, that couldn't be it. I wouldn't. Would I?

Dark shadows flashed inside my weakened mind. There was so much pain, filled with an intense cold and deep blackness that seemed to permeate every crevice of my being.

I searched my mind, trying to see through the agony I knew was the darkness of death. Amongst the abyss, a hint of light emerged; a small remembrance of a glimmer of hope.

"Hi, there!" A woman's voice chirped, snapping me from my thoughts. "Good to see you awake. How are you feeling?"

"I'm okay," I said quietly, surprised at the raspy tone of my voice.

"How's the pain?" the nurse asked, looking at her chart resting on her arm.

As she checked the bags hanging above my head, I asked, "What happened?" Unsure if I really wanted to know the answer.

Maybe that is why my father had looked so sad before, so desperate for me to wake up.

Had I tried to kill myself? Oh no, what did I do?

"You were in an accident. It is a miracle you are alive," she spoke gently. "You took a really bad fall."

As soon as she said the word *accident* my tense heart released and a wave of solace filled my whole body.

"Fall?" I questioned.

What fall? What happened? I hadn't tried to kill myself. Relief. *Thank you, God!* As soon as I thought the words, I instantly regretted them. *Why am I thanking God that I hadn't killed myself? God has nothing to do with this.*

My father shifted in his chair, causing the both of us to glance back at him; his once loud snores gave way to heavy breathing.

"You were hit by a car on a bridge just out of town. You fell into the river. The driver said he tried to find you but couldn't. He thought you were gone. Then, you were just lying there," she said as she held my wrist, taking my pulse. "It was a miracle," she added.

Memories began to flood my mind with each descriptive word the nurse spoke.

I remembered leaving the house and running for several miles until I came upon an old bridge. I remember the movement of the bridge, the shifting under my feet, but that was all I could recall.

The kind nurse leaned in to check my breathing, and I noticed a golden charm dangling from her neck. A simple cross hung gently against her caramel skin.

Noticing my attention to her jewelry she spoke, "My mother got this for me when I was a young girl." She turned it over in her hand, smiling softly. The golden charm bounced the light from the incandescent fixtures above.

Instantly, another memory of the bridge entered my mind, except now, the image was much more vivid and real. It was like I was standing there, all over again. I saw the old wood railing and its slotted base. The images continued in flashes of memories that demanded answers. I could feel it—all of it: the buckling under my feet, the sharp pain, the feeling of weightlessness. *The fall*. Then, there was the river—icy cold water rushing all around me.

Pain flooded my entire body. My hands cupped my face as I rubbed my eyes trying to remove the images of the dark creatures that began to gain traction within my mind.

"It's okay, Dear." The nurse said kindly.

Her words were like daggers in my mind. *It wasn't okay*. I almost died. *No, I did die. There is nothing okay about any of this.* I tried to calm myself, but thoughts kept rushing in like the flowing river I had succumbed to.

"Just rest," she said as she reached for the IV bag and injected something into it. "This will help," she smiled kindly, touching my arm with concern.

"Miracle?" I questioned. "You said it was a miracle. What did you mean?"

The nurse looked at me compassionately with her deep brown eyes, "It's a miracle you are alive. I see a lot of people in here every day. Some car accidents, some falls, some drownings, but rarely do we see anyone survive all you went through." She held her cross necklaces again, tracing its shape with her thumb.

I could feel my head shaking back and forth as her words began to blur, the medication beginning to take effect.

"Just get some rest," she said, her words long and drawn out.

I tried to focus on the woman standing over me. I desperately wanted to ask her more about this miracle she spoke of, and why I had this strange feeling her charmed necklace may mean something more than a religious token, but the soft touch of her hand on mine lulled me into the calming stillness of sleep.

CHAPTER 8

I woke to a room filled with people. At the head of my hospital bed, an unknown woman in blue scrubs checked my IV while a man wearing a white lab coat chatted noisily to an unknown individual at the room's entrance. He smiled at me as he noticed my eyes scanning the room. My head pounded with the bustling activity.

"How are you doing?" he said with a thick Middle Eastern accent.

As the doctor approached, the nurse wrapped a cuff around my arm, put a thermometer under my tongue, and a pulse meter on my middle finger.

I attempted to respond to his question, but only muffled noises came from my obstructed mouth. The doctor ignored my response, looked at the chart in his hand, and nodded at the nurse to order some kind of medication.

"Kara, I'm Dr. Pitts. I'll be your attending physician while you are with us here at Memorial," the doctor spoke without looking up from his notes.

For the first time since I arrived at the hospital, I noticed my father's absence from the room. I scanned the space for his boisterous snoring on the reclining chair or sports highlights playing loudly on the TV. There was no evidence of him in the room at all.

"Do you remember what happened to you, Kara?" Dr. Pitts spoke, jarring my thoughts of my absent father.

"Um, yeah I think so. There was an accident. The bridge," I

spoke in fragmented sentences, trying to piece together my shattered memories.

"That's right," Dr. Pitts said, his dark eyes looking up from his notes for the first time. "You were hit by a vehicle and fell into a river. You sustained multiple injuries, including lacerations on both legs and the right side of your body along with a femoral fracture, torn Posterior Cruciate Ligament, and a minor concussion," he paused as he looked at his chart again and walked to the base of my bed.

My eyes followed his movement. For the first time, I saw my elevated leg encased in white plaster just under my hip. I had to fight the tears that tried to emerge at the sight of my frail state. No wonder my father had looked so concerned.

"Are you having any pain?" Dr. Pitts asked.

I shrugged, trying to hide my irritation at his continued probing and poking at my injured leg.

I followed his movement as he removed a penlight from his pocket and blinded my right eye. Before I could blink, he turned it to the next.

The flash of light sent a lightning streak of pain to my brain at its intensity. A memory of a blue and white brightness clipped in my mind. Then, another and another. Continual bulbs popped in my mind as if someone was snapping my picture on the red carpet. Then it stopped. An intense light formed all around me, and I knew I was no longer in the hospital room with my doctor, but taken to a moment my mind had hidden. Within the intense light, a face emerged. Sharp blue eyes became clear around a man's face.

"Kara?" Dr. Pitts asked, pulling me back to the hospital room. The flashlight, he still held in his hand, dulled in comparison to my memory.

"Yeah," I paused, confused at what I had just seen.

"Are you alright?"

"Who was that man?" I asked the doctor as his fingers held my wrist taking my racing pulse.

The doctor dropped my hand and questioned, "The man that hit you, he was brought in for minor cuts and bruises, but was released after the police questioned him."

What? I thought, impatiently. *No, not him!*

"Okay, um… what about the other guy?" I continued, "The one that pulled me from the water?"

"I'm sorry. I'm not aware of any other man." He paused for a moment and then continued, "The policeman that questioned the driver did not mention another person at the scene of the accident. But, you will have to ask the officer handling this case. I sent him away, but I'm sure he will be back tomorrow to get a statement from you, if you are up for it. If you need anything, please let us know. I will be back shortly to see how you are doing. Please try to get some rest." The doctor made a note on his chart, smiled, and quickly left the room entering the bustling hallway.

What did he mean there wasn't another person? There had to be. Am I remembering the driver? No, that can't be right. The nurse said the driver thought I was gone, and then I just appeared. It couldn't have been him that pulled me from the water. *Then, who or what saved me?*

Just as my thoughts were being pulled back to the bridge and the beauty of my mysterious rescuer, the hospital door flung open and my father entered with two cups of cafeteria style coffee in hand and a bag dangling from his wrist.

"Oh, you're awake! Good, good," George said. "I brought some coffee. I know you like it in the mornings when you get up. But I couldn't remember if you take cream or sugar in it, so I brought both."

George placed the two cups of steaming coffee on my bedside table and fumbled with the side chair while he pulled it toward my bed.

"And, muffins," he said pulling two baked treats from the doggie bag with the hospital logo branded on its exterior.

"They said you could have whatever you would eat. And I didn't know what you like, so I just brought the basic breakfast type food," he rambled.

It was the most I had heard my father speak to me in months. My father's face desperately searched mine for approval, and when it didn't come he continued, "I think this one is pumpkin, and this one is blueberry. You like that right? If not, I can just..."

"Thanks, Dad," I spoke quietly for the first time.

George's anxiety seemed to fade with my shaky words. He allowed his tired frame to collapse into the chair behind him. His hands rubbed his tired eyes as he exhaled loudly.

"I'm okay," I said.

"Yeah." He stood and found a place next to me on the edge of my bed. "You are going to be okay Kara."

His hands reached for mine, and I let him hold them tenderly with fatherly love. A touch I had longed for since my mother died.

"I thought I lost you," he said, his eyes welling with pain.

"I'm still here," I said as I clenched his hand, "I'm still here."

CHAPTER 9

The days after my accident were chaotic and confusing, filled with unfamiliar faces and concerned eyes. My father stayed by my side, switching in-person meetings to phone conferences and even handing over a case to his assistant.

Officer Danton, the policeman handling my case, stopped in to check on my progress and said he would come back tomorrow to follow up with a statement. George lawyered up and threw out a few very concerning words like, "pressing charges," and some other legal jargon. I allowed for the concerned parent to emerge, but knew that as soon as I regained my strength, I would have to squash all thoughts of suing the man that hit me.

A few of my teachers, who were once friends of my mother, came by to bring flowers and kind words. By day four there hadn't been anyone my age by twenty years. I wasn't surprised. It was a life I had chosen to live without friends. When my mom died I had isolated myself from anyone that had meant anything to me. I just stopped. Stopped being their friend, stopped answering calls, and stopped living. I was sure they had forgotten all about me.

Knock. Knock. Knock.

The noise broke me from my burdensome thoughts as I lay alone in the hospital room.

"Yes," I muttered.

The door slowly opened and a small frame stood in the doorway.

"Hey?" a girlish voice said as she entered the room. Her

petite frame was in sharp contrast to the oversized shirt she wore, hanging low on her shoulders.

"Jen?" I said, amazed to see the girl I had grown up with, and yet had neglected for over a year standing in my hospital room.

Jen and I had known each other since the first day of kindergarten. She was my best friend. A tomboy at heart, she had an energy about her that was infectious. Jen fought for me with great strength after my mom died, even unanswered text messages and calls didn't discourage her. But, it didn't matter; my grief consumed me.

"Hey!" She said again, pushing open the large door to reveal the group filing in behind her.

"Hi," said a soft voice behind thick wavy hair. It was Teagan. She was blond, beautiful, and full of life. It is easy to see why she was the first to disappear; my despair only drowned out her brightness. I didn't blame her. The contrasting tonalities could not coexist. So I left, and she let me. I smiled softly at her and Jen as they walked into the room and stood at the foot of my bed.

"Hey Kara," a strong voice spoke from the closing door. There Kale stood with his dark bustled curls cut short against his strong chiseled face; blushed cheeks emerged from his creamy skin. *Kale.* Just thinking his name brought a rush of emotions. He meant so much to me at one time. One moment he was a friend, and then, almost overnight, he became something more. He was someone that I leaned on, trusted, and held to. He was a best friend, boyfriend, and maybe even my first love. But, then everything changed when she died. I desperately wanted him to fight for me, demanding I stay with him, by his side. I needed him to not allow my sorrow to bury me alive. But, that was only a fantasy. The reality was Kale let me entomb myself, let me hide away from everyone. As I lay in my grief, the waves came crashing in, carrying me out to sea. Kale didn't even stand at the shore and wish me safe travels.

It wasn't Kale's fault. It wasn't any of their faults. I pushed him away, pushed them all away.

Now, they were here, all of my once closest friends, standing at the foot of my hospital bed. *What are they doing here?* My mind raced.

"Hi, guys," I finally spoke quietly.

Silence filled the air. I desperately wanted to go to them, jump up, and tell them all how extremely sorry I was for pushing them away. My body ached as I arched my back and tried to move.

I winced in pain. Teagan, still highly intuitive, noticed my anguish and interjected, "You look like crap, Kara."

"Tea!" Jen said quickly.

"What?" Teagan mouthed without making a sound.

"No, it's okay. I do," I quickly added before Jen could nudge Teagan with her pointed elbow, "I'm pretty messed up."

"Yeah," Teagan nodded, her brows high and eyes wide.

Kale stepped forward, "You doing alright?"

I nodded. I could see the pain in his eyes—in all their eyes.

I didn't want to push them away any longer so I spoke, "I'm… I'm… sorry for everything this last year." I stammered, trying to find the right words between long pauses. "I became this crappy person that *I* didn't even like. I just couldn't face you guys, after…" I paused trying to find the right words. "After my mom died, I didn't want to go on acting like I was the same happy person. I wasn't, and I didn't want to pretend. I couldn't be that girl without her, so I tried to remove everything, that…well…made me…me. You guys are such… were such a huge part of who I was. So, I just cut you out of my life. I thought taking away everything and everyone would help it not hurt as much, but really, it just made it worse."

I took a deep breath before continuing, "You guys didn't deserve that. I shouldn't have pushed you away like I did." I felt a tear forming in the corner of my eye and a lump building in my throat, "I am so sorry."

I closed my eyes and breathed in deeply, trying to compose myself, not wanting the gawking eyes of my once close friends to witness my emotional breakdown.

Opening my eyes, I was surprised to see the three of them standing by the side of my bed, Teagan and Jen on one side and Kale on the other.

"*We're* sorry," Teagan spoke first, "*We* were crappy friends, too. We let you go."

"We don't want to lose you again," Jen said, clutching my hand.

"You almost died, girl!" Teagan said, standing next to Jen.

We all smiled at Teagan's lighthearted tone and her ability to alleviate the room's heavy feel.

"We aren't going anywhere this time," Kale added.

CHAPTER 10

We sat for hours together: Teagan, Jen, Kale, and I. We caught up on the latest high school drama and anything else that we deemed important to our newly restored friendships.

After they left, the room was quiet and resting came easy. Hours later, a crash of a metal chair slamming to the floor sent me jumping, and then, screeching in pain at my sudden movement. A lanky male stumbled and slunk into the room awkwardly.

"Sorry, Miss," the man said in hushed tones noticing my recently awakened state.

My jaw tightened and closed my eyes to hold back the pain as I adjusted to sit upright. Once the pain passed, I opened my eyes, my new position giving me a better view of the man that staggered into my room. He wore a traditional police uniform with a navy tailored shirt and crisp matching pants. His metallic badge reading, *Officer Danton* under the Maine State Police emblem, reflected the dimmed overhead light.

"Ms. Colten, I'd like to ask you a few questions if that is okay with you?" Officer Danton asked.

"Yeah, that's fine," I said, shifting my weight in attempts at comfort.

"Do you remember anything from the accident, Miss?" Officer Danton dove right into his questioning without hesitation.

"Umm, not really," I responded, rubbing my throbbing head. The blood pulsed forcefully with my newly seated position.

Before the officer could ask another question, I quickly interjected, "I remember the bridge, the water, and …"

"Yes, Ms. Colton." The officer urged me to continue after my lengthy pause.

Shaking my head, "…then there was just darkness."

"Did you see the car that hit you?" Officer Danton asked.

"No," I responded quickly.

"What were you doing on the bridge, Miss?"

"I went on a run, and just ended up…"

"On the bridge," the officer finished my chopped sentence.

"Yeah, I guess so."

"Okay, thank you, Ms. Colton. If we need anything else, I'll let you know. Or, if anything else comes to mind that might be important, you can contact me." Officer Danton placed a small business card on the table next to me.

"I… umm…" I stammered searching for the right words.

The officer held his notepad, he had previously scribbled on, intently waiting on my response.

"I remember this person. This man pulling me from the water," I said reluctantly, leaving out the description about the dark creatures pulling me to my death, and the saving light that seemed to surround this mysterious person.

"A man?" he asked.

"I didn't see him very well. But, he pulled me out of the water and was with me on the shore. Then, he was just gone."

"I've questioned the driver and he didn't mention anything about another person at the scene," Officer Danton said. "Can you give me a description of the man?"

"Umm, he was… his eyes were a deep blueish color, kind of," I shook my head slightly, knowing how it must sound. "I didn't see him that well. It was so bright. There was this really intense light all around him. All I really saw were his eyes." I could feel the officer's intense stare as I completed my limited description of my mysterious savior.

Through the silence, a woman cleared her throat, "Excuse me!"

Turning my head to see past the officer, we both became aware of my attending nurse standing in the entry of the illuminated door, her hands folded against her chest, and eyes honed in on the officer.

"Yes, Ma'am. I was just questioning Ms. Colten about the accident. I'm Officer Danton," he said as he reached his hand toward the guarded nurse.

"Yes, well, visiting hours are over Officer Danton. If you have any more questions you can finish up with Miss Colton during *normal* visiting hours," the nurse said assertively, arms still folded.

"We were just finishing up," Officer Danton said, closing his notepad and shoving it into his pocket.

I opened my mouth to speak, but nothing emerged from behind cracked lips. My mind raced with the words to say. I needed the pieces of this jumbled puzzle to somehow fit together, but with my limited description and vague details, it was near impossible.

Before I could find my voice the officer intuitively added, "I will look into this other man and let you know if I find anything."

"Thank you," I mustered.

The officer smiled kindly, passed by my glaring nurse, and left the room with a quick tip of his hat.

Nurse Tina Williams crossed the room and stood at the side of my bed now. She pursed her lips and shook her head slightly while she began to check the levels of my IV and other machines above my bed.

"He should know better than bothering you like that," she grumbled.

"It was okay," I said as she wrapped the blood pressure cuff around my bare arm.

She sent me a warm smile, and instantly, I saw the caring nurse emerge from behind her rigid façade. As she leaned in, I once again, noticed her cross necklace dangling gracefully against her defined collarbone.

"I heard what you said," Nurse Williams spoke softly.

"Yeah?" I asked, hoping she didn't think I was crazy for seeing a man that no one else seemed to think was there.

"You saw a man?" she asked.

I nodded.

"In a bright light?"

I nodded, again.

"Then, he was gone?"

"Yeah?" I said hesitantly, drawing out each letter reluctantly.

She nodded her head, mimicking my once inaudible responses.

"Do you want me to tell you what I think?" the nurse asked.

"Of course," I said.

She leaned in close to my still weakened body, speaking only a few words, a simple sentence that would change everything: "It was your guardian angel."

CHAPTER 11 ELEVEN

It had been almost two weeks since I came to know the bland hospital room as my home. I saw the chilly beginnings of an icy winter from behind the drafty five by eight window.

Multiple physical therapy sessions each day with Suzie, my body-builder/therapist who did not appreciate my lackadaisical attitude, helped break-up the monotony. In addition to Suzie, a college student/tutor named Dave, came by to drop off what seemed to be an endless supply of homework and offer up any help with Calculus, Physics, or anything else. I barely said three words to him and turned him away every time. My father would stop by most days, sitting with me and chatting about his latest case. In addition, a revolving group of new residency students shadowed Dr. Pitts weekly. I couldn't keep them straight. They each had a new idea about increasing my mobility, managing my pain, and determining my discharge date. The pain was the only consistent visitor I could always count on.

Truth was, I was alone. Alone in my pain. Alone in this room. I was alone, despite all the people around me. The only thing that kept me moving forward was the thought of my blue-eyed savior, my *guardian angel*, as my nurse had called him.

Every new person or new face that entered my room could be the one that saved me that night on the bridge. But, it wasn't. And, my desperation to find him only grew.

Despite my limited hospital search, no one compared to the beauty that stood over me that evening: his piercing eyes, his warm touch on my chilled arm, his saving grace for a damned soul such as mine. My mind churned with thoughts of who my savior may be. *Was he an angel as my nurse had suggested?*

My rescuer wasn't the only thing that kept my mind sprinting in all directions. Death had planted a seed of fear that had begun to take root deep inside of me—a darkness calling out from the depths of my soul. I knew the fear cultivating within was my destined fate: Hell—a place I had really never thought of before, but now, had to. It was my fate, my end, endlessly void of my mother's love.

I guess I thought it would be different. The other side, for me, would be with my mom, not the darkness that had presented itself the night on the bridge. I was a *good* person. I never really did anything wrong. Cheating on a test was far from my mind and stealing a common candy bar was inconceivable. My virtue was intact as I had only kissed my once boyfriend of over a year. Even sitting next to my mother every Sunday in church didn't seem to buy me any points in the end. In the end, I was still damned.

Then, why save me? That night a hand reached through the darkness and lifted me toward the light. I knew my impassive heart was the cause of my fate. *So then, why save me?*

Lying in the hospital bed, I knew I had to find the man behind the light, my *guardian angel* or whoever he was. Maybe he could help me find *this* light to avoid the darkness I was fated for.

CHAPTER 12

"Come on, *Lazy Bones*," Jen nudged me gently. "Let's go!" She said in a slightly deeper voice, the shoving much more urgent.

"Ugh!" I groaned noisily, pulling the covers over my head and hiding from my intrusive friend.

"Okay, now I'm not playing. Come on!" Jen shouted. I could hear her ripping open the curtains noisily. "We have to get going. We said we would meet them at eight," she paused.

Jen's bustling about my room continued to gain volume. I closed my eyes tighter under the comfort of my warm blanket, attempting to diminish the noise.

"Really? Do you know what time it is Kara? It's ten-till eight. We are never going to make it. You know I hate being late. This was your idea. 'Let's go for a run,' you said, 'Let's *hang*.' Bull! You just wanted to lay in bed all day… you lazy bum!" Jen screeched tearing around the room.

Thud! A small, yet hard object crashed into my secluded body inhibiting my attempt to hang onto the last few moments of sleep.

"Ouch!" I squeaked, "Okay, okay, I'm up. I'm up."

Shifting my weight, I pushed my tired body to sit upright on my bed. My eyes attempted to adjust to the sunlight filling the space. I rubbed them trying to hide from the light, and also to brush away the tiredness they held.

No longer hearing Jen, I knew that meant she was up to no good. The clothes rustled in my opened closet while her voice mumbled frustrations at its messy state.

I smiled at the thought of our newly rekindled friendship, which lightened my tired mood. It was something I didn't think I would have again—friends. My *almost* death had brought us back together and allowed me to see life differently, opening my eyes to what was wrong in my life. I wasn't who I was supposed to be. I had to try harder, be better, somehow. But, trying to be a better friend or daughter wasn't the only thing that I gained from the night.

I gained an obsession. *Who saved me?* It was the centralized question in my mind. Not when I would walk without pain or if I would ever run again. Not even if my new found friendships would last. Nothing else mattered except finding who saved me.

So far, my cryptic savior had remained an elusive mystery, alive only in my dreams. I yearned to find him, to search the streets for his alluring eyes. My body was the only thing holding me back.

"So, Tea told me to get you all looking cute," Jen spoke, interrupting my thoughts.

"Yeah? Where is she anyways?" I said standing and stretching noisily.

"I told her not to come. She would put you in heels and a dress if it were up to her," Jen said with a big smile crossing her face.

"She's crazy," I said. "And, where are we going? You never told me."

Jen's eyes widened, "You need to gear up. Here," Jen tossed a pair of athletic sweats and long-sleeve compression shirt in my direction and turned back to the closet.

"We are going for a run," Jen said, "And then we are meeting Teagan and Kale at that smoothie place in town after. Then we thought we would head to..."

As Jen continued to talk, thoughts raced through my mind. *We were going for a run? How is it even possible? I could barely walk!*

"I was totally kidding earlier about going for a run. I just thought we would get coffee or something. Plus, it is freezing out," I spat abruptly, not able to hide my frustration.

"Just get dressed. Trust me on this," Jen spoke tenderly as

she continued digging relentlessly in my closet.

My leg buckled and shook from my own weight. Pain arched through my thigh and down my tender knee as I attempted to undress. Frustration stirred in my gut at the pain in my limited movement. On the bed now, I loudly exhaled, pulling up the sweats and shirt over my disheveled multi-colored hair. The once bleached chopped bob, now longer and more like my mother's chestnut waves each day.

I closed my eyes, the pain continued even after I elevated my throbbing leg, and collapsed backward on the soft bed, breathing deeply.

"So, what's the plan?" I asked.

Jen emerged from the closet with a long pair of green, knee-high socks buried in the depths of my dysfunctional closet. She walked over to my desk, opened the top drawer, and pulled out a pair of long metal scissors. A cunning smirk curled across her face as she raised the scissors to the socks and cut the feet dramatically.

"Hey!" I said.

"Like you care," Jen said, still smiling.

I smirked at her ability to fully *get* me, to understand who I was, despite everything we had been through over the last year, she knew me.

Jen walked out of the room and returned seconds later with an unknown item in her hand.

"What on Earth is that?" I said in response to the odd contraption she paraded in the room.

Jen skipped over and sat next to me eagerly.

"It is the *newest* and *best* knee brace out there. My dad scored it for you. He said that all the professional athletes use it for a torn ACL and other knee injuries. It works miracles!" she beamed. "Put your leg up here," she patted her lap gently. "My dad showed me how to put it on."

Jen pulled the sock up my calf and over my tender knee, still swollen and discolored from the accident that happened months ago.

"What's the sock for?" I asked as Jen smiled back at me and gently pulled the rigid brace up my leg.

"It's a protective barrier or something like that. I don't really know, my dad just said to put a sock under the brace," Jen answered, still pulling the device gently up my leg.

The device had aluminum poles supporting the outside of the structure and neoprene material inside. Reaching down, I touched the unique padding.

"Memory foam," Jen gushed, intently fastening all the buckles and snaps that held the device to my leg. "How's that?" she asked. "Feel okay?"

Unsure of the brace, I extended my leg, stretching it beyond the bed and back down again.

"Yeah," I said cautiously.

This wasn't the first brace I had tried. In fact, it may have been the fifth or sixth, I had lost count. None of them seemed to work. They would make walking tolerable—for a few steps. Then, the pressure of the brace would send shooting pain up my thigh. This would result in weeks of therapy to try to get it matched to my stride, which never truly worked, and only caused more pain and agony with each movement. Soon, the brace would go, and the crutches would return.

Jen knew this and knew the pain that came with each new brace. Her father was one of the leading Sport Orthopedic's in the state, and I knew that it was because of Jen, and her alone, that her father gave me this brace.

"You got this," Jen said confidently, noticing my downturned eyes while I hesitantly stood.

At first, the brace was stiff. Slight pain throbbed from the weight of my body—nothing new. The true test would be walking. Crutches had been my new accessory; I refused to sit in a wheelchair or one of those boots with wheels on it, despite their amazingly mobile attributes.

Holding my arm, Jen helped maneuver me around the bed and to the daunting hallway. No excruciating pain as of yet. *This is new.*

"Okay," I said, breathing deeply.

Jen left my side and walked to the end of the hallway. Nodding her head, she motioned for me to take the first few steps. Initially, everything was fine, no alarms seemed to sound that pain was about to rock me to my core.

"Wait, wait," Jen said, walking the few steps toward me.

She leaned down, re-strapped one of the large clasps, and adjusted one of the foam pads. Jen shook her head in approval and regained her position at the end of the hall.

With each step, the pain was minimal.

"Good?" Jen asked.

"Yeah, seems good. Really good," I said, smiling larger than I had in months.

"Awesome!" Jen said taking a few steps down the stairs.

"Now, let's go," she continued.

"Umm…" I stammered. "Walking seems good, but stairs… you're crazy."

"Come on. It will be okay. Trust me," Jen said, holding out her small hand.

Taking her hand, I stepped forward. If this worked, if this brace did all that it seemed it might, I could be free.

Is it even possible? The emotional pain of the past and the physical pain of my future all cast aside, with one simple brace?

Jen and I left the warmth of my home, walked past the stone gates of the quaint subdivision, and headed down the single road into town. The much-needed air was cool against my heated cheeks. Snow lined the sidewalk, and the clouds parted, allowing the sun to warm the path before us.

Side by side, we walked slowly and cautiously, together as friends.

"Should we run?" I asked Jen, her focused face illuminating with joy as she smiled widely and nodded her head in agreement.

CHAPTER 13 THIRTEEN

Months had passed since Jen and I took that pivotal first step to my recovery. The doctors said they hadn't seen anything like it. My progress was astounding, even to me.

The winter made recovery slow, but soon the snow lifted and so did my eagerness to quicken my pace. Jen and I jogged most days. She pushed me to get out and move, despite my lack of speed. By the time the flowers began to bloom and the grass had shed its brown haze, I was running, truly running. Something I didn't think I would ever do again.

I was glad I had found running again. I loved the feeling of the wind on my face and the exertion of muscles extending through each stride. It was something I was good at before my mom died. Track was something we had shared together: meets, practices, and training sessions. When she died, I burned that part of me, like so many other things. But, now we were back together, just me and the road.

Today was like any other day. I strapped on my old running shoes and headed out the door before the sun had fully crested over the horizon. I ran my usual route through the nature trails near the ocean, around the outskirts of town, and back to *Root*, a hip café a half mile from my house.

I grabbed a strawberry and banana smoothie with an energy shot and sat at an outside table enjoying the early summer air. I let down my hair, allowing the wind to catch it in the slight breeze. I smiled as I thought of my mother; her long, chocolate brown hair, now more similar to mine, than it was before. I had been angry about so many things after she died. My appearance was one of them. I hated to look into the mirror and see my mother staring back at me. So I changed. I bleached my dark hair and cut my long locks. But, it didn't matter. My eyes were her eyes, and there wasn't anything I could do to escape them.

My smile widened at the thought of my mother, and how my appearance was reverting back to its original state, and how I was looking more like her each day. For some reason, it didn't sting as much as it had. I was happy to see her again, even if it was in my own reflection.

My knee throbbed with a dull ache, interrupting my thoughts. I propped it up on the chair next to me to reduce the intensity—*nothing a bag of ice and Advil couldn't fix.*

My mind drifted from thoughts of my mother to the bridge as it always seemed too. It was darkness either way. The pain my mother's death once caused me, was replaced with a different kind of pain—a fear induced pain. It splintered into all aspects of my life, a haunting reminder of my inevitable fate. But, through the darkness, the light that saved me always seemed to emerge.

Was it my guardian angel or merely a wonderful rescuer? I wasn't sure. Either way, I knew I had to find him. I had to find whoever saved me that night, whoever pulled me from the darkness and to the enchanting warmth of his touch.

I searched newspaper articles covering my accident—nothing. No eye-witnesses to shed light on who pulled me from the icy water, or insightful journalist uncovering my secret rescue. After I regained mobility, I hit the streets, desperate to find my own answers. Jen was right there next to me, even though she had no idea I was searching for someone. She thought I was pushing past the pain, running toward a healthier life, but I was misleading her. My intentions were on finding him.

Images filled my mind of his warming touch, the sharpness of his eyes, and the perfection of his face. His eyes haunted me with their unique beauty—different than anything I had ever seen before. They were an ocean on fire with a sapphire center and a tranquil expansion of cobalt with hints of golden flecks reaching out and pulling me into them, even in my limited memory. They say the eyes are the windows to the soul; I never understood the phrase until I saw his eyes. In that moment, I saw the one thing I never knew I was missing. The emanating light all around him—it was everywhere, all consuming. But, the light that surrounded him oddly seemed to radiate behind his eyes as well. His eyes were the light, or maybe a reflection of it. Either way, he was the key: the key to serenity, the key to finding the light, the key to my redemption.

Watching the people passing in front of me, I wondered how many other people were also destined for the darkness and never even knew it. I hadn't known anything of my fate before, thinking the life I had lived was enough for some form of peace in the end. How wrong I was.

It was a simple summer morning: women walking little ones in strollers, children riding bikes and energetically playing in their newly found freedom of summer break. Teagan had texted me late last night to meet her at *Root*, her "new thing" as she called it.

Beep, beep, beep. My phone buzzed.

"Be there in a sec," Teagan's text blinked on my outdated smartphone.

She was late, as usual; punctuality was a foreign concept to Teagan.

Looking up from my phone, I watched a pigtailed girl chasing a blond boy on a tricycle across the street. Through the girl's laughter and boy's tears, I saw *him*.

I knew right away it was my mysterious savior from the bridge. The man leaned against a light post, arms by his side. He stood still as people walked around him, going about their daily routines. He was extraordinarily tall, towering over the others around him. I could see his muscles pushing against his white shirt which clung to his biceps and chest effortlessly. His body faced my direction, but eyes did not meet mine.

Then, the mysterious man turned and locked on me. *He is looking right at me.* I froze, in both shock and utter disbelief. *I found him!*

The man's lips parted, and a flash of a memory began. "Do not be afraid," beamed in my head, the light emanating from just beyond his sapphire eyes.

As quickly as the memory appeared, it faded, and I was left staring at the man that was, without question, the savior I was searching for. His sandy blond hair, tussled in the summer's wind only added to his amazing beauty. He was the most striking person I had ever seen, man or woman—he was utter perfection.

I stood slowly. *I have to get to him.* I had to know if he was real and not my mind playing a twisted game, creating a fabricated illusion of the person I had searched for, for months. He noticed my slight movement and stiffened, pushing against the light post and standing upright. His height was even more noticeable as he stood with his chest out and shoulders back. Standing that straight and erect would look abnormal on anyone else, but on him, it only made him look more impressive.

Without taking my eyes off of my unknown savior, I stepped around my chair, pushing it to the side, and walked forward to step off the patio onto the brick-lined street.

I found him! But, who is he? Is he my guardian angel, as my nurse had suggested, or a simple hero? Either way, I had to know him. I had to meet him, talk with him, and thank him.

"Hey!" Teagan said, jumping in front of me energetically and hugging my neck tightly, breaking the hypnotic gaze my rescuer and I shared.

I squirmed in her clutches, desperate to lock eyes with the unknown man again. But, he was gone.

Without even a brief greeting, I placed my hands on Teagan's shoulders and moved her out of my view, allowing me to scan the streets for him. Again, nothing. He was gone as quickly as he had come.

"Hey?" I heard Teagan complain, but my mind was unable to focus on my friend.

Where is he?

The streets, the shops, and the park; he was nowhere to be found. I spun in circles, searching. He was gone.

Where did he go? My mind raced. *The person that saved me was here, and I saw him! And, he saw me.* My heart raced and pounded against my chest. *Now, he's gone, again.*

I felt my body move without command and sit across from Teagan. My mind was numb and yet raced all at the same time. I had found him, then he was gone. *Where did he go? Is he even real?* My heart dropped at the thought that maybe he wasn't.

"Hello?" Teagan said. "You okay?" she added noting my attention to something other than her presence.

"Yeah," I said, still scanning the people across the street from our table, hoping to find evidence of his existence.

"Sorry, I'm late. You're never going to believe this. Guess who called and wanted to *talk,*" she paused, seeing my disinterest. "You sure you're okay?"

My mind was unable to focus. All I could think of was him. *Who is he? What was he doing? Did he remember me? Where did he go? Is he even real?* The thoughts replayed over and over in my head. *I have to find out if he is real.*

"Hey," Teagan said, touching my arm with concern. "Seriously, are you okay?"

Her touch broke my repeating thoughts and brought me back to the two of us in the center of the bustling town.

"Yeah," I lied, trying to quiet my mind. "I'm good," I smiled softly attempting to reassure her feelings of my stability.

Looking into Teagan's caring eyes and gentle smile, I wanted to tell her everything about my unknown savior. I wanted to tell her about the bridge, the darkness that pulled me under, and the realization that I was destined for Hell. I wanted to tell her about the mysterious light that saved me from the demonic creatures who attempted to rip me apart.

I told myself she wouldn't understand. But the truth was, she probably would have. Both Jen and Teagan had been so amazing since my accident, but still, it was something I couldn't bring myself to tell them, not now at least, not until I found out if he was even real.

CHAPTER 14

"So, we have to talk about what you are going to do this fall?" Teagan said.

"This fall? What do you mean?" I asked.

"College. Where are you gonna go? You can't just sit around here all year," Teagan said.

"I can't?" I quickly interjected.

"No, for real, what are you thinking?"

"I dunno, I was thinking I would just take the year off. Find out what I want to do. Get my stuff together. It's been a rough year," I added softly looking down at my knee and taking the last few sips from my fruit smoothie.

Truth was, college had been the last thing on my mind. My senior year hadn't been what I hoped it would be, and finishing high school at home was definitely not how I thought it would end. I had always loved the thought of walking across the stage, receiving my diploma, turning my tassel, and throwing my hat high in the air; all while my parents sat joyfully in the grandstands. But, that dream ended the night my mother died. So instead, due to my injured leg, I graduated in the quietness of my room, reading an email my home-school advisor had sent, telling me I had passed all my finals. There were no admonishing words of wisdom for the fellow graduates, no proud-filled parental hugs, no tearful girls clinging to the hopes of future friendships. There was only a lonesome email with a simple "congrats" at the end.

"I know it has been rough, but..." Teagan said, bringing me

back to our conversation. "You can't just sit around here all year. Plus, your dad would kill you."

"Yeah, I know," I added.

I knew she was right. George would have a coronary when he found out what I wanted to do, or not do, with my college education. My lack of enthusiasm toward my future would derail the Ivy League path my father had planned for me.

"Why don't you just go to Eastern with me?" Teagan said, interrupting my thoughts.

"Eastern?"

"Yeah, Eastern Maine Community College. It's not too far, nice and small, we'd still be close to home, and it's cheap-ish…" Teagan continued to highlight the perks of her college choice.

It was something I hadn't considered, but on the surface seemed to have the answers to the problems I knew were on the horizon. And, at least my life would have direction beyond my hopeless attempts at finding my elusive savior.

"Yeah," I said.

"Yeah?" Teagan replied with a twinge of excitement.

"Yeah, it's actually a really good idea."

"Really? Ahh! We are gonna have the best time together. Oh, this is just perfect," she gushed.

"Okay, well we gotta get you registered. Let's go!" Teagan gestured as she stood and headed to her nineteen-something Toyota Camry parked adjacent to our table.

I sat contemplating the thoughts of attending the small community college, thoughts of my mother soon filled my mind. She would have loved to help with my college decisions. Sitting at the dining room table, we would have spread out all the applications to a vast number of schools. My mother and I would then choose our top locations based on education (of course) and cafeteria food variety. We would have laughed contagiously at the silliness of it. My mom would help me with every written portion of the application process as I attached my transcripts and obsessed over the possibility that I may not get in.

Maybe that is why I didn't want to go to any of the schools

George had pressured me to apply to. It wasn't what I expected it to be: a logistical strategic decision that would map out my whole future. That wasn't how it was supposed to be. It was supposed to be an exciting time of the anticipation of acceptance, and fun filled college road trips with the one I loved most, my mom. Instead, it was *only business* for my dad and loneliness for me.

Teagan opened the car door jarring my thoughts yet again, "We could hit up the library. You know no one is going to be there on summer break."

"Tea, I'll meet up with you later, I've gotta…" I stammered for the right words.

The truth was, I desperately wanted to search for him again. I had waited long enough. I had to see if I could find the man that stood in front of me only a short time before. Not knowing if he was real or a cruel joke my mind was playing on me, I was determined to find answers. College could wait. This guy, whoever he was, couldn't.

"I have this thing I gotta do. But, I will catch up with you later, and we can get me all registered and stuff," I said, walking around the car and crossing the street quickly, attempting to avoid any resistance from my bubbly friend.

"Okay, I'll call you!" she yelled, waving energetically.

I rounded the bend and headed out of town, I didn't know where to go, but I knew I had to go somewhere. Finding him was the only thing that I could think about. *What if he is the mystical being my nurse suggested? An angel? Or, would he turn out to be a simple stranger?* My heart didn't believe the latter, but I had to find out for sure.

The pavement soon changed to loose rocks, and the town slowly faded into the landscape. The sun was high overhead, pounding its rays on my already burnt shoulders. I didn't mind. I loved the warmth that it made; the way the summer blanketed you in the sun's heat, covering you up completely.

The skin on my face began to tighten, giving way to freckles dusting my burnt nose. The heat was intoxicating, the sun sending ripples of warmth flowing down my spine in slow rhythmic movements.

Soon, I noticed an odd familiarity beginning to emerge from the scenery. It was beautiful the way the wildflowers lined the dirt road. A lone cloud danced with the light of the sun in the vast blue sky. Through the clearing, I saw a rustic bridge with dark wooden beams and a narrow frame.

This was no ordinary bridge. I recognized it instantly. This was the bridge that held such dark memories, such pain, and agony. This was the bridge that almost claimed my life.

Unaware, my legs carried me to stand on the familiar boards, I grabbed the railing as I had months before, forcing the memories of that night to flood in harshly. This time, there would be no car hurling me to the water below, there would be no dark creatures pulling me under the icy water, and no magical savior rescuing me from my impending doom. Now, there was just me, the bridge, and the empty river.

The river trickling lifelessly beneath me was in complete contrast to the night of my accident. The rocks were more evident than I remembered, showing areas of the blanketed river bottom.

My head flooded with memories of the dark creatures and their ruthless intent. I tried to push past the dark images and focus on scanning the rocks below, looking for the place I first saw him. But, I couldn't. I still felt their evil presence in this haunting place.

I tried to focus and remember where I fell and where he saved me. I surveyed the banks for anything that would spark my memory.

There! I moved cautiously from the bridge, over large boulders, to below the overpass. Looking up, the height became evident, allowing me to realize the severity of my plummet that night. I had fallen over twenty feet, possibly more. The water was higher than it was now, but the fall still extreme. My injuries flashed in my mind of my broken leg and mangled knee.

"It *was* a miracle that I made it out of here alive," I mumbled to myself as I stood on the rocks.

Looking at the water, my mind flashed back to that night when the darkness encased me, the creatures pulled me in all directions, and my body failed. I began to feel the thick water filling my lungs again; the black, tar-like substance covering my throat and airways as it did once before.

My eyes shot open to the quiet stream in front of me as I gasped for air.

"Get a grip," I told myself. Perched on a large rock, I breathed the clean air into my lungs, trying to get the images out of my head.

Why did I come here? Did I think I would find him here?

"Where are you?" I yelled into the vacant scenery.

I stared into the riverbed, my memories scattered amongst its floor. I felt the darkness moving restlessly in the shallow river. It churned and agitated as if it were calling out to me. I felt their presence, those same dark creatures—they were here, again. I saw the once clear river began to change and move. It thickened and swirled, becoming muddied and dense. I felt them. I knew they were there, and I knew they saw me as well. Behind blackened waters they emerged, the dark creatures from that night on the bridge. They were even more terrifying than I remembered. The creatures twisted and moved in the pools forming between the sharp rocks. Demonic cries beckoned me to join them.

I had no idea if my mind was playing tricks on me or if the darkness had returned for me. Regardless, I knew I had to get out of here.

Running was something I didn't have the chance to do before. The darkness had attacked me at my weakest moment, the moment of my death. But, now I could run.

I pushed against the loose pavement, refusing to look back at the water I had left, and the dark memories filled with demonic creatures still so real and present in my life. I hadn't escaped them that night. They were with me all along, hiding in the shadows waiting for me to return to the place we first met.

Fear grew within me, even though I began to put distance between myself and the water, I knew I had awakened them somehow. Reminding them I was still alive must have agitated the dark creature to pursue me again. They were hungry for me, starving even. And, I had awakened them by visiting the place they had once tasted me. They wanted their meal back. They wanted me.

CHAPTER 15 FIFTEEN

I assumed my normal spot at the metal round table in the center of town. This was it; the very spot I first saw my unknown rescuer seven days, five hours, and fifty-two minutes ago—but who was counting. I had scanned the streets every day, hoping to see him again, but he never showed. I would have resumed my search this morning, like every other morning, but Teagan insisted I finally register for community college. I was happy to see her, but desperate to search for him again. After we submitted my application, I ditched Teagan at the Library, claiming George needed me at home. I hated lying to her, but I needed to find him.

As I searched again, my thoughts shifted from Teagan to Jen. She had left for school at the beginning of the summer to MSU, Maine State University, on a volleyball scholarship. It was a great opportunity, but I missed her. Teagan and I had become closer since she left, yet there was still a void that only Jen could fill.

I shook my head, trying to push past my wondering thoughts and focus on the task at hand—finding my mysterious savior. He had to be here today. I looked toward the sky, the sun was low and would soon set. I didn't have much time before it would be dark, unless… unless he wasn't real. My smile faded from the warm memories of my friends to the reoccurring thoughts of my unknown rescuer's potential fabrication. *What if he isn't real?* My heart sunk at the thought.

Looking across the bustling street, I never expected to see him casually leaning against the same light post, but there he stood.

I blinked repeatedly trying to remove the thought that my mind may have created him. I was sure to go crazy one of these days. I was stalking a man I had never met, a man that by all accounts never existed. But now, he was here, only a few yards away.

I moved quickly from my vantage point and walked along the sidewalk until I was out of his possible sightline. I couldn't lose him again, not like before.

Maybe if he didn't see me this time, he wouldn't disappear. Thoughts of the last time I saw him filled my mind. He was there one minute and gone the next. I couldn't lose him again.

I didn't take my eyes off of the unknown man as I crossed the street quickly. He rested on the post with both hands down by his side. The mysterious person was looking off to his left, same as before, except this time he did not see me. Standing behind him, yards away, on the same sidewalk made my heart flip in excitement. I had no idea what I was going to say to him, but I moved forward, intent on seeing him, disregarding any repercussions that may follow.

His muscles tensed, and he shifted his body slightly. I froze. His back flexed as he moved effortlessly toward the busy street. I followed unknowingly. My rescuer's pace quickened, gliding with elegant, graceful strides, crossing the street in a few effortless bounds. I tried to match my stride to his, but I was losing him. *I had to get closer.* He began to put distance between us, and thoughts of his previous vanishing act played out in my head.

My walk changed into a full run, and soon I had removed the gap between us. My heart raced in excitement at our proximity. He was right there. I could almost reach out and touch him. The elusive man that saved me that night on the bridge was within reach. *I found him.* He was no longer a person leaning on a lone street post, a mirage only to disappear moments later. He was moving and breathing. *He is real!*

After we crossed through the grass courtyard, he paused on the other sidewalk before stepping into the road. I waited and watched as he bent down, one knee on the asphalt and the other at a ninety-degree angle. His back, still toward me, moved rhythmically with each breath he took. On the ground beneath him, I was able to see a person lying there.

What is happening?

Pedestrians began to take notice of the individual lying in the street. It soon flooded with people gasping and moving in all around. The crowd pushed me further from my mysterious savior. A burly man stepped in my line of sight, struggling to see beyond him was useless. Desperation began to well within me. I had to get out of this crowd of bystanders. I had to see him again, retain a line of sight so he wouldn't disappear. I had to see what was happening.

I moved through the crowd, parting the bodies to see him. Then, I saw him, still perched next to a woman lying on the ground motionless. The strong frame held her head in his hands, softly and gently. Dark crimson hair flowed from the woman's head and down his strong arms, gently brushing the street below them. The woman was lifeless, her milky skin drained of all color.

He reached out to her and touched the side of her face intently. A white and blue pulse of light moved from his hand to her cheek. *What is that? Did anyone just see that? What is that light?* The crowd did not respond to this unknown energy passing between my savior and the woman. In fact, they didn't even seem to notice him at all.

Within seconds, her eyes fluttered and I saw her feet begin to twitch, then move, straightening out from underneath her.

Without hesitation, my savior lowered her head back to the ground, stood quickly, and moved away from the woman who began to regain consciousness. No longer could I call him *my* rescuer or *my* savior. Now, he was someone else's too.

What just happened? My mind raced. Through the onlookers, he began to move again. Unnoticed, he passed through the crowd beginning to encroach upon the stricken woman. His head down, he glided through the street, unseen by anyone other than myself. He ducked into a narrow alley behind the local hardware store, and I quickly followed, leaving the woman and bustling crowd behind.

What had happened back there? Who is this guy? The questions pounded against my head, demanding answers I could not give.

The alley gave way to a private courtyard in the center of

four buildings. The air was open and clear, despite the close confines of the small space. There were a few picnic benches lining the exterior walls and an archway of ivy leading to the center of the garden. I ran my hand along the blue and yellow blooms lining the stone pathway. The back wall of the garden had thick greens weaving between broken bricks and rusty pipes. His perfect frame sat in pure contrast against weathered masonry.

I froze, trying not to move a single muscle, my mind attempted to focus on who was sitting before me. *I found him.*

The man lifted his head, revealing his powerful eyes. He didn't move, frozen in shock or disbelief, I couldn't tell. He looked almost as surprised to see me as I did him. Our eyes locked. I couldn't look away, nor did I want to. Heat flushed through my body, starting deep within my gut and moving to my blushed cheeks. I had found my elusive savior, the one who pulled me from the darkness. *It's you.* I wanted to shout.

I had dreamt about this moment—what I would say when I found him and how I would thank him. But now, I just stood, every muscle transfixed by his vehement sapphire eyes. Even my words held still behind closed lips.

He looked deep into me, the same look that I had seen the night he saved me: the same magnificently brilliant eyes. His full crimson lips parted slightly as if he were about to speak, but no words emerged.

My body began to twitch in my stationary state. First, it was my leg. The pain in my knee breaking the hypnotic lock he had on me. I struggled to fight past the ache that radiated from my knee to my upper thigh, desperate to not fracture the connection I felt between us—looking away would surely do that. I had to soak it in, every last drop of it, until the moment he disappeared again. I knew it would come. One minute he would be there. The next, I would be alone.

"It's you," I managed to squeak out through quivering lips, my words shaky and voice rusty and soft. As if my words initiated a reel pulling my feet toward my unknown savior, I approached him. Just short of his strong body, with his eyes level with mine, he was silent.

What is he thinking? Who is he? What am I doing? My mind raced with questions first, then insecurities. He stood slowly, looking down at me with his piercing eyes.

I towered over most girls and guys for that matter. Most people looked up to me, but now I was looking up to this extraordinarily gorgeous man. I longed to reach out to him, to feel his skin against my own. Then, I would know if he was real, or if I was dreaming this freak encounter. I had to find out. Instead of touching him, I found my own wrist and pinched myself slightly.

My eyes instinctively followed my attempt to jolt me out of my fantasy. I half expected to wake up, full of disappointment and anguish, alone in my room.

Closing my eyes for the first time, I breathed in and out deeply. My heart ached at the unknown. I didn't want to see the empty brick wall in front of me. So I stood, eyes closed, for what seemed like hours. I took another deep breath, trying to brace myself for the inevitability that he surely disappeared into the recesses of my mind again, or to the thought that he never truly existed at all. I lifted my face tentatively, hoping he had not vanished again, yet fully expecting his absence when I opened my eyes.

My eyes opened slowly to see him still looking at me, a small smile crossed his face. It was absolutely gorgeous, making my knees weak.

"Hi," the word escaped my mouth foolishly and hung in the air between us.

His smile widened, revealing brilliant white teeth behind rose lips, illuminating his already bright eyes. I bit my lip slightly. I knew I had made a complete fool of myself.

To my complete astonishment, he spoke. "Hello."

His strong voice had a raspy tone sending a warming hum over my entire body. From a distance, he was incredibly handsome. But, up close there was no flaw I could find on his perfect form. *Who is this mysterious beauty?* My mind raced as we stood in silence, I felt myself getting lost again in the intenseness of his eyes.

His words interrupted the spell he had on me. "A-kahr-a," he spoke, moving closer with each syllable.

He gazed intently down at my innocent face, and reached his hand toward me, brushing my cheek gently with his fingers. A shock emanated through his hand onto my skin with a warming touch. I could feel the heat of his breath covering me in its perfection.

Unable to think, I quickly corrected, "It's just Kara."

My mind was mud, thick and deliberate. The only thing I could think of was the touch of his hand on my skin.

Unmoved for what felt like a lifetime of bliss, made waking my clouded mind that much more difficult. But, I had to move past the softness of his hand against my face and the luring sweetness of his breath if I wanted answers to the questions that plagued me. I had to will myself to trek through the muddled questions within my head and past the thickness and haze of his touch in order to get answers.

What is happening to me? I was standing with the man that saved me. I had found him. This was him, my mysterious rescuer. *But, why now?* I had searched for months and nothing, and then I found him. *Why? And, who is Akahra? Why did he call me that?*

My mind raced violently, demanding answers. *Who are you? What are you?* My mind begged my mouth to speak, to find answers to the questions that pounded within my head. But, my body was in full submission to his touch, as innocent as it was.

"I know," he spoke in reference to the correction of my name. "Hello, Kara."

My mind was unable to hold on to any form of reality. I desperately wanted answers, needed them, but couldn't get the words to form within my congealed mouth.

Who are you? The question rang loudest in my head, yet was unable to break the silence of our proximity. His hand dropped from my face, breaking the hold he had on me the instant his skin left mine.

As if he read my mind, he answered, "I am Evangel."

I knew he could not just be a man as I had labeled him to be. His uniqueness was all around me. He was magnificent, beautifully exquisite in every way possible. His illuminating, saving light was unseen now, yet, somehow the presence of it lingered in the air, just out of view—a blindfold soon to be taken off, exposing the luminosity I remembered.

"Evangel?" I questioned, trying to focus my spinning mind.

"You can call me Evan," he said, responding to my poor pronunciation.

The answer to one question only brought on more and more.

Who is he, really? I knew he couldn't be human; he had to be what I only dreamt of, never logistically considering the possibility of his true nature. *Is he my guardian angel? Is Evan an angel—my angel?*

"I, umm…" stammering, I tried to express the thoughts that ran through my mind desperately trying to escape. "Are you…" I attempted again, desperate to find out who he really was, yet still unable to speak the words.

Evan stood still and unmoved. He was a wonderfully carved statue as I stumbled through my attempt at mere conversation.

"Are you an angel?" I blurted from my stammering lips.

As soon as the words left my mouth, I knew how ridiculous they sounded. Whoever this was, he would surely laugh in mockery at my stupidity. He would describe how he was only a passing bystander, a man that happened to be in the right place at the right time. Sinking my head and hiding my face from what I assumed to be his judgmental gaze, embarrassment welled within me.

Before I could, before I could run and hide forever, he said softly, "I am. I'm a Shamar."

"Shamar?" I questioned.

His eyes looked into mine again, "I am a keeper, a watcher, a guardian…" He paused, then continued, "An angel, as you call it."

After a moment, I said, "Why?"

There were so many *whys*: *Why did you save me? Why are you here now?* Questions filled my head, only to have the singular word emerge from my elementary lips.

"I mean, why…" my voice trailed off.

"Why did I save you?" Evan interjected.

Nodding faintly at his intuitiveness, I desperately wanted to know his response to the many *why* questions that spun inside my head.

"You are my Charge, the one I was summoned to guard and protect," he said. "I was called to you the night on the bridge, to pull you from the darkness. I was called to save you."

Astonishment rushed over me. My nurse was right. It was my guardian angel. *He* was my guardian angel.

"You are very special. You are the Akahra," Evan continued.

Akahra? There was that name again. *What did it mean? What is it, and why is it so like my name?*

As if Evan heard the questions sounding off in my head, he answered again. "You are the Last One."

The last one? What does that mean? My mind spun in confusion. This was all so foreign and dizzying in its complexity. *I am the last one of what?*

One question answered by Evan only uncovered another, leaving no room for the basic concepts. I felt the world around me spinning and twisting ferociously. The fundamental elements of gravity holding me to the earth became shaky and rocky.

Who is this guy? An angel? Angels aren't even real or were they... He looked nothing of the iconic images I thought of to be angelic. He said I was special. The *last one?* He must be mistaken. There was nothing special about me. *And, I'm the last one? The last what?*

The questions continued to barrage my fragile mind as I reached for the brick wall beside me, no longer feeling that I had any ground to stand on. My head spun with question after question.

Evan, standing before me, began to slip away into a tornado, pirouetting manically around me. My legs buckled, and I felt myself falling to the hard ground. Instantly, a feeling of warmth encircled me with strong hands around my body. I quickly slipped beyond the two of us to a blackened still of calmness and comfort.

CHAPTER 16 SIXTEEN

I awoke to a dark room, my eyes fluttered in adjustment to the stream of light from the hallway. I lay in my bed under a quilted blanket. My shoes neatly sat in the room's entry.

How did I get here?

The last thing I remembered was meeting my mysterious rescuer. I had an amazing encounter with the man that saved me from the darkness, a man who wasn't really a man at all, but an angel named Evan.

Why did he called me Akahra? What or who is that?

As I sat up, my hands went to my throbbing head, pulsating with each pounding heartbeat.

How did I get here? The question demanded an answer that I was unable to give. An uneasy feeling swept over me while I kneaded my temples with my index fingers, intensity trying to eliminate the pain that grew with each passing second.

What if this was all a dream? A sweet, intoxicating fantasy, a disillusioned fragment of a meeting I longed for so desperately. *What if it wasn't real? Could it have been a dream?*

It had to be real. Evan had to be real. Determination eddied within and I quickly stood. *I have to find him!* With my quick movement, a bolt of pain shot from my knee to my thigh. I felt the stiffness of my tired joints throughout my entire body. A bottle of pain medication sat on the bedside table. It would help the piercing pain felt between both temples and my knee. After swallowing the two large pills, I collapsed back on the bed, my head finding its place on the pillow.

Where would he even be? It took months to find him the first time, and now he was gone, again. *Where did he go?*

Within minutes, the pounding discomfort throughout my body had dulled. I jumped in the shower allowing the heat to provide even more relief to not only my mind but my weakened knee as well. The steam became my sanctity within a cloud of soothing vapors.

Once out of the shower, the questions of how I had gotten back to my room and where Evan had gone spurred a desperate search for answers. My head no longer spun and the throbbing had all but ceased, only determination remained. *I had to find him!*

As I walked downstairs, the isolation of the quiet home hit me, my mother's absence still so greatly felt—a feeling that never truly went away. In the kitchen, I noticed something stuck to the refrigerator door. Across the front of the folded piece of paper in my father's handwriting was my name. I tried to shake the lonely thoughts while I investigated the kitchen for any evidence that my father had come and gone while I slept. I saw a half empty soda next to the sink and a candy bar wrapper crumpled on the counter. He had come and gone while I slept, without as much as a *hello*. It was hard not to be hurt.

I removed the money and threw the note and candy wrapper into the trash. I didn't have to read his words to know what it said. My father would be gone for a while, and I was alone—again.

Back up the stairs, I entered my quiet room, hoping to find any evidence of how I had gotten home after my encounter with Evan. My desk in the corner of my room was clean and organized, same as I had left it except there was a letter on its surface. It was from a university I had applied to months ago before agreeing to attend community college with Teagan. Opening the letter revealed acceptance to another Ivy League school; Yale, Harvard, Princeton, and Duke. I had my pick.

George had pushed for me to apply to all the top schools around the country. The truth was he didn't care what school I went to, as long as he could say that his daughter was attending a prestigious university. I knew George's heart was eager for me to follow in his Harvard footsteps. He was excited about the possibilities. I was not, to say the least.

George might literally die when I told him I was staying home and wouldn't be attending any of the schools of his choice. "Waste of talent" and "unused potential" were phrases my father would use when he heard of my collegiate decision to stay local and attend a community college.

I tucked the letter neatly with the others in the file cabinet under my desk. I knew the disappointment he would feel when he found out my secret, but I didn't care.

The desk chair squeaked as I leaned back, putting tension on its wobbly legs. The antique analog clock read half past nine in the evening. I had been asleep for hours. My father must have left some time before I came home or when I slept. *But, when?* Still unable to remember how I arrived in my room, I reluctantly tried putting the thoughts behind me to get some much needed rest. Curling up with a book was sure to put my wandering thoughts at bay and allow sleep to come easily. I searched my desk for the historical thriller I had just recently begun to read.

Unable to find the book on the surface of the wooden desk, I searched the contents of its rickety drawers. Amongst notepads and pens, I stumbled upon my mother's Bible I had rescued from the donation boxes the night before my accident.

I turned the worn leather cover over repeatedly in my hands, trying to uncover the mysteries the unknown book held.

"What was so special about this little thing?" I spoke quietly to myself.

I opened the cover and flipped through the thin, gold trimmed pages. It told me nothing of its life-changing abilities or *special powers* my mother claimed it had.

Quickly, I found the note my mother had left me nestled in the center of her Bible. Instead of opening it, I placed it gently on the desktop, still folded with crisp edges and handwritten script on its front. I didn't want to read it now. I couldn't take the roller coaster of emotions, with little ups and more elaborate downs that I knew would come from reading her note. Yet, somehow knowing her words were close meant that she may be too. I knew it was silly, holding onto a small piece of paper attempting to keep the essence of my mother near. But, it was all I had.

As I continued to flip through her Bible, I was about to cast it aside and regain my search for the novel when my mother's handwriting caught my eye. I found her words written in the margins in blue ink and a yellow highlighter marking the verse her commentary reflected.

For Kara, was all that she wrote.

Reading the verse, I instantly understood why my mother had selected this one for me. It was one I had heard often from years of sitting in church and from my mother. It was a verse no one could escape, a phrase that was surely displayed in every Christian's home, as it was ours.

I read John 3:16 in almost inaudible tones, "For God so loved the world that He gave His only begotten Son, that whoever believes in Him should not perish but have eternal life."

"Eternal life, what a joke," I scoffed at the idea of a belief in eternity.

My mother believed in this *eternal life* and where did that get her. She was dead. She was gone, forever. There was nothing *eternal* about that.

Flipping through the pages, another highlighted section caught my eye. I read from the same chapter.

"Most assuredly, I say to you, he who believes in Me has everlasting life. I am the bread of life. This is the bread which comes down from heaven that one may eat of it and not die. I am the living bread which came down from heaven. If anyone eats of this bread, he will live forever and the bread that I shall give is My flesh, which I shall give for the life of the world."

The pink highlighter noted the verse to be one of my mother's favorites. The words on the page seemed so foreign to me, despite my many years in the church. *How is this cryptic jargon something my mom held so dear to, when it makes no sense to me?*

A few pages later, I noticed the same familiar yellow high-lighter with *Kara* written in the margins of John chapter eight, verse twenty-four.

"Therefore, I said to you that you will <u>die</u> in your <u>sins</u>; for if you do not *believe* that I am He, <u>you will die</u> in your sins."

The underlining gave my mother's emphasis to the words which seemed to leap from the worn pages. My mother's handwriting scribbled in the margin was now not as simple as my name; instead, they housed a painful prayer that I was unable to resist reading.

Please, Lord, don't take Kara from me before she learns the truth. She will die in her sins, I know that. Please, Lord please, show her the light, so death cannot steal her from me.

Her words were crushing. How was I so transparent to the mother that had died over a year ago? How did she still know me, even from beyond the grave?

Tears trickled slowly from my eyes as I read her words over and over again. I couldn't help but hear her voice whispering in my ear, not only praying to God but to me as well, begging me to believe what she had for so long.

It was not foreign to me. How could it be? I grew up in church from Sunday school classes to Wednesday Awana meetings. It was my mother's life and in turn my own. But, there was a huge difference between the two of us. She loved the church, loved her faith, and I didn't. We were similar in so many things, but in this, we were complete opposites. *But why? Why did I not follow her?* I did in so many other things. *Why not follow in her faith as well?*

Now, after my accident, I could no longer claim ignorance to the afterlife. I knew my fate, and *life*, illustrated in the verse, was not how it ended for me. The darkness was my destiny.

I looked back to the scripture, and the underlined section, *you will die*, repeated in my head. I *was* going to die. And my death wouldn't be the same as my mother's. Death was different for her. *Can it be different for me too?* Evan had said that I wasn't "destined for the darkness" and that is why he saved me. Maybe he was right, somehow. Maybe it wasn't my fate, or at least, it didn't have to be.

Maybe I didn't have a curse on my soul. Maybe there was still hope for me.

But, maybe not. Maybe I was destined for the darkness and that is why they returned the other day at the bridge. They knew it too. It was just a matter of time until we met again.

Negative thoughts crashed around my mind. I shut the Bible and slid it back into the side drawer. I knew it was too late for me. Too late to erase the words read tonight, too late to save my soul, and too late for any form of redemption.

I had tasted death, or rather, it had tasted me. And, there was nothing sweet about it. There was no escaping the darkness, that night on the bridge, or the next.

My cheeks soon became damp with salty tears. I lay on my bed hoping sleep would ease the depravity I felt welling within my chest. As I drifted off to sleep, I tried to push back the dark memories and focus on Evan and our meeting, but all I could see was an all-consuming blackness.

CHAPTER 17 SEVENTEEN

Hours later, I awoke in a cold sweat, not able to remember what had startled me awake, jolting me out of my bed and sending me pounding back down in an unknown terror.

The room was black with only a glimmer of evening light shining behind closed curtains. Taking a deep breath, I tried to remove a blackness that seemed to cloak my memories. An uneasy feeling churned deep within my stomach, sending the hair upright on the back of my neck and causing chilled goosebumps to emerge on my arms. Even though the dreams origins were unknown, my body seemed to remember as it shook with fear.

What was the nightmare about? What's the last thing I can remember?

I had read my mother's Bible, laid down, and had fallen asleep. *What did I dream about that has me so shaken?*

I tried to search my mind. Sifting through the blackness was difficult, but soon, flashes of the nightmare began to play in my head. Like an old movie projector spitting out a new reel violently, I began to remember.

The bridge. I was standing on the planks, holding onto the rail desperately, as a growling began in the distance. Then, in an instant, a cloud of darkness began to encircle me on the bridge, starting at my feet and moving up my body to my chest. Tornadic smoke crept up my body in a whirlwind of activity. Frozen, I clung to the bridge, hoping my hands would hold, and the dark cloud wouldn't cover me completely. But it was no use. Within seconds an oblivion of complete nothingness overtook me.

That was it. There was no boogie man or masked hillbilly yielding a screaming chainsaw. There was only darkness.

Daylight couldn't come soon enough. I quivered under the heavy blanket, which I had curled up with on the upholstered window seat, looking out at the night sky. I fell asleep waiting for the first indication of the morning's light. When I awoke this time, it was almost noon; the sun was hot on my face, and my neck was stiff from my choice of sleeping arrangements. Stretching, then quickly getting dressed, I rushed downstairs and out the door in under a few minutes.

I had to find Evan. I needed answers. Within minutes, I was out the door and on my bike heading into town. Desperate to find him again, images from my nightmare replayed in my mind, pushing me to peddle harder against the uneven road.

CHAPTER 18 EIGHTEEN

A short bike ride into town allowed me to think of Evan, putting the horrors from my nightmare behind me. I peddled hard, desperate to find him again. I needed answers. I needed help from the darkness. But, maybe even more, I just needed him.

Arriving in town, I was surprised to see the usually busy streets, calm and empty. Two people entered a shop in an old building around the square. A few cars parked along the road adding to the desolate feeling in the air. It was a ghost town.

The sun overhead beamed down with the intense brightness of a full summer day. I tried to hold my gaze, to look directly into the sun. Even though you were not supposed to stare at it, I did anyways. My eyes begged me to close their thin lids, seeking protection from the bright rays. Unable to hold it any longer, my eyelids forced themselves closed, saving my eyes from the burning they had begun to feel. A few watery drops emerged from the corners of my eyes, soothing the sun's stinging power.

The light, still bright under my closed lids, made me think of Evan and the intensity surrounding him that night on the bridge. His light was similar to the sun, that even though it hurt to look at, you longed for it just the same.

After my eyes adjusted, I scanned the streets in search for Evan and his light. But, I couldn't find him anywhere.

After hours of searching and finding nothing, I decided to head home. Walking my bike slowly, instead of peddling the short distance, seemed to reflect my downward mood.

"Hey!" a deep, low voice spoke from behind me.

I spun around quickly, my mind raced at the person I might see. *Evan? Did I find him again? Or rather, did he find me?* My heart raced as I kicked the stand to hold the bike in place and turned to see the man behind me.

Kale stood, smiling widely at me. My heart fell at the disappointment of not seeing Evan.

"Oh, hey," I said, obvious regret plastered over my sunburnt face.

"Well, good to see you, too," Kale said, with a hint of irritation cloaked by a twinge of arrogance that I found oddly attractive.

"No… Hey!" I said in an attempt to sound more enthusiastic.

Truth is, on any other day, I would have been excited to see Kale. He had been distant since my hospital stay, with limited interactions only a few text messages here and there. I had missed him and the friendship we shared, even the closeness we once had. We used to be everything to each other before I threw it away. Kale hadn't completely disappeared. He was still here, still a friend in my life, even if it was on a microscopic level.

Every now and then, I would think of him, of how things used to be when we were together. He was the first boy I had ever held hands with, dated, or even kissed. Kale held such a strong place in my heart.

My thoughts quickly went to a time we shared such a *first*. It was my freshman year of high school when everything you thought you knew from previous years of education came crashing in on you in a hierarchy of mean girls and adolescent boys.

Teagan was beginning to find who she was in the opposite sex. "Boy Crazy," Jen called it, who had no real interest in anything other than volleyball. My curiosity for boys floated somewhere in the middle. Kale had been one of my best friends since we were eight. He had moved into our quaint subdivision that year, our parents instantly becoming friends. We too became close, playing together almost every day. As the innocent years of *capture the flag* and *hide 'n go seek* faded, our friendship only strengthened.

Middle school had posed a challenge with the separation between boys and girls emerging. At the start of eighth grade, Kale had begun to show interest in me as more than a friend. Hard as it was, he still was my best friend, and I didn't see him in the same way.

The beginning of freshman year was different. Kale had gone away to camp for the summer, and when he returned, everything had changed. His once lanky body no longer held the frail, thin appearance it once had. The evidence of muscles was not the only difference; his once boyish, round face was now longer and leaner with a square jaw and enhanced cheekbones. Kale was different, he had grown up, and I wasn't the only girl that had noticed.

It was our first school dance, and he had asked Sandra Miller, a well-endowed, curvy blond who had blossomed years before her peers. She was every girl's worst nightmare and every boy's fantasy. Jealousy grew within me the entire night while I watched the two of them hold each other on the dance floor. I can remember thinking that he was gone forever, that he would no longer be *my* Kale, but now someone else's. Before the dance had ended, I walked home, unable to stand seeing Kale with her for another minute.

To my surprise, Kale had chased after me. We stood alone on the dark sidewalk for minutes before either one of us spoke. And then, before he said anything, before I told him how I wanted to be the one dancing with him that night, before I could say anything at all, he kissed me. It was my first kiss, followed by the first time I had held hands with a boy, as we walked home together. From that moment on, we were inseparable. We were happy, maybe even in love.

Standing in front of him now, the memories of that night seemed so present, yet extremely distant, separated by a time that we could never get back. The girl I used to be, I honestly didn't recognize her. She was so extremely naive to the world she thought still had *fairytales* and *happy endings*. Those things didn't exist. And, any future happiness with Kale died when my mother did.

The questions of why I had pushed him away and allowed our premature love to dissolve filled my mind.

"How ya been?" he asked, walking over and standing next to me on the narrow sidewalk.

"Good," I shrugged, "Pretty good, I guess." I fumbled with

my words as he moved closer, allowing someone to pass by us on the sidewalk, his arm grazing mine.

With Kale's nearness, a twinge of pain emerged under my chest, an ache echoed from a time when his touch would have made my heart skip in excitement, instead of the sadness it now felt.

"Sorry," he said, noticing our proximity and stepping away quickly.

"So, how have you been?" I asked.

"Good," he answered. "Going to state with Jen in the fall. Looking forward to it, I guess. It's school. You know me and school. But, Jen said she'll help me get through the class junk, and there's a pretty good intramural lacrosse team that I wanna check-out before orientation stuff. I'll probably head up there in the next few days and check it out."

"Sweet, wait… with Jen?" I asked confused by the way he fit Jen into his sentence.

"Yeah," he said.

"Oh, cool. I didn't know that."

"She didn't tell you?" Kale asked.

"No?" I questioned.

Why *hadn't* Jen told me Kale was going to the same university as her? Jen and Teagan always told me of Kale's latest sporting achievements or flops for that matter. We would laugh at the lack of true athletic male talent at our school, Jen always claiming total domination over any sporting team she could get her hands on. We would laugh for hours at their inability to let a girl win without faking a twisted ankle, weather interference, or some other lame excuse.

Why didn't she tell me about Kale? I had talked with her the other day about school, and she made no mention of him. "State was fun," Jen had said. There was nothing about Kale going to school with her. Surely she knew, or maybe that's what Kale was telling me.

Awkwardness occupied the air between the two of us as I mulled over my lack of information.

"I better go," I said, as I made a quick exit and continued

home in thought as to why Jen hadn't told me about Kale.

Something seemed off and unlike Jen, or Teagan for that matter, who would update me almost daily on literally everyone from our senior class. Not to have mentioned Kale's college decision, and it being where Jen was attending, made it that much stranger.

As soon as I entered the front door to the house, I sat at the kitchen counter and called Jen, sure to get an answer as to why she hadn't told me Kale was joining her at the university. The voicemail picked up to her usual chime of *leave a message at the beep.*

"Hey, it's Kara. Talked to Kale… you should have told me… it's cool, though. Well, give me a buzz so we can catch up." I hung up, not expecting my phone to ring back moments later with Jen's name flashing on its iridescent screen.

"Hey, I just left you a message," I said quickly before she could talk.

"Yeah, I'm so relieved. I thought you were gonna be ticked, that's why I didn't say anything. You're not mad right?" Jen questioned after a moment's pause.

"Um, no, of course not. Why would I be? I think it's cool you guys have each other there," I said.

"Oh, good," Jen exhaled loudly. "Kale wasn't sure how you would take it. And I didn't want to make you upset. It isn't serious or anything, but… it's cool we will be going to school together. I mean, then we at least have a chance at making it. School can pull people apart, and we didn't want that. Oh, I'm so glad you are cool with us being together. Well hey, I gotta run, but I'll call you later. Bye, girl!"

Click!

The phone went silent, my mind numb to the one-sided conversation we just had.

Quickly, I sent a text with four simple words, "We need to talk!"

Within seconds, the phone buzzed back with, "Be right over."

My mind raced at the thought of Jen and Kale together—a couple. *How long had this been going on? Why didn't she tell me about it?*

So many questions stirred in my head. I wasn't sure how I was supposed to feel. My best friend dating my ex—something didn't feel right about this.

CHAPTER 19 NINETEEN

A knock on the door jarred my thoughts from their questioning state. *Kale and Jen. Together. Boyfriend and girlfriend. A couple.*

All the labels were strewn out in front of me; no matter the title I put on them, it was offsetting. They were my best friends, and Kale was once my boyfriend. *This broke some kind of code, didn't it?* I thought, standing to answer the door.

Were they keeping it from me? For how long? And, why?

"Coming!" I yelled, approaching the door and opening it quickly.

"Hey! Thanks for coming over," I said.

"Yeah, what's up? Your message seemed kinda urgent, and I was just heading into town. What's going on?" Teagan chirped.

Teagan sat at the kitchen island as I grabbed her a drink from the fridge and leaned my body on the cool stone slab.

"So, I talked to Jen," I spoke, drawing out each word deliberately.

"Oh," Teagan said popping open her soda and taking a long swig. "She told you?"

"You knew!" I blurted out uncontrollably.

"Yeah, well, it wasn't my place to tell," she said defensively.

I rolled my eyes and turned to grab myself a soda. Teagan interjected, "Hey, don't get mad at me. I told her to tell you, but she didn't want you getting all…"

"All what?" Anger welled within me as I spun back to face

Teagan. I could tell this was a secret that had been going on much longer.

"Well," she said motioning to me as I manically took a long drink of my soda and began to pace around the open kitchen floor-plan.

"How am I supposed to act? Everyone has been keeping a secret from me, and for how long?"

Teagan's silence told me everything I needed to know. It had been going on for a long time.

"How long?" I repeated.

"It's been awhile," Teagan vaguely answered.

"How long?" I said firmly.

"Okay, it's been since you got hurt, and we started talking again."

"What?" I said, shocked.

"Listen, they had just started talking and didn't want to say anything if it wasn't going anywhere. Then, I guess it went some-where, and they didn't want to hurt you. You were just, I dunno, not in a good place. And, we just were getting our friendships back together. No one wanted to mess anything up."

"So everyone lied to me… for months?"

My head spun, I knew it must have been something more than what Jen had projected it to be on the phone. They were seri-ous—very serious.

"Does she love him?" I asked from the silence, not wanting to even allow myself to utter the words.

After a moment's hesitation, Teagan answered, "Yeah…" she paused and then spoke with heavy words. "And, Kale loves her too," she said slowly so the words wouldn't hurt, as if speaking them softly would help their sting.

Betrayal filled my head and heart. Jen was the one person that I counted on now, that I fully trusted. Sure, Teagan and I were close but not as close as Jen and I. We were even closer now than before my mom died. And, Kale, well that was why he didn't have much contact with me, why he had kept his distance. He had Jen.

"Why didn't they just tell me," I asked, already knowing the answer.

Teagan had made it known. My frail state had sent them into hiding, pushing my friends away, yet again. Dropping my head to rest on the cool granite, I felt my newly restored friendships slipping away.

Teagan put her hand on my shoulder, attempting to comfort my fragile heart. She didn't understand the severity of their actions—their lies. *They hid this from me, all of them.* But, it was more than the lies that hurt. A piece of my heart I held to from before; a possibility of rekindled love, a hope of how life was without death, was now gone. I would never have a friendship, or even love with Kale again. Teagan's touch just mocked the failing trust I had in her—in all of them.

"Don't," I said, brushing off Teagan's kind gesture with the shrug of my shoulder.

Reluctant to let her or anyone see I was hurting, I attempted to mend my snub, "It's really no big deal. I'm fine."

"You sure?" Teagan questioned.

"Yeah, for sure. No big deal," I said, "I'm totally beat. I'm gonna just crash."

"Alright, well, if you wanna talk I'm here for you." Teagan paused, "You sure you're alright?"

"I'm fine," I lied, as I ushered her out the door, quickly shutting it behind her.

I collapsed onto the floor behind the closed door, my hands covered my eyes trying to hide the images my mind crafted of Kale and Jen together: pictures of Jen laughing at his immature jokes, Kale holding her hand as they walked to class, and Jen kissing his chiseled check. It was all just too much.

Such a weak heart I had. *Why can't I just laugh it off?* My emotions were overtaking at times, and this was one of them. Kale and I hadn't been together for over a year. *Why did it hurt this bad?* Deep down, I knew there was no longer any lingering feeling between Kale and me, and there was no reason I should be hurt. But still, here I was, crumbled on the floor, obviously distraught for a love I would never share with Kale. It was a friendship broken by not only time but new love, and lost all the same.

Defeated at my inability to control my emotions, I went upstairs and fell into bed. The weight of the world rested on my chest as it rose and fell with each labored breath.

Why is this world so hard? Why does everything hurt so much?

Tears didn't come, as much as I would have loved the emotional release. Instead, the thoughts of broken friendships and torn love twisted and churned into bitter defeat. Soon only the darkness remained.

CHAPTER 20 TWENT

From the first moment I saw Evan, the dreams began: the warm promise of his touch, his tender smile, the perfection of his light. Unfortunately, my dreams also consisted of something much darker.

Each dream began differently.

Some began with Evan standing across the street as I first saw him. He was perfect, just as I remembered. Light emanated from behind, covering him in a fantastic brilliance. My arms outstretched. I longed to feel the warmth of his light. But, before I could reach my mysterious savior, the darkness entered my dream turning it into a twisted nightmare. There was an unknown dark creature lurking in the shadows, stalking Evan. I tried to call out to him and warn him of the menacing beast, but my voice could not escape my quivering lips. Soon, the darkness was all around him with the dark creature leading the hunt. Wrapping up his legs, the darkness began to snuff out his light, suffocating him in the process. *No!* I tried to call out to him. But it was useless. Within minutes only the darkness remained. Evan and his light were gone.

Other dreams began with the darkness, a twisting tornado of menacing wind roaring to life in the distance. I stood, frozen in fear. As it neared, the single cyclone broke into three uniquely dark entities within the tornadic movement. These entities morphed into animalistic creatures, viciously bounding toward me. Seconds before they reached me, the blackened clouds parted to allow for a single beam of light to penetrate the main creature's frame. On impact, the beast reeled, crashing to the ground in defeat. The other two monsters disintegrated when the single beam of light burst from the clouds illuminating the entire valley, covering everything in its all-consuming light.

Light or dark, dark or light, either way, one overcame the other.

Tonight was no different.

I was on the bridge and could see the water agitating below. Black ripples mixed with the cobalt water wildly beneath me. There was no placid sunset, only a darkened sky with clouds twisting eerily to the heavens. Gripping the bridge railing tightly, I knew what was to come. It was the same that night, and every night to follow.

A low growl pulled my attention to the forest just beyond the bridge. Within an instant, a dark creature emerged from the woodline. It screamed and roared, barreling down the dirt road toward me. The creature's hell-bent eyes and massive frame sent a shiver of fear down my spine. Even from my distance, the bridge's footboards shook with each hardy lunge. The creature's raging eyes stared at me through our distance, gnashing teeth glistened with intent as it continued bounding toward me.

I closed my eyes tightly, bracing for the attack I knew would follow. When it did, the pain was instantaneous. I flew into the air and over the railing. Falling slowly, time seemed to stop; I hung in mid-air, just above the icy river. Out of the dark water a hand emerged, and I felt it grip onto my ankle.

The nightmare's validity had me overtaken with fear. *It's just a dream.* I tried to tell myself.

The water roared to life below me, smacking at my exposed feet with the pain of a thousand knives. The hand gripped harder, digging barbs into my supple skin, pulling me to the frosted water below. I scratched at the air, frantically trying to hold onto anything that could save me from the creature pulling me closer and closer toward its evil abyss.

Wake up! Wake up! My mind pleaded. There was no pinching me awake from this evil, no escape from this hell.

Unable to escape, the satanic hand pulled me into the water.

I struggled to keep my head above the surface, but the water quickly changed into a black tar wrapping itself around me like a vine crawling upward.

As the water encased me in its darkness, I thought of Evan. In real life, not this dream, this was the moment Evan would reach down and save me from death. But, without his light, the darkness would cover me completely, filling me to my brim. Tonight, I would then fade into a dark cold, an emptiness that left me alone in my room shaking with fear when I awoke.

I had to cling to the hope of Evan's light; his warmth that saved me that night, maybe it could reach into this realm and wake me from this horror.

Hope welled within me at the possibility of Evan saving me in my nightmare, that he would come and rescue me again, pull me out of this ultimate destruction. I thought of his warm touch, his urgent sapphire eyes that demanded I join him in the light.

The tarlike substance coiling around me began to reel at the thought of Evan's light entering my mind. Not wanting to relinquish the hold the darkness had on me, two creatures sunk their talons deep into my calf.

I lifted my head and screamed in pain, allowing more of the icy water to fill my already full lungs. It was then that I saw the ominous clouds above. Through them, I searched for a glimmer of light, a small star in the sky, anything that could pull me out of my dream's fearful embrace.

Then, I saw it behind the dark clouds: a faint light glimmering softly amongst the night's sky. Focusing my eyes, I saw the light grow brighter and stronger. Moving closer, the light reached my head and over my body, covering me in its protective power. The light traveled down my body toward the dark creatures still holding onto my legs. Their grips relinquished. The cold sting housed within their touch slowly faded. Wrapped in light, a calming warmth permeated my fears. The torturous dream did not have its dark hold on me any longer. Reaching toward the light, I demanded my mind to awaken.

Wake up. I pleaded one last time.

In that moment, I sat up sharply in a cold sweat, tears running down my cheeks, gasping for air.

My hands went to my lower legs that ached from the creatures' dream induced hold. The realness of the nightmare made it difficult to concentrate on what was happening. My quivering hand jerked away quickly, shocked by the cold that radiated off my upper leg and the tender abrasions of open wounds. I felt a wet, thick substance on my fingers, and brought my hand to my face in an attempt to see the slick element in my low lit bedroom. Unable to see anything, I switched the lamp on that sat on the nightstand beside my bed. The light from under the limited shade allowed me to recognize the substance I moved between my fingers.

Blood. Crimson, thick, blood.

An addition of a black substance mixed with the vibrancy of red covered my fingers and dripped down my hand.

Looking down at my legs, I saw the deep claw marks, and fresh blood mixed with an unknown, toxic black material. Horror filled my whole being.

What is going on? What is happening?

Then, the pain began. First, it was a slow, dull ache. Then, it progressed and intensified, radiating from my calves to my knees and upper legs. I could feel the darkness filling me up.

Quickly, I grabbed the throw blanket next to my bed and frantically wiped the blood and blackness from my legs. Removing the tar-like substance allowed for the pain to dissipate slightly. Black and crimson hues stained the blanket's fabric. I clung to it, in disbelief. The chill of the creatures' touch still felt on my exposed limbs. An aching, dull throb of fresh lacerations pounded in my calves with each beat of my terror-stricken heart.

I tucked my feet under my covers and pulled the blanket over my legs and around my body, attempting to alleviate the chill and pain that pulsed within them.

What just happened? I was dreaming. It was only a nightmare. It had to be. But the creatures attack in my dream hurt me, really hurt me. How is this possible?

My mind was racing. I rubbed my hands on my head and

tried to forget the nightmare that just unfolded. A sickening feeling welled within me. This was not just a bad dream with shadows or things that go *bump in the night*. It was more than that. There was a real and present darkness out there, a pure evil that was coming for me—coming to finish what they started on the bridge.

"It was just a dream," I said aloud in the empty room, as if saying the words would make it true. "It was just a dream," I repeated over and over. I lay in my bed, my body trembled waiting for morning to come, begging my mind to believe the phrase I knew to be false.

This was no dream.

CHAPTER 21

The first hint of light peered through my drawn curtains, illuminating the room and shining onto the place I once considered *safe*. Still trembling, I sat with the covers tucked tightly under my chin, my eyes ached from keeping watch the remainder of the night.

What happened? What is this darkness and why is it after me?

Thankfully, the questions were the only things that continued that night, not allowing sleep to come. I had fought valiantly to stay awake, desperate to keep the monsters to their corner and the nightmares at bay. When my eyes begged for relief and demanded sleep, I kept hold of the pain, though now dull, that I felt on my legs. It was a hurt that came from the nightmarish creatures which had broken into my reality, ripping into me from my dream. The veil was torn. The dark creatures had left their metaphysical world and found a hold in mine.

But, how is it even possible?

I had to find Evan. He had defeated the darkness before, saving me that night on the bridge with his powerful light. Maybe he could keep the dark creatures in my dreams to the limitations of my mind. Or, better yet, maybe Evan could eliminate them completely, sending them back to where they came from.

I had to find him. I had to find my savior again. I needed my guardian angel, now more than ever.

My body desperately wanted to bask in the sun's warmth that flooded my room. I was amazed at how urgent I was for it and how often I had taken it for granted. The sun's warmth encased me as I stood, allowing the light to invigorate my bones.

I quickly dressed; it was urgent I find Evan. Rushing out the door and hurrying into town, my search for him began again.

Where is he? Would I even see him again? I had to find him, I needed Evan. I tried to think of the last time I saw him, where he was and what he was doing. If I could understand what Evan was doing in town the other day, maybe I could find him again.

As I walked by a small clothing boutique, I noticed how close it was to the alley where I first met Evan. Inside the small shop, I hoped to find clues that would direct me to his whereabouts.

The shop had an array of items from purses hanging neatly on decorative hooks to colorful knit scarves draped over rustic chairs. A random collection of shoes caught my eye in the corner and a faceless manikin stood in front of the window.

"Can I help you with anything?" a voice spoke from behind a weathered table, layered with ornate jewelry. The petite woman had vibrant red hair that curled erratically in all directions. She stepped around the counter and offered to show me some of her newest items.

There was a familiarity to the woman, but I was unable to locate her in my already jumbled mind. I had seen her before, I was sure of it.

I followed her to a collection of shirts and stacks of tailored jeans before I attempted conversation.

"This shop is really great," I said.

"Oh, thank you," the woman said, "I'm Julie."

"Hi, I'm Kara. I can't believe I haven't been in here before."

Julie just shrugged.

"You've got some great stuff," I said, admiring a navy dress hanging on a handmade rack. After a few lingering minutes, I continued, "Have you been here awhile?"

"A few years," Julie said as she folded a pair of jeans from the stack next to me.

Julie fluffed her hair, tossing her crimson curls over her shoulder. A flash shot through my mind, and instantly I knew I had in fact seen this woman before.

It was the woman on the street that day: the woman Evan saved. The red hair, her delicate frame, her pale skin—it was defiantly her.

"Can I ask you something?" I said softly, walking to the woman who continued to fold the pile of stone-washed jeans.

"Sure," Julie said putting down her work and turning to face me.

"Were you that woman that collapsed in the street the other day?"

Pain filled her face instantly. She quickly turned and moved to the front of the store.

I paused searching for the right words, "I'm sorry; I just thought I saw you the other day. And, I wanted to see if you were okay. *If* it was you?"

"It was," she said quietly, turning back to me after a long pause.

"*Are* you okay?" I asked.

"Yes," she nodded, "I'm fine. I just had a little scare, that's all."

I longed to ask Julie more questions, but she was no longer the inviting woman I first met.

"I'm sorry, I shouldn't have asked. You just looked really familiar, and I thought I saw you the other day. I guess I just wanted to see if you were okay. I'm sorry," I said.

"No, it is okay. It was just a very scary day. And, everyone has been coming in to check on me. I thought that maybe you were here to actually buy something. But, I guess you were just curious too. Everyone seems to be," Julie said.

"Small town," I shrugged, trying to give some justification to the busy-bodies that buzzed her store with questions.

"But, I really was looking for a new shirt," I lied, trying to regain her trust.

I suppose I could use a new top.

The truth was I hadn't been shopping for new clothes since Jen had taken me to the city with her to prepare for school. Teagan joined us as the fashion consultant. We shopped at a large supermarket chain for all the basic college dorm necessities, and then, went to the mall to find the clothes needed for the upcoming school year. We had a fantastic time together, just the three of us. It was before I knew the truth. They had lied to me about Jen and Kale's relationship. It was all a lie.

"Oh, really, you want to *actually* buy something? Great!" Julie said, her demeanor warmed instantly.

I followed her as she guided me to a table with assorted tees. Looking through the casual tank tops, long sleeve button downs, and blouses I repressed the memories of my last shopping trip filled with girlish giggles and friendly voices. I had to focus on finding Evan, and Julie might have the answers.

"It was a stroke," Julie said, breaking the silence. "The other day, I had a stroke."

"A stroke? Wow, and you're here. I mean... you're working...you're okay?" I said, unable to hide my surprise. "It just happened the other day?"

"Yeah, well, I was lucky, I guess. Plus, someone has to run this place. Seeing how we are so very busy," she said with heavy sarcasm, motioning the empty store. "I am just glad I'm alive," Julie added.

"I know how that is," the words rushed out before I could hold them back.

"You do?" she questioned.

Before I could answer, "Wait, wait. I thought I knew you from somewhere. You are Lily's girl, right?" Julie asked.

"You knew my mom?"

"My little girl was in her class. She loved her. Lily was the best teacher, and *so* sweet," she said.

"She was," I added, my mind instantly going to the mother I missed desperately.

We both smiled as our minds filled with memories of Lily.

"You had a close call yourself, didn't you?" Julie asked.

"Yeah, it was a little while ago. But, yeah, I guess I'm sort of lucky too," I said while choosing a white, loose-cut tank from a stack of basic colors. I held it up for approval. Julie nodded with a smile.

Walking over to the counter, "We are both in the club now," Julie said over her shoulder.

My eyebrows furrowed in her reference to a *club*. Julie came to stand behind the antique cash register and entered the information from the hand-made tag, not yet looking up at my bewildered expression.

Julie looked up and smiled widely. "The, *we-should've-died* club," she said, giggling slightly. Her smile quickly faded and anxiety filled her eyes as the weight of her own words sunk in.

Julie seemed to feel the same way I did when thinking of how I almost died and how quickly this life was almost over. We both did have something in common despite the *death club* Julie had pointed out. A heroic, other worldly being had saved us both. *But, did she know that?* I had to find out if she saw anything or knew anything about her rescuer. Maybe she saw Evan or even knew where I could find him.

"So, did you see anything?" I blurted out awkwardly, "I mean, like when I was in the accident I saw this really bright light. I read that some people see that when they, you know, die… or almost die. I dunno, just wondering if you did too," I paused realizing how ridiculous my statement must have sounded.

Julie looked at me with question, then concern.

"Sorry," I said, "I shouldn't have said anything. I just… I've never known anyone that is in this *we-should've-died* club." I laughed uncomfortably.

"No, it's alright, I was just thinking," Julie said putting the shirt in a paper bag with the store's logo on the front. I slid a folded twenty dollar bill across the counter and smiled kindly.

"I don't remember a light," Julie said. "But, I do remember a warmth that overcame me. It was like a warm hug. Wow, that sounds crazy. I can't believe I just said that. I haven't told anyone about that. You must think I am completely nuts?"

"No. Not at all," I said, gathering my change and sending a comforting smile in the direction of the kind woman who knew nothing of her savior except the warming touch I too remembered.

"Well, it was nice talking to you," I said.

"You too. Come by anytime and visit, or if you need to talk, I'm always here." Julie said, waving goodbye as I left the shop.

She was a sweet woman, but she did not remember Evan. It was a dead-end, leaving me without any idea where Evan could be.

Why did she not remember her savior like I did? And, where can I find him? Where is he?

Thoughts of Evan's presence ran through my mind. *What were the similarities between Julie's encounter and my own?*

"We should have died," I said Julie's comment aloud.

Instantly, I knew where I had to go to find him. I knew where Evan would be.

CHAPTER 22

Despite my discomfort, I was determined to find Evan here. The large automatic doors opened and instantly the immaculate facility brought back painful memories. The juxtaposing smells of latex and bad cafeteria food wafted past my nose sending a shiver of anxiety down my spine.

This is where I awoke, broken and bruised, after my accident, and where my mother took her last breath. It was a building encased in death. Mankind's fatality poured out a highly circulated ventilation system roaring overhead, pushing cold gusts onto the back of my neck. I wanted to run, escape the feeling of death looming in the claustrophobic corridors. But, I had to find Evan. I was desperate. There was no other place to go, no other options. It was the hospital or back to square one: meandering town square in hopes of seeing a glimpse of him again. I couldn't go another night without finding Evan and seeking his protection.

As I walked past the neon *Emergency Room* sign, I remembered my mother. The ER bustled that night: a young child cuddled under his mother's arm, coughing uncontrollably, an older man had a large cut on his arm that was in desperate need of stitches, and a woman breathed heavily, clutching her pregnant belly while her husband paced frantically around the crowded space. My mother had come by ambulance, and I had followed the speeding vehicle.

Standing in front of the ER counter, I felt the same feelings from that night come rushing back in.

I demanded the receptionist tell me where my mother was. Soon, the ER doctor pushed through the steel doors, motioning me to join my mother in her curtained room. We sat together on the hospital cot while monitors beeped and chimed with life. In that moment, I truly thought everything would be fine, that my mother would be alright. Finding her on the kitchen floor unresponsive was terrifying. She had slipped or become light headed for some reason. I didn't want to think it could be something serious. If I had only known that almost a year later I would be sitting in the exact same hospital, yet instead of listening to the machines teaming with life, I would hear a steady tone indicating her death.

Today, the ER was not the same bustling environment my mind remembered. Instead, it was quiet and orderly.

An older woman sat behind a reception desk. "Can I help you, Miss?" she asked kindly.

"Umm…" I thought carefully. I knew I couldn't say I was looking for my mysterious angelic savior. I would be committed to the psychiatric floor before I could recant.

"What floor is surgical?" I managed to ask.

"Down the hall to your right. Take the elevator to the fifth floor."

"Thanks," I said as I moved toward the elevator. Once there I illuminated the *up* arrow and contemplated why I had even asked to go to that floor.

Once inside the metal enclosure, the overhead light began to flicker. An uneasy feeling turned my stomach. I had never had a particular liking to the dark; but ever since the bridge, I was downright terrified of it. I had to get out of this black box.

My hand went to the third button as it illuminated, but I wasn't quick enough, so the slow ascent and flickering lights continued. My heart began to quicken. The transition between the third and fourth floor seemed to take minutes instead of seconds. With every flicker of the overhead light, it seemed to take longer to regain its full power, leaving me in darkness as the elevator inched along. Then, it came to an instant halt just past the fourth floor, sending my hands to each side in attempts at remaining upright. The lights held for only a second before sending me back into complete darkness. Except for this time, they didn't come back on. I waited in the black space, my heart pounding against my chest, hoping the elevator would continue to the next floor. It didn't.

I punched the buttons for each floor hoping one would get me out of this confined space. It didn't work. I felt the walls closing in on me. Then, I heard it. At first, it was a low rumble just below me. *Maybe the elevator is trying to start up again.* But, it didn't move, and the noises only continued. The rumble gained in strength. It was just below me. Through the rumble, a growl became clear, not from one, but two of something. My heart knew what my head didn't want to believe. *The dark creatures are back!* My stomach dropped to the bottom of the shaft and my heart leapt from my chest.

What is happening? My hands flew to the buttons again. I punched it repeatedly hoping I would find the emergency button and have the doors open to secure my escape. The noise continued with a loud bang on the ceiling. The dark creatures *were* back.

"Open! Open!" I commanded the doors still pounding on the buttons.

To my relief, they opened to the fifth floor and light filled the elevator. My legs hurled me toward the bright hall, my body lunging forward without thought or hesitation. Behind me, I saw the overhead light in the elevator resume its power, blinking only once, then fully lit. There were no more sounds of any dark creatures. The doors closed, and the elevator continued onto its next floor without me.

My chest felt tight. *What just happened?* I looked around trying to find answers to my fearful encounter, but I only saw empty corridors. *It's just my imagination.* I tried to tell myself, over and over again.

Eventually, it worked. My breaths evened and my racing mind steadied. If my previous desperation for Evan wasn't enough, now it had become imperative.

Unfortunately, there was nothing. There was no Evan, no sign of him anywhere, just empty halls and closed doors.

What did I expect to see, him sitting beside a dying man's bed or holding an elderly woman's hand? Why am I even here?

Questioning myself, I wandered into the waiting room trying to find a soda machine or candy bar dispenser—anything to divert my attention of my complete failure and inability to find Evan.

Against the back wall of the room, a woman clung to a beaded rosary, her mouth moved slowly in prayer. A man sat in the chair below her. He held her waist and concealed his face into her bosom, his shoulders rising and falling quickly between obvious sobs. It was easy to recognize their pain, I had been in their shoes not too long ago. Not wanting to disturb the strangers, I slowly left the quiet room. A part of me wanted to reach out to them, comfort them somehow. My fear held me back. I had no grounds to comfort their aching hearts while mine still lay shattered in a million pieces on the floor.

Not taking my eyes off of the couple through the textured glass, I almost ran into a stretcher with a woman lying motionless, tubes coming from her nose, mouth, and arms.

"Sorry," I mouthed to the two male staff members. With my hands in the air, I stepped back allowing them to move in front of me. As they passed, I saw Evan trailing behind the patient. I froze in shock and disbelief.

Evan didn't acknowledge my presence. His focus was on the patient they wheeled into the room to my right. He walked by me, not looking up from the woman that moved ahead of him.

My heart raced with excitement. *I found him!* I had found Evan again.

My eyes followed him into the waiting room I had just left. Still frozen in shock at finding him, I stood in the doorway watching as he moved to stand over the grieving couple. Evan placed his large hands on their shoulders, and a faint light grew from underneath his gentle touch. The man once cradled against his wife sat up and wiped his wet eyes. The woman looked up from her beaded charm and surveyed the room in wonder.

They didn't notice Evan's presence, even though his hands still rested on their shoulders. *Why didn't they see him?*

As Evan left the waiting room, the elderly couple calmly sat together on the upholstered loveseat, holding each other gently.

They no longer showed any pain in their once troubled eyes, and an unknown peace surrounded them.

Evan turned to exit and, for the first time, noticed me standing outside the now serene space. He seemed shocked I was there, unaware of my presence while he had helped the grieving pair. I couldn't shake the disbelief I felt. *Did I really find him? Is he really right in front of me again?*

"Hi," I said softly, uncomfortable in his intense stare.

"Hello," Evan responded as he passed by me.

The elevator chimed, two people walked out, and Evan stepped inside. Not following, Evan's brows narrowed in confusion while I watched the doors begin to close. My ears rang at the remembrance of the claws scrapping the metal box. I couldn't will myself to move. As much as I wanted to follow Evan, my feet would not follow him. Soon he would be gone again. *Move!* My mind begged. But I remained still. Just before the doors closed Evan's hands obstructed their movement.

"Aren't you coming?" he asked.

"I… um…" I stammered and stumbled over my words.

The elevator's alarm sounded as Evan continued to hold the doors open, his forearm flexing in the tension. Hesitantly, I stepped inside the enclosed space.

"Are you hurt?" he questioned.

The door shut loudly at his release. I jumped at the sound.

"No, I'm fine. I was…" I couldn't find the words to say.

I'm stalking you! I had to find you. I'm desperate to see you again.

None of those would do.

"I was visiting a friend," the lie escaped before I could find another excuse.

Smiling widely, a soft, knowing snicker escaped his soft lips, "A friend?"

My lie hung in the air. It was obvious we both knew the truth in my visitation was not for a friend. I wanted to tell Evan that I had been searching for him since the moment we met, before that even. I wanted to beg him to never leave again, to stay by my side and protect me from the darkness I felt all around me. But, I stood, gazing at his perfection, fully aware of my own insecurities.

The intense eyes of the man I longed to find, now standing over me, waiting for me to explain our meeting, made me feel as if the walls of the elevator were coming in on me. No longer was I afraid of the dark creatures hiding in the shadows. Now, I was terrified of his rejection.

The air became clammy and stale, panic ignited. I was desperate to escape, both the piercing eyes of Evan and the confines of this space. I would have thought that being this close to Evan would have been heart-stopping, stomach flipping, and electrifying. But, instead, it was completely terrifying.

As soon as the doors opened I felt myself lunge for the clean air outside of the metal enclosure. In the hospital's main entry, my rapid breathing continued: eyes staring, tears falling, people dying.

I have to get out of here!

I pushed through the revolving door to reach the serenity of the fresh summer air. As the warm breeze hit my face, I exhaled loudly. After a few deep breaths, my heart dropped. I completely forgot about Evan. I had let him out of my sight, again. *No!*

Spinning around the open commons, I searched for Evan desperately, only to be completely devastated at his disappearance. *He's gone, again. I let him slip away!*

"Are you alright?" a strong voice said.

I spun and found Evan's eyes. Relief hit me like an unexpected wave. My knees buckled, and I could feel myself begin to fall at the whiplash of emotions.

"It is okay," Evan said, grabbing my shoulder to hold me upright.

Unable to control my emotions, let alone my mouth, I blurted, "I thought I lost you again," I said, dropping my head into my hands.

I felt like I was on an emotional roller coaster and unable to find my center. Dizziness filled my head, as it had the first time I met Evan. *Why did I feel like this around him?* It was as if the Earth itself was tipping over and pouring me out.

With his hands on my shoulders, I felt a warmth begin to pass between us. My muscles relaxed and I could feel myself melting into his touch.

No! I almost said aloud, shaking my head I stepped away from Evan's peaceful embrace. As much as I longed for his touch, I did not want to slip away again, wake up in my bed alone, unable to remember how I had gotten there or where Evan had gone. I couldn't give into his calming touch, not again. I had to push past the head-spinning, earth twisting effect he had on me. I had to find my footing on this unstable ground that surrounded Evan.

"I'm fine," I breathed deeply, trying to regain my composure and allow the oxygen to awaken my dazed mind. "I'm okay," I heard myself repeating over and over again.

"Here, sit," Evan said, his hands guided me to a wooden bench under a weeping willow tree.

As my head and heart steadied, I noticed the long branches of the tree dusting the ground, enclosing us in our own little cocoon. Within the sanctity of the willow branches, with Evan by my side, I finally felt safe.

CHAPTER 23 TWENTY-THREE

The light streamed through the scattered leaves dancing effortlessly under the cloak of the downcast willow.

After moments of sitting in silence I spoke, "I went searching for you. I didn't know where you would be. I looked in town, at the *bridge*, and then I came here. I thought it would be okay, that I wouldn't let this place get to me. But, it just has so many painful memories."

"It is alright, Kara," Evan said tenderly.

"Why didn't anyone else see you?" I asked after we exchanged glances. "The man and woman in the waiting room, and the woman on the street yesterday." I paused not sure how to proceed. "They didn't even know you were there. How do I see you, when no one else does?"

"I don't know," he answered, quickly dropping his eyes and breaking my intense stare. "Usually humans can't see us unless we allow them to."

After a long pause, Evan's words sunk in, "I take it you weren't allowing me then?" I spoke; unsure I wanted to hear his response.

"It's my duty to protect you—unseen." Evan said, "But, you *are* different. You see me when others don't."

"I get it," I said, allowing the weak thoughts of my unworthiness to twist in my mind.

He didn't long for me the way I did him. He didn't want me to find him. Searching every day, desperate to find him, I never thought that once I did, he might not want to be found.

"It is just the way it has to be," Evan said after a few agonizing moments.

I heard him loud and clear. My search for him was successful, but what I hadn't ever asked myself was what I wanted to find. Did I want to find Evan, the duty bound, other-worldly being that saved me? Or, did I want to find the fantasy I created, a feeling I manifested deep within that made me think I yearned for him? Was it all a lie I told myself—an illusion crafted in my desperate attempt to pull beyond the depression and darkness I was afraid to fall back into? Was it a creation of redemption I thought I could find in the arms of an angel?

Thinking of the darkness brought the memories from the previous night to the forefront of my mind. The dark creatures had come for me last night, and they were no illusion. They had bridged the gap from my nightmares and entered my reality, and I had the marks on my legs to prove it.

"I wanted to find you to ask you something," I said reluctantly.

Evan nodded as I continued, "After the accident on the bridge, I have had these dreams, well, nightmares, of the darkness that night, and of your light that saved me."

"You remember that," Evan interjected calmly.

"I remember everything. The darkness that pulled me under, the creatures, the light, your warmth," I paused, looking down and then back into Evan's eyes.

I searched his face, desperately trying to read his thoughts.

"The nightmare… I dunno… the darkness in my dreams came alive, somehow. The dream felt so real. The pain was so real. Waking up, I had these scratches on my legs. They were ice cold. It felt like the dark creatures had crossed a plane or something. That they had stepped out of my dream and were… *are* coming for me."

Evan's eyes fixed on mine, "Can I see them?"

My brows creased with the unusual question.

"May I see the marks?" Evan said quickly.

I nodded and rolled up my pant leg without verbal approval.

The marks were a faint pink against my white skin; there were no traces of the black substance from the night before.

Evan reached down and touched them gently. His right hand held my calf while the other brushed the scar with his fingers. Warmth radiated off his soft skin.

"It was so fresh last night, there was so much blood and a…" Shaking my head I didn't want to finish the horrible memory.

"Tar-like substance," he said, finishing my statement.

"Yeah?"

"You should be alright. Your body is already healing itself," Evan spoke coldly, releasing my leg and sitting upright with his back against the bench.

What? I am anything but alright.

"I should go," Evan said.

"Oh…okay," I stammered.

Evan quickly stood and walked out of the serenity of the willow and disappeared into the low hanging sun as I sat there, *like a fool*, letting him leave.

Frustration filled my mind. I was desperate to find him after the night I had, and now I was alone again, with the evening less than an hour away. My expectation had been so great, as if my *knight in shining armor* would sweep in and save me, again, from the dark creatures. But, that didn't happen.

As I sat alone, the willow leaves began to cast dark shadows on the ground around me. The shadows formed hands with long splintery claws moving and twisting toward me. *Is my mind playing tricks on me again, like in the elevator, or are they back to finish what they started at the bridge?*

I knew I had to get out of there. I had to get home. Not that it was any safer there. Truth was, only one place felt safe, and he had just left.

CHAPTER 24

The room was dark and cold. I tucked the covers under my chin, wrapped my arms around my legs, and pulled them into my body. A force was conjuring around me; I didn't have to see them to know it was the dark creatures from the night before.

Last night had been a terrifying experience. The earth shattering dream had ripped the veil allowing the darkness to bridge the gap between my nightmares and the real world. They were no longer just in my dreams. They were hunting me and ruthlessly seeking out my soul for their own maleficent devices. Foreboding feelings of the dark creatures lurking in the shadows of my room were overwhelming.

Through the stillness, I heard a sneering whistle coming down the walls of my room. Claws scratched amongst a single shrill cry of an unknown monster. Then, silence again.

Am I dreaming again? Did I fall asleep? Not being able to remember closing my eyes sent a shiver of concentrated fear down my spine.

"This has to be a dream," I told myself.

My dark room made it difficult to see anything beyond my footboard. *Are they gone?* Through the stillness, a chatter emerged from the unknown creature. Then, the shrill returned. It was accompanied by clicking, unlike anything I had ever heard before. My stomach dropped in fear as I realized it was not just one creature I was hearing, but two.

Amongst the blackened room I heard the two beasts snap

and growl between communicating clicks and hisses.

There are two of them now! I had to know what was coming for me.

Desperate to see into the blackened room I pushed against the plush bed, inching to its edge. As my eyes adjusted, forms began to emerge into monstrous bodies with jagged teeth and piercing red eyes. Their smell instantly hit my nose, sending me recoiling to the head of my bed and safety of my pillows. I covered my mouth, trying not to make a sound or cry out in complete terror.

Please be a dream, my mind begged.

But, I knew the truth. This was no dream.

The chattering increased to a snarled laughter, getting closer with each passing second. My inability to see them only added to my fear.

I tried to think of the light the way I had the night before. It had worked then, pulling me from my dream, maybe thinking of the light and all its beauty would pull me from my living nightmare.

Images from the night on the bridge filled my mind. At first, I could only think of the blackness that surrounded that night. Then, I remembered the light. It seemed to breathe with each movement it made toward me, changing and churning in new brighter tones each passing second. It almost seemed alive. *But, that can't be possible. Light is not living.* I searched my mind more for further details on the light. Its beauty still amazed me. The intense white hues with strands of golden rays amongst faceted beams of opaque blues and purples reached from the heavens to my submerged body. It was truly magnificent the way a light contained such intensity at first glance and such beauty at its depths.

A scratching noise from the base of my bed yanked my mind from the pleasant thoughts of the light to the dark reality I was living. The howling wind outside my window intensified as the creatures moved closer, no longer taunting me against the far wall of my room, but now only feet from my bed. The sound of scraping nails on the wooden board at the foot of my bed creaked with the creature's weight. Tapping from a single claw on the metal accent rang against the eerie stillness in the air.

"Think of the light, think of the light," I commanded myself quietly behind chattering teeth.

But, I could no longer envision the light's beauty with devilish eyes staring into me from their perched position at the foot of my bed. The glowing, red eyes entranced me. I barely noticed the weight of the other creature on my bed. I lay immobilized in fear. Knowing what the creatures truly wanted only added to my horror. They wanted to devour my soul. They tasted it the night on the bridge, and after last night's dream, they were craving it again— starving for it even. It was my soul versus the darkness, and there was no real question who would win.

Both creatures barked and bit at one another, still at the base of my bed. My muscles twitched from their tensed immobility aggravating the beasts and turning their attention back to me. They moved over my legs and hovered over my stomach; the weight of their bodies indenting the mattress below me, pushing me closer to its inner coils. Holding my breath, I longed for the creatures to think I was already dead. But, that trick would not work on these dark forces. They crept as two unified figures outlined with a small amount of light coming from the streetlight outside my window. The larger of the creatures took the lead, crawling up my chest and resting its strong paws against my insignificant body. The animal's paw was wide and rough in texture. I could feel barbs on each pad as the weight of the creature pushed me deeper into the sinking bed.

The creature's weight made it hard to inhale completely. Taking quick gasps only added to my angst and terror. I lay unmoved, stunned at the sight of the creature's faces emerging from the darkness of the night. It was unrecognizable. There was no animal on earth or ever created with such repulsively hideous malformations. It was a being of sheer evil: muzzle and fangs of a wolf, talons of an eagle, piercing eyes of a sadistic feline, and the mass of a silverback.

An icy chill spat from its open mouth. I gasped in horror at its frosted fetid breath, my nose overcome with its putridity. My mind and body began to panic, driving my limbs to thrash wildly and body writhe under the weight of the large creatures. My attempts at freedom were unsuccessful and only roused the two beasts. One creature crowed in maniacal laughter at my futile attempts to move. The other snapped at its partner, growling deeply while moving closer to my vulnerable body. The creatures' putrid breath, a spewing pit of rotting death wrapped in a wintery wind, stabbed my cheek as they both moved in for the kill.

This is it. This would be my end. There was nothing that could stop these great nefarious beasts.

The *light* could. It saved me before, defeating the darkness in its brilliant power. But, there was no light here. There was no light to save me and cast the evil away; no guardian angel, no Evan.

Maybe any light will chase them away, even that of a common bulb.

Moving under the weight of the creatures, I stretched for the lamp beside my bed. My long arms reached the insignificant lamp and with a click the light bulb, the space illuminated, momentarily blinding me.

The once dark room was now extremely bright, my eyes clamped shut at the sharp contrast. After a few seconds, they adjusted, and I was able to see how the light had filled the room. *The creatures are gone!* Relief quickly left when I saw them cowering in opposite corners of my room. One creature was huddled on the top of my dresser, hiding from the light. The other cast to the opposite shadowed corner. The serenity of the lamp's light covered my head creating a circle of protection around my bed. I breathed a sigh of relief. *My* light had chased them away. *I am safe.*

Then, the light flickered. *No!* Its power began to diminish. With a pop, the bulb and light became non-existent, and the room instantly became black again. My heart sunk.

I searched for another source of light, but there was none.

A shrill cry erupted from my blackened room. The creatures were enraged and moved with unrelenting intent, lurching forward and reaching my bed in only seconds. Their bodies twisted and moved like the dead branches of a tree's, reaching over my bed and onto my body. I could feel the cold emanating from the two monsters perched on the footboard. A wretched paw reached for me through, what I could have only assumed, were the depths of Hell.

Overcome with desolation, tears began to fall down my cheeks.

I closed my eyes tightly, trying to turn all my thoughts to Evan, the same way I had in my dream. Maybe it would work the same way, pull me into Evan's light, and chase away the darkness.

The creature pressed its weight against my ankles as one barb pierced my leg, injecting sheer agony into my body.

Not able to hold in the pain, a scream erupted from my lips. I tried to focus my thoughts toward Evan again; his eyes, the intense light around him, and the hope he held in his gaze.

The second dark beast speared its spur deep into my lower calf. Pain surged through my lower limb. Amongst the pain, I felt the darkness burrowing into my body; injected by the creature. I screamed out in agony as I felt another attack on my opposite leg, higher than the first. The same burning poison rushed through my blood, moving up my torso. The excruciating, venomous pain of pure evil radiated through my entire body.

A boiling torment coursed through my veins.

"Evan!" a scream escaped my quivering lips.

Saying his name was the only thing I could do to not succumb to the pain. I didn't have much longer. Soon the poisonous darkness would consume every atom within my body, covering my cells in the thick black tar. The gluttonous creatures would leave my soul, the ripe fruit underneath, for their own edible desires.

Amongst the affliction, I heard an unknown noise coming from outside of the house. I was unable to focus on its origin as the creatures reared back, ready for their final deadly blow. I closed my eyes, waiting in horror. Nothing.

Not sure why the creatures did not attack, I tentatively opened my eyes.

Before I could process what was happening, the room began to tremor forcefully, shaking my bed and sending my lamp crashing to the floor with a sharp crack. The creatures released the hold they had on my lower body, reducing the poisonous injection. They too looked to the source of the sound outside my window that continued to boom with force.

An intense light shown through the window, once only lit by a small streetlight, now ignited in brilliance. Its frame and panes shook violently, radiating up the wall and toward my bed, allowing me to feel the vibrations.

Soon the entire room was convulsing violently.

An earthquake?

Pictures fell, and books hit the floor. The room quaked with great power. Plaster hit the floor as a crack split the back wall in two.

If this is an earthquake, it is off the Richter scale. But, something deep within told me, this was no earthquake.

At the end of my bed, I saw the creatures recoiling and turning in on themselves. They seemed terrified of whatever continued to rattle and shake my room, increasing in power with each passing second. It was as if a jet plane was flying right over the house. My hands covered my ears in protection. The booming noise roared with power. The room quaked even more than before as the light burst into the room, collecting in the corner. With its arrival, the boisterous noise intensified beyond reason. I sought refuge at the head of my bed, cowering in fear. My ears burned with a ringing pain from the intense noise, my hands unable to protect them. The room continued to illuminate and tremor aggressively.

This is no jet flying overhead. It is landing in my room!

The light began to concentrate into a ball. It was as if the sun itself was materializing in my room. I felt the ardor of warmth and the blinding light.

This was the saving light I had longed for. This *light* was the same light that saved me on the bridge, and that was with Evan.

A new feeling of fear welled within me as I felt all of my insignificance and utter frailty. This fear was different from the feelings I felt from the dark creatures. That fear was an abyss of emptiness pulling me into its blackness—an oblivion of despair. This new *fear* was one of desperation and my incompleteness in the *Light's* wholeness and perfection. A feeling of my iniquities flooded over me; how unworthy I was to be in the room with this magnificent light.

The ball of light faded slightly, and I was able to see movement inside of the unknown object. Morphing from the spherical shape into a figure, a man hunched over and crouched became apparent.

The light began to fade.

The figure rose with strength, a blue-white hue emanated in a crescent shape around the mysterious body. I couldn't see a face or features, but a man emerged with what looked like flowing wings of light behind his strong form. It was as if an egret had just landed.

The light dissipated, slowly dissolving into the silence of the room. The figure's wings glided behind him as he reached the foot of my bed, towering over me. I shook at the unknown. All traces of the dark creatures had gone, cast back to where they had come, but still, fear is all I felt.

Immobilized from the magnificent sight standing before me, I felt tears falling down my flushed cheeks—one lone droplet, followed by many.

"Do not be afraid," he said calmly stepping toward me, "they are gone."

With his words, I recognized Evan in his angelic form. He was absolutely stunning.

I desperately wanted to run into his arms, flee to the protection of the one that just saved me, but the power I had just witnessed had me shaking in fear.

I hid my eyes from the angel that stood over me, glowing from the light which had once filled my room with such vibrancy.

How can I look upon a face of such perfection?

"It is okay now," Evan said as I felt the weight of his presence on the bed next to me.

His arm outstretched over my hunched shoulders and held me in his warming embrace. I allowed myself to fold into his heated body. With each rise and fall of his chest, my fears subsided and my manic breathing matched his calming rhythm.

Evan's hand left my shoulder and touched my chin gently, raising my eyes to meet his. The other went to my cheek, wiping away the tears that fell uncontrollably. Through blurred eyes, I saw

Evan, back to his human form. The light was no longer surrounding him but glowed behind his reassuring eyes.

As he cupped my face, a calming warmth pulsed from his angelic hands to my fragile body. Under the warming comfort of his touch, my legs began to twitch with a pain I had suppressed. Noting the discomfort in my eyes, Evan followed my gaze and met my injured legs. A searing pain began to surge from my wounds as his fingers gently felt the marks left by the dark creatures. The agony of their strike flooded my mind.

Evan pulled my legs closer to him, resting them on his lap. I noticed a familiar tar-like substance mixed with the vibrancy of fresh blood scattered in scratched patterns along the tops on my exposed skin. Evan gently touched the agonizing marks, sending a warming release to the aching pain.

"It will be alright Kara," he said leaning into me as he continued to heal my injured legs.

With one hand on my leg, the other went to my face again. My tears pooled under his touch. I saw a blue hue of dulled light begin to grow under his palm, followed by the same steadied warmth I felt on my calf. Evan's eyes closed and jaw tightened, sending a stronger pulse of warmth from one hand to the other, filling my entire body. Willingly, I gave into the calming peace that invited me into its warmth. Slowly the pain and Evan faded away, and all went black.

CHAPTER 25

I blinked repeatedly in an effort to wake my tired eyes. I pushed against the pillows attempting to sit but was met with a strong hand on my chest, gently urging me back to the comfort of my bed. I rolled on my side and found Evan next to me. One hand elevated his head, jutting his sandy hair in all directions.

"Hello," Evan said.

My eyes clamped shut at the single word he spoke. It felt like lightning in my battered mind. My head pounded with thunderous throbs. I attempted a forced smile, but only managed to wince at the slight facial expression.

"How long was I out?" I said, rubbing my temples with both index fingers.

"A while," Evan said. "It's not yet morning," he paused, "we have a few more hours."

I nodded my head under my hands while thoughts of the night began to fill my already full mind: the dark creatures attack, so much fear, the light, Evan's saving presence. He *was* an angel!

I looked to the back of my room where he manifested. There was no evidene of his announced entrance. If I had any doubts about his angelic nature, they were chased away the moment I saw who he really was.

My mind raced in confusion. Everything inside of me told me that there was nothing more than what we see; nothing more than the here and now. But, what I saw, what Evan *was*, changed everything.

Evan had told me he was an angel. But, truthfully, I had no idea what that meant. I did not know what an angel really was, or what one looked like. The plump cherubim seated naked on a cloud was the religious icon I had engraved in my mind. Now, I knew the truth. It was a mockery of who Evan truly was and the power he held. He was breathtakingly grand, and I was so minuscule next to him, so insignificant to such an amazing being.

I turned and looked at Evan, dropping my hands slowly from my face images of his angelic form was all I could see. I would no longer be able to see him for the human form he held. He was more than the most beautiful person I had ever seen. He was my savior. He was my angel. And I was just a human. I was nothing next to Evan, nothing next to an angel.

I knew now why Evan did not want me to find him, why he seemed so distant at the hospital. He was a magnificent creature of light, and I was someone destined for the darkness. How stupid I was to think that he might look at me any different than what I was—human, fragile. Nothing.

No longer able to look into his eyes, I turned from him. My feebleness exposed.

"Are you alright?" Evan asked.

I didn't answer. I couldn't. Desperately, I longed for him, a needing for him deep within my being, a yearning for Evan I never knew could exist. My mind told me how foolish I was to even think that such an amazing creature could feel the same urgency I felt for him.

Not knowing what to say and not wanting to lie to Evan, I shrugged my shoulders in defeat. I was sure my transparency was evident, allowing him to see this lowly child pining for him amongst the night.

"Let me know what is troubling you," Evan said.

"It's my head. It's pounding."

"Here," Evan said.

Extending his arm across my body, he moved my hands from my head and touched my forehead gently. A warming hum wrapped around my mind, releasing the vise instantly.

"Thank you," I said softly. "Not just for this," I pointed to my head, "but for saving me tonight, and for before, too." Evan smiled softly, and I continued before he could speak, "I'm sorry you had to come."

Evan's eyebrows furrowed in confusion, defining his chiseled features all the more. "What do mean?"

"I know you don't want to be here," I said, turning from him. "You can go. It's okay."

"Why would you think that?" Evan said quickly.

"The other day at the hospital you didn't seem glad I had found you," I said. "I just don't want you thinking you have to be here. Just tell me how to get rid of those *things*, and you can go. If that's what you want?"

"It's not what I want," Evan said.

Does he feel for me the same way that I feel for him?

"I know you said I'm your *Charge*. I get you *have* to save me or keep me safe. But, I…" The words were so hard to verbalize. I desperately wanted Evan to want to be here with me, not because he had to or because he was *called* to, but because he too felt something more for me than duty.

"You *are* my Charge. But, there is nowhere I would rather be, than here with you," Evan said, leaning toward me slightly.

The words were rich and filling. Evan's eyes looked deep within my own as we lay next to each other on my bed, only inches from each other. I felt the warmth emanating from him, radiating comforting pulses to my chilled frame.

We didn't touch, even though I longed for him to reach out to me. We sat in a calming silence. It was peaceful being next to him. My soul seemed at rest, relaxed next to his.

"I am sorry about the other day," Evan said. "I wanted to find answers to why the creatures were after you. It upset me that I wasn't there to protect you; that they were able to hurt you. I should have kept a closer watch, but…" Evan paused, "I…"

As we lay there, close enough that I could taste his sweet intoxicating breath on my lips, Evan searched for the words to speak. I couldn't help but think that maybe he felt something more for me too. Maybe he wanted to be here, next to me, as much as I wanted him to be.

"You can tell me," I said, trying to encourage him to continue.

Evan's eyes looked deep into mine, calling me into him, begging me to join them in their peaceful serenity. I longed to go to him, curl into Evan's warm embrace, wrapping myself in his arms. But, even more, I longed to push my lips onto his, tasting their nectarous aroma, feeling the softness of their blush appearance.

Evan spoke breaking my wondering thoughts of his lips, "I am your protector. And you are my Charge."

"Is that all I am," I felt the words boldly escape my mouth.

Evan smiled and collapsed onto the pillow behind him. His smile was wide as he gazed at the textured ceiling above us. A hushed laugh seemed to hang in his mouth, while his smirk remained.

"Sorry," I said leaning back on my own pillow as he did.

"It's not," Evan said after a moment of silence.

"Huh?" I blurted out at his strange response to my apology.

Evan clarified, "It is not the only way I see you."

I couldn't speak.

"You are not *just* my Charge," Evan said in hushed tones.

I desperately wanted to ask him to continue, to probe his thoughts further, but I was frozen, unable to speak. We lay in silence as my wondering thoughts of his feelings for me continued.

Maybe he did feel something more for me. Maybe I'm not the only one feeling this strange connection.

Either way, my heart was elated at the idea that hung in the air. I allowed the thoughts to dance in my head until I couldn't take the silence any longer.

"Can you tell me about the creatures?" I asked. "What are they?"

"They are the Naphal, creatures of pure darkness and complete evil," Evan said rising from the bed and walking to the window to sit across from me on its tufted seat.

My eyes narrowed at the unfamiliar word as I sat up on the bed across from Evan.

He continued almost immediately, "The Naphal are the *Fallen Ones*. You would call them fallen angels."

"They are angels too? Why are they after me?" I asked quickly.

"No, they are not angels anymore. When they chose to turn away from the *Light*, they became complete Darkness. I don't know why they are after you," he said. "They rarely pursue humans, but it could be that they too sense you."

"*Sense* me?"

"Yes. You are very special, Kara."

"Yeah," I said with heavy sarcasm. *There is no way I'm special.* The angel calling the human special was sure to be a mistake.

"You are," he paused before continuing, "You're the Akahra, the *Last One*."

"Akahra? Wait, the last what?" I questioned.

Evan shook his head, "I can't tell you that. Just know you *are* special, and I'm sure the Naphal are aware of that. The Naphal can take many different forms. They are trying to scare you."

"They were trying to kill me," I said abruptly.

Evan shook his head in agreement, "The Naphal are ruthless creatures and will continue to hunt you until…" Evan stopped and looked out the window behind him.

"Until what?" I asked, even though I already knew the answer.

"Until you are no more," he said.

"Why?" I asked quietly, wrapping a blanket around my shoulders and rising to stand beside Evan in the small alcove.

"Why do they want me? If I am so special, why do they want me dead?" I asked.

"If you are no more, then…" Evan trailed off again, "then they win."

"They win?" I asked, "Win what?"

"A war is going on every day. It is a war for the souls of mankind. If you die, they win, and the game would end." Evan said, taking a deep breath and continuing. "Most humans never know about our world. They never see the *Darkness* or the *Light*. Your al-

most death on the bridge exposed you to both sides. Your eyes were open. You are able to see all of it now and with that, they are able to find you. The Naphal must have sensed you when you died before I brought you back," Evan said.

"And, when I returned to the bridge, searching for you, I must have awakened them, somehow," I interjected.

"It's very possible," Evan said looking back at me as I stood across from him.

"Why did you save me?" I asked.

"Because that is not what was meant to be. That death was not your fate. You are not damned to the Darkness, Kara," Evan said, looking at me deeply with his intense eyes. "You are destined for the Light."

"The *Light*?" I questioned.

Evan's light was the only light I had ever seen or known.

"Why do you fight it?" Evan asked interrupting my thoughts. "Why is it so hard for you to believe when you have seen the *Light* in me?" he asked again, neglecting any judgmental tones.

"I don't know," I said softly.

Why am I fighting it so much? Why is it so hard for me to see what my mother knew so clearly and what Evan emits? Why is it so hard for me to see this Light?

"I see *you*, and that is something that is hard enough to grasp… anything more than that, well, I just don't have it in me," I said after a moment.

A fact that was simple but monumentally true. I had no idea why I couldn't accept the thought of something grander, a divine *Light* source. I saw the Light, but still, I was unable to believe in it. I wanted to have the reins to *my* life, the way to *my* path. I was not ready to let go to someone else—not yet at least.

It wasn't like it was even that simple. Wanting to believe and actually believing were two different things. I wanted to believe, I really did. But, believing in what? God?

I needed to know more, see more, maybe then I would believe and be able to trust fully in the *Light* I saw in Evan.

"So, what now?" I asked, standing in front of him, my eyes

meeting his.

"Now, I protect you. I keep you safe. As long as I am near you, the Darkness cannot harm you," Evan said. "I will not let them hurt you again."

"And the *Light*?" I questioned.

"The *Light*," Evan smiled widely as he stood tall, towering over me and looking down on me tenderly, "I will help you find it."

CHAPTER 26 TWENTY-SIX

While the sun rose over the trees, we watched the light slowly illuminate the world around us. Everything came alive with the sun, from the chirping of the finches to the blooming flowers turning their stems toward the new light. But, I couldn't enjoy its beauty. Ever since the bridge, the brighter the day, the more I thought of the night, and the horrors that played within it.

For now, the dark creatures had faded into the past where I hoped they would stay forever, never to show themselves again. Evan kept watch, a guarded statue frozen in time, staring at the empty sky. He no longer held the illusion of the man I saw. He was an angel, my protector against the dark creatures hell-bent on killing me.

The warmth of the sun wrapped around us as we sat on the wooden steps leading to my home.

"You will be safe during the day," Evan said, standing and slowly stretching his large limbs above his head.

"You're leaving?" I asked quickly, standing next to him, the wind blowing my hair in all directions.

Aware of my own stiffness, I also stretched and reached toward my aching knee.

"Are you alright?" Evan asked turning and lowering himself to look at my leg more directly.

"I'm fine," I said. "It's just my knee, still hurts every once in a while."

"From the accident?" Evan asked.

"Yeah, but I'm okay," I smiled at him, trying to squash the concern he held in his gaze.

"Do you have to go?" I asked.

Evan walked a few steps down the worn porch in order to look at me directly.

"I must. But, I won't be long. Nothing can harm you during the day. You will be safe," Evan tried to reassure me with his caring eyes.

I nodded in agreement. I wanted him to stay, not only for his security but for the feelings I felt when I was around him.

"You *could* stay," I said with uncertainty. "If you wanted to."

Evan smiled softly, "I would, but I need to find answers to why they are after you, and if anything can be done about their presence."

"Okay," I said, nodding again slowly.

Evan lowered his head to mine and whispered in my ear, "I will be back to you soon. Do not worry, Kara."

My heart raced at his proximity. He was so close the heat of his breath warmed my neck and sent a fire of allure throughout my body. His face lingered next to mine even after his words ended. I felt Evan's hand on mine, squeezing it slightly. He walked away sending my heart reeling for more of his touch.

With a gust of the wind, he was gone, vanishing before my eyes.

Exhaling loudly, I collapsed on the steps underneath me, my heart raced in all directions. My breathing was rapid as if I had just finished an intense run. *What is he doing to me? Why does he make me feel this way?*

His closeness, the smell of his body next to mine, the softness of his hand on my skin, and the intenseness of his eyes made my heart reel in elation and my stomach flip in anticipated excitement.

Unable to hold onto the pleasant memories of Evan's touch, daunting images of the dark creatures began to fill my mind. All the anxiety and fear Evan had masked came crashing into my fragile mind. Flashes of the dark beasts standing over me, pressing into me, digging their blackened claws into my skin and injecting their evil toxins played over and over again in my head.

My breathing increased again, but this time, it wasn't because Evan had placed his hand on mine or whispered in my ear; it was the memory of the Darkness and an intense fear encircling my mind. I pulled the sweater up to my neck and tried to avoid the unusual chill that was in the air, evidence left by the creatures that pined for me, I was sure.

"Hey!" George yelled.

I jumped at his greeting as he emerged from the familiar silver sedan and shut the door loudly behind him.

"Where have you been?" my father shouted before digging into the opened truck for his suitcase.

"Umm, I…" I stammered, unsure of what he meant by his question and shocked at his unexpected arrival.

"I texted you and called you all last night and *this* morning," George said, now standing in front of me, hands on his hips, eyes glaring in full fatherly authority. I had never seen my father like this. He was flustered. He was mad!

"I, umm… oh, my phone must be dead or something," I responded.

"Well, I was worried about you," he said putting down his bag and bending over to hug my neck as I sat, still in shock, on the porch steps.

"You were?" I questioned.

"Yes, I was. I'm your father. You had me worried. My meeting was canceled, so I jumped on the red-eye and headed home. I thought we could do something together today," George said.

"Really?" I responded in disbelief.

"Of course," he said.

"No, I mean, yeah, that would be great."

This couldn't have come at a better time. After the night I had, I didn't want to be alone.

"Okay," he said, smiling. "Well, let me run in and get cleaned up, then we can head out and get some breakfast. I'm starving."

"Sounds good," I said, smiling back.

As we walked together into the dark house a shiver rippled down my spine. The memories of last night were palpable.

My father, unaware of any residual energy, said, "I do have to head into the office this afternoon and work on some stuff."

"Okay, Dad. I'm just glad we can hang out this morning."

"Good. Give me a minute, and we'll head out," George said, dropping his briefcase and heading upstairs.

Breakfast at Jill's Café in town was a sweet relief to the weight I felt hanging in the air around me. George talked about his work. I didn't listen. I couldn't focus on his words about case briefs or weekly meetings.

"Is everything okay with you, Kara?" he asked finally noticing my inattentiveness.

I shrugged but knew my father would not be satisfied with a simple gesture.

"I've been thinking about college," I lied; college was the last thing on my mind.

"What are your thoughts? I think you would really enjoy Harvard," George said between bites of his pancakes dripping with syrup. Before I could detest he continued, "I know, I know. It isn't your first choice. But if not Harvard, then what? We need to have a plan here"

Oh no, what did I start?

I filled my fork with as much food as it would hold and crammed it into my mouth in just enough time for my father to notice and roll his eyes.

"What are you thinking, really, Kara?" George pushed.

I swallowed the large bite and took a long drink. After I couldn't stall any longer I said, "I...I think I am going to go to the local college."

George didn't answer. He didn't have to. I knew what he was thinking. *Waste of talent* and other negative ideas about my decision.

"If that is what you would like to do. I will respect it," he said behind a steaming cup of black coffee.

"What?" I said, shocked.

"You want me to have a different option?"

"No, no. I just thought…"

"You thought I would demand you go somewhere else?" George said calmly.

"Well… yeah, I guess I did."

He didn't answer right away. There was a bit of pain that seemed to be hiding behind his blank face.

"I want you to be happy. That's all," he paused. "A year ago, yes, I would have put my foot down about the whole college thing. But, now…things are different. We are different. I truly just want you to be happy." George smiled, his dimples evident behind his cup. I couldn't help but return his expression.

After I finished my omelet, I searched for the right words to ask something I had been thinking about since I found the note my mother left me.

"Dad?" I asked between sips of my vanilla latte.

"Yeah, Hun."

"There is something else that has been bugging me. Or not bugging me but… I…"

"What is it?" he asked with concern.

"I found this note Mom left me," I said.

"You did!" He said, sounding rather excited at my discovery.

"Yeah, it was right before the accident."

I could feel the air quickly leave the room, my father's face dropping with the mention of my accident.

"It's just…" I fumbled with my words, trying to find the right way to ask the question I had always wanted to know.

"Well, the note, I found it in Mom's old Bible. And, well, you never really went to church with us or anything like that. Mom talked a lot about what she believed, but she never said anything about what you believe. I guess I just wanted to ask you what you think," I said. "Like when all this is over, what else is there?"

George was never one to talk about his feelings or beliefs. When my mother died and he distanced himself the way he did—the way we both did—I stopped caring what my father thought. But, after the accident on the bridge, George and I had attempted to mend our torn relationship. It had been better. And with his kindness surrounding my college decision, I thought now might be the time to ask a question I had wondered for years.

After moments of quietness, George finally spoke, "I never really thought about it before your mother died. I always thought she had her faith, and that was fine. I was glad she took you to church with her, but it just wasn't something I was interested in. Then, when she died," George paused after weighted word. "Everything changed. Instead of being indifferent to God, I hated Him for taking her from me—from us. I guess I still hold on to that a little—that anger. Why would God take someone so special? Why would He take away *your mother* and *my wife*, in that way?"

I completely understood the anger my father had for God. It had been so easy before, not thinking about God or anything spiritual at all, no worry of death, no worry of the Darkness, or hope of the Light. Now, death was at my door, pounding relentlessly for me. I had no other choice but to think about answering it.

Looking down at my cup, I wanted to comfort my father, to reach to him and tell him everything would be okay. But, I didn't know it would, and I couldn't lie to him.

When I fell from the bridge, hit by the car and forced to the water, death had come, and it wasn't something I would have ever longed for. Death was sharp and bitter, painful and aggressive. Not the comforting warmth of encompassing light my mother described it to be.

Heaven hadn't been my end, and I supposed it wouldn't be my father's either. He didn't have the answers I was searching for. He was just as lost and broken as I was.

Through choked words, my father continued, "Your mom, I like to think she is somewhere perfect without pain or sickness. Heaven, I guess. I like to picture her painting in a field of wildflowers with nothing else around her but the open sky and a colorful canvas," George paused. "She loved to paint; she loved nature and getting away from the bustle of town, she loved… a lot of things."

George's words trailed off, his face sunken from the painful memories running through his mind—the same that ran through mine.

Images of my mother sitting in our back room, overlooking our natural yard, paint brush in hand. Her fingers stained in blues and purples as she moved the bristles across the large canvas.

I reached toward my father and grabbed his hand in mine in an attempt to comfort his troubling mind.

"I'm sorry I brought her up. I shouldn't have, I was just …"

"It's okay," he said, choking back any bit of emotions he might have let slip out. "Well, I better get back," he said. "I have a conference call this afternoon and should get to the office and prepare."

"Yeah, of course. You go; I'm just gonna sit here a minute and then walk home."

"You sure?"

"Yeah, I'm fine."

My father was in such deep pain about my mother's death, a resenting pain that turned into anger. I guess it is easier to be mad at *someone*, like God, rather than accept that the one person that meant everything to you was gone.

But where did that leave me? Alone, and without answers.

I sat alone at the table. Something deep within told me that no matter what was going to happen to me, with the Darkness that haunted me or the *Light* I longed to find—either one would consume me. It would engulf everything about who I was, either for better or for worse, for good or evil, for Light or Dark. It was all up to me to choose, but why couldn't I? *What is holding me back? Why can't I just accept the Light and go toward it?*

It seemed so elementary. I didn't want to end up in an eternity of darkness, but, how was I supposed to find the *Light* when all I saw around me was complete blackness?

CHAPTER 27

The walk home from breakfast was long and quiet, not near-ly as short as it seemed most any other day. My father's car passed and honked while he left, and I entered our subdivision. Smiling widely at him was a ruse for the both of us. As soon as his car drove out of sight, my smile faded, and the weight quickly returned.

Breakfast with George left more questions than answers. I had hoped that I would ask him what he believed and he would un-cover a secret passion I hadn't known existed. His life that he had lived with my mother, shared in the joy of their faith, could have been his reality. But, that was not the case. In truth, his belief was one of hatred and anger to the one he thought took his wife away.

About forty yards from our home, I noticed a large figure sitting on the porch steps. Eagerly I ran to meet the man I expected to find.

"Evan!" I called, waving eagerly.

As I approached, I instantly knew it was not Evan.

The man stood tall, extremely tall, with a dark shirt and equally dark hair.

He took a step from the shadows where his face was visible in the afternoon sun. His charcoal hair was in sheer contrast to his ir-idescent skin. His eyes as black as the night called out to me, pulling me into their cavernous appeal. His magnetic face, strong chin, and muscular frame reminded me of Evan. But, he was different as well. Evan's skin was a golden tan, rich from the sun's rays. Whoever this was, his skin was pale, devoid of any interaction with the sun at all. The differences continued as I neared. I noticed the man's eyes even more. They were spheres devoid of all movement and depth, while Evan's eyes had intricate leveled hues of blues and golden flecks. Visually, they seemed to be the complete opposite. Whatever Evan had, this man lacked. And what this man had, Evan did not.

As I approached, the man reached out to shake my hand. "Hello," he spoke with a strong voice chiming with a hypnotic tone. His eyes drew me further into their orbit, leading me down a path I willingly followed.

"Hi," I said with a questioning ring in my voice, uncertain of the man before me.

Hesitantly, I grabbed his outstretched hand, sending a chill down my spine. I felt the wintry frost of his palm against mine and waited in silence for him to introduce himself.

"I'm Helel," he said after a moment, still holding my hand in his massive grip.

"I'm Kara," I said, intentionally releasing my hand from his.

"Yes," he said, a smile twisted across his face. The unknown person stared down at me, allowing the uncomfortable silence to build.

"Can I help you with something?" I asked.

"Sorry, where are my manners? I am a friend of Evangel's. I wanted to meet you, Kara," Helel said, with a cunning smirk curling around his beautiful face. "I have heard so much about you," he continued.

"Oh," I said, unable to look away from his dark eyes. "You have *heard* about me?"

Without answering, Helel began to circle me, looking over my body with his piercing eyes. I felt like I was the prey, a wounded animal being sized-up and evaluated before the predator's next move.

"You are very special, Kara," Helel said. "But you already knew that, didn't you. I am sure Evangel has told you all about how *unique* you are. You two have gotten close, haven't you? You care for him... and him you? Oh, I can see it in your eyes. It's true." Helel circled again. "Huh, well, that is a twist in the story, now isn't it? Evangel, the good little follower, binding to a human. I didn't see that one coming. I mean honestly, he is devoted to humanity and all, but this, it takes it to a whole new level of insubordination. *He will not like this,*" Helel said clicking his tongue against his teeth and shaking his head slightly in disapproval. "Poor little Evangel, becoming the one thing he has fought so hard against."

"I don't know what you are talking about," I tried to respond.

"Oh, sweet, innocent, Kara you don't know what I am talking about because you are nothing. You are not special. You are merely human."

"I thought you said…"

"Oh, I said you were *very special*, did I? You see, that is kind of subjective, isn't it. No, no don't be upset. I think you are great, *special* even. But, Evangel, he is a good little soldier. 'Yes, sir!' kinda guy. He is not going to give that up for a human." Helel continued his attack, "Oh, you didn't think that he…that you two? Maybe he hasn't shown you. You see he isn't really all that *human,*" he leaned in and whispered the words. Standing tall again he continued, "Talk about special. Evangel, now, he is something."

Passing by me, only inches from my vulnerable body, he reached his hand to me and traced a thin line from my abdomen to my arm seductively.

"You see, *I* do think you are very special Kara. You are a unique creature, beautiful, captivating..." Helel said.

His subtle touch made me lean into him as if his finger was a string pulling my unwilling body toward him—my flesh hypnotically moved closer. My mind, not affected by his allure, screamed at my body to move and run from Helel.

"Well, we can discuss all this another time. I really must be going," Helel said.

Before I could will my body to move, he leaned his face into mine, "But, I'm sure I will see you again," I felt his chilled breath on my skin. "Very soon, I'm sure." Helel lingered, smelling my hair, then shoulder. Her rested there for a moment before pulling away.

As I stood in fear, I could hear his laughter under his breath as he walked away slowly. I didn't turn to see him leave or acknowledge his invitation. My head was spinning with fear.

What is going on? Who is this guy? Is he like Evan too? How does he know Evan? How does he know me? And, what was he talking about? The thoughts raced through my mind as I quickly entered my home.

Once inside, I locked the door behind me. I couldn't stop the questions saturating my mind, making my stomach flip with nervousness.

Who is Helel? What does he want?

Moments later, a knock startled me. Unsure of the guest outside, I peeked through the stain glass panels decorating the wooden door. Relief washed over me at the person outside my door. I quickly opened the door to see Evan standing in its entryway.

"Come in, come in," I said ushering him inside the quiet house.

"Hello," Evan greeted. "Is everything alright, Kara?" Evan asked, noticing my urgency to shut and lock the door behind him. "Your heart is racing."

"I thought you might be someone else," I said.

"You were expecting someone?" Evan asked with a hint of reservation.

"No, No. I just thought it might be your *friend*, again," I said turning toward the kitchen and walking to the counter. "He gave me the creeps."

Evan stood in the doorway; a perplexing look crossed his brow. His jaw clenched making his strong facial muscles protrude.

"You want water or something?" I asked, turning back to face Evan.

"Who visited you?" he questioned abruptly.

"He said he was a friend of yours," I breathed in deeply, trying to push away any ill thoughts I might have formed about Evan's *supposed* friend. "He said his name was Helel," I added.

Evan's eyes widened and jaw clenched.

Earnestly, he rushed to me and grabbed my shoulders running his hands down my arms.

"Are you okay? Are you hurt?" Evan said, quickly scanning my entire body with an intensity I had not seen from him before.

"What's going on?"

His hands moved down my arms and held both my hands in his. The warmth of his touch pushed away all uneasy feelings I had earlier felt about Helel and his presence outside my home. The comfort of his hands pulled me into him.

"Your hand!" he said, jolting my pleasant thoughts of Evan's caressing touch back to the two of us.

Looking down, I saw nothing. Evan turned it over and over in his own hand, examining it meticulously.

"What?" I said.

"Did he touch you?" Evan asked, still turning my hand over in his own.

"Um, yeah, he shook my hand and my..." I said, feeling where Helel had traced his fingers across my stomach. "Why, what is going on?" I asked.

"He *Marked* you," Evan explained as he ushered me to sit on the wooden stairs behind us.

"Marked? There is nothing there," I said, examining my own hand.

"It is not meant for anyone to see. The *Mark* is a beacon allowing Helel's creatures to track you," Evan said. "Does it hurt?"

"No. Wait. What do you mean *track me*?"

Evan looked up from my hand, holding my palm within his strong grasp. Seeing the concern in his eyes only added to the fear that had begun to stir from Helel's presence.

"He wasn't your friend, was he?" I said, already knowing the answer.

"No," Evan said, "This might hurt a bit."

"Hurt?" Confused I looked down at my hand.

Evan placed one hand under my own and the other on top of my exposed palm.

What is going on? Who is Helel? Why did he Mark me? There were so many questions that I longed to ask, but before I could begin the conversation I desperately wanted to have, a burning pain pulsed through my hand. It was a warming dull ache at first, then it quickly intensified to a burning that felt like I had grabbed a hot coal.

Searing hot agony pulsed through my *Marked* hand.

I bit my lip in order to hold back the scream trying to escape. The scorching on my skin moved into the muscle of my palm, gaining in burning strength, gradually moving along the backside of my hand and up my forearm—a boiling, bubbling and growing in ferocity with every second.

I could not hold back the distress I was under any longer. A scream erupted from my confused lips. I tried to pull my hand away from Evan's burning touch, the source of my pain clear. Evan gripped my hand firmly not allowing me to pull away from the fire he induced. I squirmed in agony, my body thrashed desperately trying to free myself from Evan's grasp.

Why is he doing this?

My eyes pleaded with Evan's to release me. His eyes flashed a blue haze that emanated from his eyes toward mine. As the light reached out to me, a calming radiance washed over my body, and I willingly allowed the tidal wave of tranquility to cover me. For a second, I forgot about the searing pain in my hand and arm. I was lost in his transcending eyes, lost in a sea of peace.

His eyes blinked, breaking the pacific tether formed between us. With Evan's calming release, I felt his hand let go of mine.

"I am so sorry Kara," Evan said. "I had to remove the *Mark* before they could find you. I'm so very sorry I caused you pain."

I looked down at my hand and saw three connected crescents. The glowing red emblem branded into my quivering palm was like nothing I had ever seen. My breath quickened and my heart began to race.

"The *Mark*?" I said softly.

Evan, perched in front of me, touched my cheek with his hand, tracing his fingers over my smooth skin. A pulse of warmth ran over me, calming me once again.

"It's alright now. The *Mark* is gone," Evan said.

The smell of his sweet enticing breath called me to melt into his strong frame. My soul urged me to reach out to him, pull Evan close, and never let him go. Before I could, Evan stood and helped me to my feet.

"What is that calming thing you do?" I asked feeling the heat on my cheek, still radiating from his touch.

Evan only smiled, and I knew no answers were going to follow.

"Please, tell me what is going on Evan," I asked deeply concerned, standing only inches from his firm chest.

"Come. Sit with me," Evan said, grabbing my hand and guiding me to follow him into the empty family room. Saying nothing, I sat next to him on the sofa. Evan's large frame reclined in its corner.

Evan spoke, "Helel is a Naphal. He was the first that disobeyed the Creator and because of that, cast out of Heaven. He found quick refuge with mankind. Soon his dark deception integrated humanity, and they choose to trust *Helel* rather than the Creator."

"Adam and Eve?" I questioned.

"Yes," Evan continued surprised at my limited knowledge about his world.

"Many others fell with Helel. I lost thousands and thousands of my brothers. It was a very dark time. With their disobedience, many of the Naphal's were diminished with the Great Waters."

Evan paused in an attempt for my mind to keep up with his story.

"Noah and the ark? The flood?" Evan questioned in reference to the Great Waters he spoke of.

"I don't understand. What does Noah and the Ark have to do with the Helel and the fallen angels or Naphal?" I asked in complete confusion.

"The time of Noah was when the Naphal roamed the earth, ruling over the humans and twisting creation into their own destructive game. The flood came to purify everything, destroying the fallen and all they had done to damage the world."

"Wait, I thought the flood was because people were wicked?" I asked, remembering my early Sunday school lessons.

"That was part of it. Humans had become horribly corrupt. They had begun to worship the Naphal. When they claimed the daughters of man for their own, they created abominations that attempted to destroy the world," Evan said.

"It didn't work," I said. "I mean, the fallen didn't die. Not all of them at least."

"No, not all of them," Evan said. "Helel and his remaining followers were forced to live in hiding after the Great Waters. Initially, the Naphal tried to rule over man, posing as a god of water, sun, or earth. That too faded, when the pursuit for man begun and any form of divinity disappeared. Now, man only worships man."

Evan paused and took a long breath, "Helel uses this for his own benefit. You see, if no one believes in anything, then he wins, and man willingly walks toward their death. Helel wants to capture as many souls before the End comes. He can sense it is near, and he will do whatever he can to prevent it or prolong it."

"Wait, wait, this is all too much," I said, "Helel is a fallen angel? A Naphal? And, he is not only just any fallen angel, he is the first. Like Satan or the Devil?"

"That is correct," Evan said.

"But, I thought that was Lucifer. That he was the *Devil* or something like that?" I asked.

"The name Lucifer arose after the translation of the original scriptures from Hebrew to Latin. Lucifer in Latin means *Morning Star*. Helel means *son of the dawn*, or *Morning Star* when translated from Hebrew into Latin the name Lucifer originated. Lucifer has come to be the name humans know him as, but his true name is Helel."

Rubbing my head, there was so much information to take in, so much that I didn't know.

"So, Helel, is really the Devil?" I said as I stood and began to pace. "And he *Marked* me, why?" I asked, "How do I play into all this?"

"You are extremely important, Kara. You are the one that holds the key to the *End*."

Evan stood and firmly held my arms, stopping the manic pacing I could not control on my own.

"The end of what?" I questioned, drawing out each word.

"The end of time itself," Evan said. "You start everything in motion, or you don't."

Confusion filled my mind again. *How am I able to control the end of time? Nothing he said makes any sense.*

"I don't understand," I said.

"If Helel stops you, then the End will not come," Evan said, as we both sat back down on the sofa.

"If Helel stops me from what?" I questioned, "and isn't' it a good thing that the *End* doesn't come?"

"If he stops you from finding the *Light*," Evan said, scooting closer to me on the sofa. Placing his hand on my knee, he continued, "The *End* is not a bad thing. At least it doesn't have to be."

"It doesn't?" I questioned. There was nothing about *the End* that didn't sound horribly bad. I had seen the apocalyptic movies. *The End* was never a good thing. "How is the End *not* a bad thing?" I said abruptly.

"You humans think you know everything. Yet, there is no real understanding of the world out there. No real truth to it. You all just go around thinking you have all the answers and what you don't, you make up. Time is one of man's fabrications. It is infinite, but you have no comprehension of that because you are so self-consumed. *The End* is not the end at all. In fact, it is the exact opposite," Evan said.

"I'm sorry, I didn't..." I stammered at Evan's intense outpouring of emotions. "I just don't understand!" Frustrated, I stood again. For the first time, I noticed how the room had now become dark as the sun began to set outside.

Evan stood too and held my unnerved body in his tight, yet gentle grasp.

"I'm sorry," he spoke softly now only a few inches from my face. "It is so very hard to try to tell you something that you were not designed to understand yet."

"If you could just show me, then I could understand," I begged.

Evan smiled softly, "This is something you have to find out on your own. Faith is believing without seeing. It is trusting in more than yourself. It is not just you Kara. It is all humans. They are so desperate for control that they fight the truth with their whole being. And, that fight and the need for control, will be their demise. The *End* is not a bad thing when you let go of yourself and plunge into a sea of belief. The *End* becomes a beautiful and a glorious anticipation."

Evan's words spun in my head trying to find fertile ground.

How can I let go and rely on something that I have never truly known? I'm just supposed to jump in the deep end of belief not knowing how to swim and hope to not drown.

"It will be alright, Kara," Evan said, touching my cheek gently pulling me back to the two of us.

His subtle embrace soothed my racing thoughts, melting my skin into his. I closed my eyes and bathed in his close proximity. Nodding slightly, I had no idea if it would be okay or if I would be okay. But, in Evan's arms, under his touch, everything else seemed miles away.

Knock. Knock. Knock.

"Kara! Kara! Are you in there?" a girl yelled from behind the closed door, yanking me from the serenity of Evan's embrace.

"Kara, its Tea, open up!" she demanded.

CHAPTER 28

Teagan stood with her hands on her hips glaring at me through the newly opened door.

"Where have you been? I have been texting and calling you all day!" She exploded, unable to hide her irritation. "And then I called your dad…" she paused, "Yeah, *your* dad!"

Standing in the entryway, I was shell-shocked by Teagan's verbal barrage. I had completely forgotten about the outside world and left my phone plugged into the wall outlet on my nightstand.

Teagan continued, walking past me rolling her eyes, "Thankfully he told me you were alive! And, home. Or, so he thought. And, here you are fine, just avoiding me?" she asked, plopping down on the kitchen bar stool completely unaware of Evan standing in the living room behind her.

"No, it wasn't that, I just…" I tried to find the words to explain the craziness that surrounded my day.

I hadn't told Teagan, Jen, or anyone about my mysterious savior that night on the bridge; let alone the fact that I had *found* him. And, oh yeah, he was an angel. It wasn't something you sent in a text message.

Interrupting my thoughts, Teagan continued, still unaware of Evan who now sat on the couch, lounging his long legs over the coffee table, "I know you were hurt by the whole Jen and Kale thing, but, you can talk to me." Teagan paused, "I know it must have really bugged you. I mean you were like really into Kale, even if it was a long time ago. I know it must have hurt…"

"No, it's not that," I interjected before Teagan could continue the embarrassment.

Walking behind Teagan, I stood by the arm of the sofa where Evan sat quietly, observing the girlish interactions that played out in front of him. He shot a playful smile my way, making my cheeks instantly flush with embarrassment.

Teagan still seemed oblivious of Evan presence.

Didn't she see him? How could she not? His presence was electrifying, I could see him. *Can't she?*

"Oh, really… it didn't bother you at all," she said spinning around in her chair to face the two of us.

I raised my eyebrows and motioned toward Evan. Nothing.

"What? Don't give me that look, Kara," Teagan said, turning her back to me and heading into the kitchen, still unaware of Evan, "I'm ticked, you totally blew me off. We were supposed to meet up tonight. And, okay, I was kind of worried about you, too."

She can't see him.

Looking down at Evan, he was smiling widely, almost laughing out loud.

Quickly, the words Evan had said under the willow rushed into my mind. He wasn't allowing Teagan to see him.

I sent my pointed elbow into his shoulder, making him jump slightly and then stand next to me. I shot him a glare that begged him to expose himself so that I would avoid the prolonged embarrassment by my friend's girlish rambles.

Evan cleared his throat and nudged me back playfully.

Teagan spun around from digging through the fridge. Shock filled her eyes as her mouth dropped open in disbelief at the man standing next to me in my living room.

"Okay?" Tegan said, looking extremely confused.

"I'm sorry Tea, I've just been busy with *other* things," I said cryptically.

Teagan walked by me with an intense gaze that said she thought she knew everything that was happening, any question of how she had not seen Evan earlier seemed miles from her mind.

Now, only pubescent teen notions of a guy and girl alone in an empty house were obvious in the way she looked back and forth between the two of us.

Without hesitating, I decided to jump on board with her illusion, taking full advantage of her speculations and usher her out of the house as quickly as possible.

"Hello," Evan greeted Teagan, halting my attempt at her exit.

"Hello," Teagan mouthed, mocking his formality. "Wow! You are insanely tall," she added abruptly.

"Yeah, I think he knows that Tea," I said quickly with a hint of irritation. "This is Evan."

"So…you and Kara, huh?" She gave him the once over, looking him up and down before sending me an approving nod.

"Okay, then…" I said, "Don't you need to get going?"

Not allowing an answer, I guided her out of the living room and out of the house quickly.

I shut the door behind us, and spoke in hushed tones, "Sorry, I didn't mean to push you out, it's just…"

"Hey, no biggie. I get it," Teagan said smiling widely, "Oh man, he is hot..." Teagan fanned herself dramatically. "Who is he?"

I shook my head, laughing softly at her outward display. "I'll call you later," I said encouraging her to venture beyond the porch steps.

"I've never seen him around here before. He's a college guy, right? Is he home over break? No... Oh! Did his parents just move here? No, we would have defiantly heard about *him* moving in…."

"Tea," I stopped her, "he's a friend."

"Oh yeah, a friend. *Right*." Teagan said, "I'm not an idiot, just give me something."

I shook my head.

"Come on, girl," Teagan continued, "Are you guys…"

"Good-bye!" I said, attempting to sound stern.

"Text me," Teagan mouthed.

I watched her leave, then took a deep breath and opened the door. Evan was standing in the entryway.

"Sorry about that," I said slipping into the home.

"Its fine," he said quietly, the corner of his lips twisted upward in his attempt to hide a smile.

With my back against the hard door, Evan took a few steps toward me. My heart raced. I longed for him to reach out to me, to hold me in the darkening hall, kiss my unknowing lips. I yearned to feel his warmth against my skin and breathe him in completely. My cheeks began to blush as the thoughts of Evan's touch raced through my mind.

His eyes bore into mine, deep into my being in a way that only caused the lustful thoughts to continue. The space between us felt energized, electrified with a current that drew us toward one another, even more. His deep blue eyes speckled with a golden movement of the stars. My heart reeled to his. I longed to just touch him, his strong chest only inches from me.

Pushing my back off the door allowed me to stand closer to him. My hands boldly went to his athletic frame and rested there for a moment. I felt his heart racing under my palm. I moved my hands slowly from his chest, my fingers trailed down to his arms and over his protruding biceps, to his defined forearms.

I could not help myself. I had to feel his energy, his warmth—I craved it.

To my elated surprise, Evan did not pull away. I felt his muscles twitch under my touch, his eyes holding fast on mine as I moved my hands along his body.

Soon, my hands found his and we interlocked our fingers, intertwining ourselves together. My eyes drifted from his eyes to his soft, supple lips. They parted to speak but words didn't follow. Looking back into his eyes, I knew he wanted this too. The yearning I felt deep within, I saw reflected in his eyes. His hands held firmly to mine, his thumb tracing my own in affection. I longed for his lips to touch mine, pressing passionately against my own, allowing me to completely disappear into his embrace.

Evan read the lustful intent housed within my eyes and pulled away quickly. His hands dropped and he took a few steps back. A deep sigh escaped his lips and he turned, disheveling his hair and clenching his jaw. He seemed so distraught. *Why is he fighting this?*

I stood in the entryway, mentally telling myself to breathe, something I seemed to have forgotten.

With his retreat so did the illusion I had fabricated. The hope of our embrace shattered into a million pieces as Evan now seemed miles away.

Evan shook his head slightly. He seemed to be fighting a question I never asked. A troubled look crossed his face, and my heart sunk at the distance he was putting between us.

Evan's back was strong, his muscles bulged and flexed. His hands tugged at his head, then clung to his neck.

"I'm sorry," I said.

Turning to face me, I was able to see the pain in Evan's eyes.

"I shouldn't have... I just..." I fumbled with my words.

Our simple embrace was nothing but innocent. Yet, there was more to it, something deeper and greater than I could have imagined. Most of all, it felt completely right to me.

We stood in silence for an unknown time, staring at each other; the darkness of the night fell in around us. My mind wanted to stay in this moment, but my body twitched in fear at what I knew came with the night.

Will they come again tonight? Will they find me now that I've been Marked by Helel?

Unable to push the troubling thoughts away I asked, "Will they come tonight?"

"No. They won't come while I am here," he said.

Evan was still extremely troubled, fighting something deep within himself that was completely unknown to me.

Thinking of the *Mark*, Helel's words rang in my head, *Evangel, becoming the one thing he has fought so hard to avoid.*

What did he mean by that? What did Evan fight so hard to avoid? Me? Am I somehow a reason for his pain?

"What about the Mark?" I questioned, looking down at my hand which no longer held any residual evidence of the cryptic emblem.

"I was able to remove it before it could fully accomplish its purpose," Evan said calmly, gently feeling my palm where the Mark once was.

"Purpose?"

"It would have released a signal, allowing every Naphal to find you. There might have been too many for me to hold off until dawn."

Concern filled his eyes, as well as my own. My eyes were heavy, and my body ached from the tension of the day and previous night. Too many thoughts raced through my withered mind. The only thing I knew for sure, I didn't want Evan to leave. Not only for his protection but for the force that drew me to him. I was tired of straining, tired of wanting.

"Will you stay with me?"

"Of course."

"My dad should be home soon," I said motioning him to follow me.

Thoughts of our closeness only moments before rushed in as we walked up the stairs to my room. I had to push them aside—push the thoughts of our hands intertwined, the warmth of his body, and the steadiness of his breath. I had to put it away so that Evan would stay.

Evan sat next to me on my bed, his large frame making my queen seem insignificant.

"You need to rest," Evan said.

But, trying to sleep was not as easy as it sounded. With each passing second, the darkness seemed to move around us, each new noise jolting me from my momentary slumber.

After many attempts, and what felt like hours, I said, "I can't sleep." I fully felt the weight of my exhaustion but was unable to rest. "I see the creatures every time I close my eyes. I feel like they are playing with me, tormenting me. I can't see them, but they are there, aren't they?" Evan nodded.

A crash outside my window sent me jumping in fright as a tree limb scratched my window pane.

"I am right here. Nothing will hurt you," Evan said, lying next to me he reached out and pulled my body into his.

Resting my head on his warm chest, I felt the rise and fall of each breath. His strong arms held me close, stroking my back gently.

Exhausted tears started to fall.

Why am I crying?

But, it was futile fighting it. My weakness prevailed, I succumb to the emotional fears left by the dark creatures. Tears continued. There was nothing I could do to protect myself from the Darkness, nothing I could have done to avoid the collision on the bridge, and nothing I could have done to save my mother. I was a spinning top ready to tip, and my emotions were flying everywhere.

My life was upside down. Everything had changed. The world was not the simple place of childish dreams. It was a dark world with demonic forces and angelic beings. It was a world of death and destruction, a world of pain and agony, and there was absolutely nothing I could do about it.

"You are safe," he said. "You are safe, now."

Within seconds, a wave of warming comfort passed over me and filled me with peace. I knew the source was Evan, and I willingly gave in, drifting off to the stillness of sleep, resting on Evan's strength, wrapped in angelic arms.

CHAPTER 29 TWENTY

As I rounded the path I had taken so many times before, the memories of last night flooded my mind.

Images of Evan's warming touch, the harmonious movement of his breath under my tear stained cheeks, and the comforting caress on the small of my back.

As Evan had promised, there were no dark creatures that came for me in the night; his presence alone had kept them at bay.

When I awoke, I knew the fragility of my emotions would have made me look weak and infantile to Evan. I hated that I cried, allowing everything to pour out of me that way. I had bottled it all up, from my mother's death to the dark creatures, and everything in between. The tears ripped out of me, dragging along all those old feelings I had tried to dam up: feelings of sadness and pain from my mother's death, trepidation and an unknown desperation for Evan— all those emotions became a crashing tsunami of flowing tears.

When I awoke, I felt the baggage weighing on my sore eyes, remnants of salty sobs left my checks chapped from sustained moisture.

Evan was not there. My insecurities didn't blame him. I found a note in his absence, indicating he would return before nightfall and for me to *rest*.

I ran harder against the uneven trial, trying to push past the emptiness of waking alone. This wasn't the easiest route, but one I had taken often with Jen during my months of recovery.

The shadowed path behind me had begun to show hints of light flickering through the leaves. The view beyond the trees revealed a massive cliff and ocean below. Once I reached the security of the sun, I rested, both arms on the wooden railing, stretching over the only barrier between looking at the water and falling into it.

I breathed in deeply, regaining my composure, allowing every bit of air to fill my tired lungs.

After waking to an empty home, I had texted Teagan to meet in town and catch up. I was desperate to fill the time without Evan. We had grabbed lunch at the same café my father and I had eaten the day before. Teagan probed me to disclose who the mysterious man in my home was last night. I deflected and directed the conversation toward her impending love life. We talked for hours, laughed even. It gave a sweet reprieve to the troubling truth I was living.

I had no idea who I was. *The Akarah? The last one?* I had no idea what those concepts meant and how they related to me.

The *Light* was another metaphysical notion I could not uncover.

But, it didn't matter. All I thought of was Evan. He was all I really wanted. I did not want to be the *Last One*, the *Akarah*, *Marked* or anything like that. I just wanted Evan.

My thoughts faded when I saw a man sitting beyond the security of the railing. He rested on a large cluster of rocks that overlooked the churning water below. His back was to me, arms gripped tightly pulling his knees to his chest.

Drawn to him, I knew it was Evan. It didn't matter that I couldn't see his face, his beauty emanated from his intense perfection. Without hesitation, I scaled the rail and climbed cautiously to him. Rocks slowed my pursuit, but soon I came to stand next to Evan's seated position. His eyes were distant, almost as if he didn't know I was there. His molded face was lit with the glowing golden hues of the sun.

Evan looked up at me, his sapphire eyes tenderly encouraged me to sit and take in the beauty before us. I tried to speak, to say something that would make him smile, to see the glistening of white teeth through his blush lips making my knees weak and my stomach flip, but there were no signs of the carefree smile I craved. His eyes were pained and saddened.

As I found my seat next to him, I couldn't help but think of Helel's troubling words again. *You are nothing.* Maybe Evan had finally realized what Helel had so easily identified and what I knew to be true. I was an insignificant human, and he was a magnificent angel. Maybe that was what was troubling Evan. He finally realized the truth about me. *I am nothing.*

Evan released his legs, allowing them to find their resting place on the rocks below us. His size still amazed me as his long limbs spread before me.

The landscape was captivating, with white capped waves crashing onto the rocky shore below. A spray bloomed high in the air, creating a mist that rose toward us, dissipating just before it reached the edge of the cliff.

We sat for hours in silence, watching the waves crash below and hearing the birds chirp within the canopy behind us. I wanted to reach out to Evan, but my own uncertainties and fear of pushing him away again held me back. The night before, I boldly grabbed his hand in my own. We were close. Close enough I could have reached my lips to his. But, before I could, he retreated. I did not want that to happen again. I sat quietly, allowing thoughts of my own weaknesses and frailties to snuff out any bit of positivity in the air.

I felt Evan's intense stare and turned to face him. He took my hands in his without taking his eyes from mine. The intensity of his eyes searched for the answers to questions that I never asked.

"I'm glad you're here," Evan spoke from the stillness around us. "It is almost evening; the sun has begun to set."

Evan, still holding my hands, looked back to the fading sky. I knew the light would soon fade to darkness and the sun would slip behind the trees creating an elaborate wheel of colors, fanning from pale yellows and oranges to vibrant lavenders and blues. Soon only a glimmer of light would remain.

"It's beautiful," Evan spoke.

My words came out raspy and weak, "Yes, it is beautiful."

He closed his eyes slowly and lifted his nose into the air,

breathing deeply, filling his lungs completely with the sweet evening's breeze.

He exhaled loudly, and then spoke, "If you could only hear what I hear, see what I see. Then…" he paused, shaking his head he looked down at his hands still holding mine tightly, "…then you wouldn't deny it. You couldn't."

His words held the weight of an unknown sadness.

"I don't hear anything," I said quietly.

"I know."

Evan's eyes pleaded with me, begged me to hear whatever he heard. His hands released mine, and I soon felt the weight of his arm on my shoulder, pulling me into to his strong frame.

Under his arm, I looked up toward Evan and was amazed at how close we were. He embraced me, holding me tightly into his muscular body. An intoxicating aroma of sweet, crisp rain, just out of reach, filled my nose. I had never smelled anything as intoxicating.

Sensing his body beginning to tense and pull away, I asked, trying to keep him close, "Tell me what you hear?"

There was a long pause, "You have to open your mind and expose yourself to what is around you. You have to allow yourself to feel deeper, breathe deeper, *love* deeper than ever before."

My heart leapt at the word *love*, and I fidgeted in my skin. I tried to calm myself but was unable.

Evan sensed my restlessness and his embrace tightened, "Be still… deep within. Listen to everything around you and connect to it," Evan spoke passionately. "Hear the waves crashing below us. Listen to the second right before they hit the rocks; the water moving so hastily toward them, so anxious to reach their eminent end. Feel the moisture in the air from the water's resonating existence. Taste the distinction of salt on your lips and the grit of its presence on your skin."

I felt the words as he spoke them; everything around me was becoming clearer. I moved my tongue over my bottom lip and tasted the salty aftermath. Smiling slightly, I touched my fingers to my lips, thinking I would feel the salt that I had tasted, but there was nothing, only the rough beginnings of chapped skin.

I was amazed that I had never stopped to look at the world the way he did.

"There is so much more that you cannot even begin to understand," he said.

"Then tell me," I urged.

"It is not just the waves, or the rocks, or the air… it is so much more than that; the wind wisps past us singing a beautiful swirl of musical interludes, the last bit of light in the sky harmoniously screams for attention, and the sound of your breath amongst the night only adds to its symphony," Evan paused and then continued. "It is all around us, within us, and through us."

My head spun in Evan's cryptic, yet poetic words. It was a wonderful thought that everything moved and roused around and through us; the world beating to an unknown maestro. But, I knew that was not true. It couldn't be. Science was behind everything and hearing the sound of the wind was poetic, nothing more.

I smiled slightly at him and said, "That's beautiful," like an idiot and looked away quickly.

"Beauty only masks its true greatness. It is the most wonderful sound, a bit of Heaven spilling out onto Earth. It is the closest we will ever be to *Him* here."

Evan continued as I attempted to open my mind and hear his words fully, "The sun setting is a chance for all of Creation to marvel at another magnificent day, and they sing, rejoicing in it. That is what I hear… the most glorious song ever sung. *Creations Song*," he smiled widely and quietly laughed to himself.

"But, it is horribly tragic as well," pain filled his face and his smile faded. "It is just one more reminder of a home I have not seen in a very long time. A reminder of a peace so many will never know."

My heart ached for him. How horrible it must be for Evan to be here on Earth. To feel and see so much, when we as humans easily miss it all. He could see the movement of everything, the reason the sun rose and set, and yet this place wasn't his home. It was ours, and we didn't care.

Looking deep into his alluring eyes, I saw purity in truth. His words were not merely poetic but real—a living movement, breathing and twisting all around us. And, here I was, barely able to taste the salt on my lips. I lowered my head in defeat in my inability to hear what he heard: the longing sound of hope, wonder, and excitement. The thought of *Creation's Song*, as he called it, begged me to understand everything deeper. But, it was just out of reach.

Maybe Evan is the Light I am searching for? Maybe there is nothing deeper to it. Did I find the Light? Did I find it in Evan?

CHAPTER30 THIRTY

The sun rose from the dark cobalt water; Evan shifted, snapping me awake with his movement. We had talked through the majority of the night; the darkness staying just out of reach.

"I'm sorry, I must have dozed off," I said.

Evan smiled gently, still showing the pain within his eyes I saw before. He looked off to the almost rising sun. Most of the sky was still dark. Slowly, it began to change and lighten creating a wheel of color from vibrant purples to intense pinks. As the night hung on, the remaining stars glistened in the darkened sky. For a moment, there was peace, both the night and the day living together in harmony. The blackness of the night didn't chase away the day, and the sun didn't make the stars flee. They existed together, peaceful and still, even if it was for that one second in time. *Why can't I have that? Why did it have to be one or the other?*

Deep down, I knew that wasn't what I really wanted. I didn't want the darkness and light to co-exist. I didn't want the darkness at all. Truth was, I was afraid. Afraid that waiting for the light was like waiting for the sun. That even though you saw the sky changing colors and the darkness fading away, there was still that moment of hesitation before the sun came, that moment that you could choose to either walk toward the light or back into the darkness. *But, why can't I choose? Why can't I let go of hanging onto that one moment?*

Evan and I sat and waited. When we felt the heat of the day encircle us, Evan shifted and turned toward me. He reached into his pocket and pulled out a chain with a cylindrical charm dangling from the golden necklace.

"Wear this and nothing will harm you," Evan said.

He leaned close to put the chain around my neck. I longed for Evan to remain close, but he pulled away quickly.

The charm rested in the hollow of my neck. Turning it over in my hand, I saw the uniqueness of the stone. The gem was a magnificent glowing jewel, deep blue in color with highlights of golden pearls dancing within the intricate stone. It was stunning, more exquisite than any diamond or sapphire I had ever seen, and somehow a magnificent combination of the two.

"It's amazing!" I said, wrapping my arms around Evan's neck in gratitude.

Again, Evan pulled away quickly at my quick embrace. Placing his hands on my shoulders he pushed back gently. Confusion crossed my brow. My hands went to his, still holding my shoulders, not allowing him to put distance between us. His hands against my skin sent a feeling of yearning for a deeper touch. His thumb moved along my collarbone, tracing its rigidness to the smoothness of my neck. Soon his fingers found the charm, and he turned it over, examining it for himself. My cheeks flushed at his closeness. Evan's hand dropped the charm and trailed down my arm with a soothing progression before finding my hand.

"I have to go now," Evan said tenderly as we stood together.

"Yeah... I should... me too." I stumbled, cumbersomely tripping over my words, "I better get home. My dad might start to worry. If he's even home."

The quietness of his eyes and stillness from his lips made my stomach drop with an uneasy feeling. His gentle touch, something that would otherwise send my heart into a spin, only made the sickening feeling well inside of me. *Something is wrong.*

Evan pulled me close, hugging me tightly, holding me in his strong arms.

I looked up at him as he forced a slight smile. This was no loving embrace. There was something more to his closeness. *Something's wrong, I can feel it.*

"I *will* see you again, Kara," Evan said with raspy and forced words.

"What? What are you talking about?" I said quickly.

His mouth opened slightly to speak, but he didn't. His hands released mine, and he slowly stepped back.

"Please, tell me what is going on?" I urged, stepping closer to Evan.

"I have to leave you now," Evan said. "I must go."

"Why?"

"You *don't* understand. If you could just see the *Light*, see the truth…" Evan pleaded, holding both my hands now.

"I do, I do," I responded. "I see it in *you*."

"I know, and that is the problem. You are so blinded by me, you can't see *His Light*," Evan said. "I'm just a reflection. I don't hold any light; there is nothing bright about me at all." Evan continued, "The moon doesn't emit light. It may seem bright when everything around it is black, but there is nothing bright about it. I am the moon made to reflect the true *Light* of the Son."

"Wait…" I said, "This *Light*? Are we talking about God?"

"All this," Evan motioned to the space around us. "It has nothing to do with me. I am just a messenger. Someone sent to show you the right path, and instead, my feelings for you have gotten in the way. And now, you can't even see past me. I am blinding you, Kara, blinding you from seeing the truth," Evan said with passionate defeat.

I tried to process what he was saying, but my head was spinning.

"This is *my* fault," he continued, "I allowed you to see me, to talk to me. But, the truth is, I couldn't stay away from you. I didn't want to. And now, I have ruined *everything*. I am so very sorry, Kara. This is not how it was supposed to be. You have a bigger destiny, a bigger design, and it does not include me. I am sorry I did not see it sooner. I should have never…" his words trailed off as he dropped my hands and turned.

After he spoke the words, I knew that I wasn't the only one feeling the connection growing, the chemistry titrating between us.

No longer able to hold back my feelings I spoke, "No! No,

this is right," I grabbed his arm and spun him around to meet my face. "*This* is the most *right* thing I have ever felt."

"But, it is not what is supposed to be," Evan said.

"Then what *is* supposed to be? Tell me, and I'll do it. Then, none of this will matter, and we can be together," I begged.

As I spoke the word, *together*, Evan's face filled with anguish. My heart dropped.

Seeing his discontent, I expanded, "If…if that is what you want?"

Holding my hands in his, he spoke tenderly, "There is nothing more I want in this world than you."

My soul soared within me, and my heart reached to him in mutual affection.

"But, Kara, that is the problem. This pull I feel toward you; I thought it was because of you being my *Charge,* a connection so that I could protect you better. But now, I know it is not that simple. This tether I feel pulling me toward you is something much greater. I know you feel it too."

"I do," I interjected quickly leaning into his body and reaching my head to his earnestly.

"But, it is distracting you, Kara. It is not what is supposed to be," Evan said. "This connection, whatever it is, is not allowing you to see the truth. To see your future, what you are destined for. You *have* to see the *Light*, it is the only way. And, I am blocking you. With me here, there is no way you will find the truth. I have to leave or everything will be for naught," he said.

Evan held my hands tightly sending pulsing warmth toward me. A calming wave began to wash over me.

I dropped my hands, "No! Don't do that. Don't make everything calm and okay." I paused, feeling the weight of the conversation, before making one final plea, "Don't leave."

Evan leaned into me with one last embrace. His lips met my heated, blushed cheek, and lingered. Warmth washed over me, instantly. I was no longer able to feel anger or pain, everything became placid.

"No! Don't go!" I wanted to scream out to him, but his calming haze held me, even when his arms released.

Evan whispered in my ear, *"My beloved is mine, and I am my beloved's."*

Before I could respond, Evan turned and slowly walked toward the tree-lined path. His strong frame slowly faded into the evergreens with a vaporous gust of light. Then, he was gone. I felt my soul crumble and wither within. *No!* I wanted to cry out, but my body wouldn't move, the warmth still encased around me from his touch.

I stood quietly alone on the rocky cliff, clinging to the one and only thing I had left of Evan. The charm he gave me still felt his warmth, dangling against my neck. With the charm in my hand, a wave of Evan's warming peace pulsed through my body. Behind the tranquility, sadness dwelled in his absence. Even the calming powers Evan endowed within the jewel could not banish the emptiness I instantly felt without him.

CHAPTER 31

I found myself aimlessly walking. My solidarity was all-consuming. I was a ghost of my old self. And still, I looked for him.

Evan had been gone for weeks now. There was no sign of him anywhere. No sign of his magnificent light or saving presence. The only evidence he had even existed was the charm dangling against my skin.

I crossed in front of the courthouse and patrolled its perimeter. I was back where I started, searching the streets for my mysterious savior. Except now I knew I would not find him. He no longer wanted me to, regardless of how diligently I looked, he was gone.

He wasn't on the street corner waiting to rescue a lone pedestrian, although I looked. He wasn't at the bridge, and even though it was terrifying, I went there daily and sat on the bank watching the water churn eerily below. He wasn't at the hospital or under the willow whose leaves had fallen and branches hung low, reflecting my mood. Regardless, I looked everywhere I thought he might be.

The dim lights cast a shadowy haze around the exterior of the town, sending a sharp shiver down my spine. With his protective power encased in the charm around my neck, the dark creatures kept their distance but were always present—lurking in a dark alley, hiding behind a large Sycamore, or peering in my window. They were all around me. Hidden in the shadows, the creatures knew they couldn't touch me, at least for now. It was a waiting game I knew would eventually end. Somehow, the creatures would break the protective spell Evan had locked away in the charm. Then, my demise would follow.

I rarely slept. When I did, I would awake to the smell of rotting flesh filling my room. It was a new level of torment, waiting for the moment when the beasts could forge through the charm's power and overtake me.

Last night had come just as it had before, fast and hard. The creatures were ready to push the boundaries of my protection, terrifying me in the process. First, it was the noises outside my window. Then, I heard the dark creatures in the darkest corners of my room. They stayed there, mostly. Their bodies were just out of sight, red eyes were the only visual indication of their attendance. But, last night, unlike the many others, two creatures left their corners and began to circle my bed, snarling between one another. Their bodies were so close to mine that their massive outlines became visible. The pair's aggressive behavior shook my bed with each horrifying pass.

After hours of their torture, I thought about taking off the charm and ending their sadistic game. It would have been easier that way, to let the creatures finish what they started on the bridge. But, I couldn't bring myself to take off the necklace. I was even more horrified of what would come after the creatures attacked. *What will become of me if I give into the Darkness?*

I could feel myself slipping away again, turning into a person who wanted the pain of this world to disappear. I had known her before: the girl I had been when my mother died. I could feel myself slipping back to the person that hid from everyone, back to the person that almost killed herself. I didn't want to be that person again, yet I didn't want to fight anymore either.

I left the sanctity of the courthouse and began to meander down the lone, dark streets of the town. Hours passed.

After some time, my knee began to ache, begging me to sit and rest. I found refuge on the wide flagstone steps of an old gothic building. I buried my face in my hands and tried to push back my troubling thoughts.

I reached into my coat pocket and felt the piece of paper I had desperately held onto—my mother's note I had found in her Bible months prior. It had once found its place within my desk. Now, I carried it with me everywhere, trying to keep a connection to her—to anyone. I had Evan's charm and my mother's note. They were the only things remaining from the two people who I had loved and who had left me alone.

Careful not to rip the delicate page, I unfolded her note written on ornate stationary with hand painted lilies. It's once white finish now resembled parchment with ripples scattering its surface. A few water-mark tear drops added to its tarnished appearance.

My mother's words were an elegant calligraphy of eclectic handwriting scripted in black ink. Her words only confused me. They were as coded as they always seemed. I longed to talk to her and ask her what she meant. The dim light overhead cast shadows on the note making it hard to read. Still, I searched for a hidden meaning I may have missed.

The Light is in you. I have seen it. My mom's words jumped off the page.

What does she mean? The only light I had seen was Evan's and other than the sun nothing else compared. *How is this Light in me?*

I felt the heat of wet drops begin to pool in my eyes, and then fall down my cheeks slowly. This was the last thing I had intended. With the sleeve of my coat, I attempted to wipe away the pain. But, it was no use. The tears began to fall, slowly at first, then uncontrollably saturating my face completely.

There was no more strength left in me, no ability to hold back the tears. They had fallen the day Evan left, and the next, and the next—they never stopped.

My breathing slowed along with the tears, allowing me to continue reading the cryptic lines of my mother's note.

Please just believe and fully give into it, please Kara, please. I could almost hear my mother's voice pleading with me from beyond the grave. *Find the Light, my sweet girl.* I read behind blurred eyes.

"Tell me what to do!" I found myself yelling at the paper.

My throat tightened as I pleaded, "Please. Please. How do I

find this *Light*? Please help me find him. Please, Mom, help me find you."

A few lone tear drops fell to the paper below, blurring my mother's writings.

The streetlight, high above my head, faded and flashed in the night's sky. I looked up, into the iridescent fixture, to see the last bit of electricity slip from the lone light. A warm breeze filled the cold space around me, before the light emitted its final glow and plunged me into darkness.

I closed my eyes, expecting the dark creatures to emerge from the darkness that I now bathed in. Nothing came. When I opened my eyes, I was surprised to see a single light illuminating over my head. Transfixed, I stared into the ornate wall unit.

"Find the *light*," I said inaudibly.

Evan had said the same thing to me when he left, and my mother had written those words in her note. How did they both know I needed this *light*? And, how did they know of it and I didn't? *What am I missing?*

Still looking up at the light covering my head, for the first time, I noticed the building behind me. The large stone walls reached the charcoal sky above, spitting its icy bits of water down on me. Above the old cathedral door, I read, *I am the Light of the World.*

A church. How perfect. I thought sarcastically.

A chill filled my bones and shook me to my core. I tried to pull my saturated jacket around my body in an attempt to retain any remaining heat, but with no success. The option of walking the streets all night seemed lunacy, making the building that much more inviting.

"It's only a building," I repeated over and over under my breath, barely audible.

Haunted by the memories of my past, I sat unmoved on the steps of the cathedral. The last time I had been in a church was my mother's funeral. I had promised—or more cursed—that I would never step foot in another church again. And now here I was, desperately contemplating the sanctity of its massive walls. But, I had nowhere else to turn.

Slowly, I got up from my stoop, the weight of my damp clothes held me like tacky cement to the hard steps. Even they didn't want to go inside. I knew I couldn't sit here any longer. It was only getting colder. Thinking I could call Jen or Teagan, I reached into my pocket for my phone and quickly dialed Teagan. But, before she could answer, I ended the call. *What would I say; she is miles away at school?* My father—I could call him—if he were home.

I was alone. No other fear had been stronger than being alone. It was the fear I lived with daily. Everyone I had ever loved had left me. My mother died, my friends were away at school, my father was consumed in his work, and Evan was gone.

Why did Evan leave?

"You are blinded by me," he had said.

Before Evan disappeared he told me how much he cared for me. It sounded as if he might even love me. *But, then why leave?*

Helel's words answered the question in my mind, as it always seemed to, reminding me of my obvious insignificance. *You are nothing. You are not special. You are merely human.*

My heart knew it was true. Evan had left because I was nothing. I wasn't this special *key*. I was just human. Weak. Frail. Broken. *No wonder he left.*

Shaking my head, I tried to remove the images of Evan's final goodbye. I couldn't think of it, not now. Now, I had a decision to make: enter the church or stay amongst the darkness?

I was a statue standing in front of the church's entry. My heart pounded with trepidation as my hand reached for the brass doorknob.

Why am I so nervous? It's only a church, right?

But, I knew it was more than that. It was a part of my life that I didn't want to go back to, a part filled with pain and disappointment. My mother's funeral was just a portion of that pain. The entire concept behind those doors and what lay inside had me internally quivering.

I knew what it was, it was life—real and true life. Something I was completely void of now. I had tasted it before when my mom was alive. Her eyes lit up every time she talked about church and what it stood for.

We'd sit in the front row every Sunday. I sat close to her so I could hear her voice singing above the congregations. The church lifted her spirits, even when the cancer was at its worst. I never understood why. It was only a facility, a building with people milling around, a glorified business that called itself *Holy*. But, to her, it was more.

Standing there, with my hand on the old rusty knob, I couldn't help thinking of her waiting for me inside, wearing her blue dress with the yellow flower pattern. She would be sitting alone with the Hymn book across her lap, legs crossed at the knee, tapping to the song played by the pianist.

The image faded as I dropped my hand from the doors entrance and took a step back. Shaking my head, I fought the thoughts that began to flood my mind. No longer did I see the images of my mother sitting in the pews motioning me to join her. Now, I saw the memories of a shadowed church: an open casket in front of a crowd of faceless people dressed in black lace and dark suits, all with downcast eyes.

I shook my head harder. My hands covered temples and pulled on my disheveled hair in an attempt to dislodge the horrible memory. I wanted to hold on to the initial image of my mother, bright eyed and teaming with life, sitting in the pew wearing that blue dress. But, I could only see her lying in a box, washed of all color and life—dead. Flowers adorned her side. Memorials plastered on the walls next to fresco paintings sharing in my grief.

My mind unwillingly recalled the difficult memories of my unforgiving past. I couldn't shake them. I was there, walking down the dark aisle. Stoic faces looked up as I passed by them. Shadows towered behind the mourners, reaching the top of the cathedral ceiling, enclosing the pews in tented horror. Before I knew it, I was standing in front of her body. Her lifeless frame: lips fixed, eyes closed, hands folded across her chest. The only color from the muted coffin was her flowering blue dress and golden cross necklace entangled in her permanent clasp.

A movement came from the church door, snapping my

thoughts back to my decision to enter the church or stay on the dark steps.

I stepped back in shock and dropped my hands trying to act as unassuming as possible. The door swung open and out walked an older woman pulling her homemade knit sweater around her frail body. Concern filled her caring eyes at the sight of me. With my tousled appearance and wet eyes, I can only guess what the woman was thinking. She stood there for a minute, looking me over with apprehension.

"You coming in, Dear?" she said gently.

The woman held the heavy door with her wrinkled hand, motioning with her head for me to go in, "Go on in. It is very dark, and oh so cold."

She pulled her sweater close to her body and guided me through the church entryway. Looking over my shoulder, I watched her walk down the dark steps and off into the night before the heavy door slammed behind me.

I spun to check my surroundings. Somehow, I had allowed myself to be ushered into the one place I feared more than the dark creatures. Clenched fists at my side, I attempted to hold back the residual pain from the memories still so fresh in my mind.

The pews were wooden and worn with a decorative design chiseled into the ends. I sat quietly in the back, breathing deeply, trying to regain my composure from the emotional barrage I had just endured.

My mother always said this place had all the answers to life's questions. Maybe it could help me with the answer I was so desperate to find. Maybe it could help me find the *Light*.

CHAPTER 32 THIRTY-TWO

I sat on the hard pews, closing my eyes, I saw it all again. I was skipping down the long corridor to Sunday school, my whistling echoed through the hall.

"Kara, come on, class is about to start," a pigtailed Jen called from the open door.

I ran to catch her, interlocked our arms, and hurried into class. We sat on a carpeted rug in front of our teacher who began to lead us in the classic children's song, *Jesus Loves Me*.

The high pitch childlike chimes quickly morphed into a monotone hymn of collected notes. No longer surrounded by happy sounds of youthful excitement, I soon sat amongst adults in somber worship.

"Mom, psst…" I nudged my mother who sung next to me, "I don't understand. What is *peace like a river*, and how can it *attendeth my soul*?" I whispered as quietly as my nine-year-old self could.

"Shhhh," A woman turned and placed her twisted finger in front of pursed lips, her eyes pinned on the inquisitive child that I was.

The memory retreated as I removed my hands from my eyes, and saw I was no longer in the company of an angered, elderly woman shushing me in judgmental tones, or my mother as she hummed a sweet melody. I was alone.

I still felt like that small child again, but this time, my transgressions were not as minimal as speaking during church. I was a defiant child that disobeyed and turned her back on God.

A soft sound arose from the front of a wide stage. I noticed a few musical instruments strategically placed around the raised platform with a lone microphone in the middle. The hum grew louder, and I could see it was coming from an acoustic guitar held by a man, at the right of the stage. He played another note, then paused to plug the guitar into an amplifier beside him, and approached the mic. The music grew, bouncing off the walls and landing next to me in the back of the church.

The musician, in his mid-twenties, had dusty brown hair that flew wildly in all directions. His small frame began to rock slowly to the newly forming beat. I didn't recognize the song, but why would I? If it wasn't a classic hymn or one sung in Sunday school, I wouldn't have known it anyways. The melody was modern and sounded like something I would have heard on any secular radio station.

The tune faded out allowing the lyrics to ring through. The man's raspy voice had a rawness to it that was pleasing. His words told of broken roads filled with a hopelessness and some sense of redemption. The weight of his words sat heavily on my chest, resonating deep within; I knew my life was one broken road after another.

Over the last two years, my life had spun completely out of control. With the death of my mother, I had lost everything I thought I knew about faith and hope. When I saw her suffering the way she did any possibility of life unending, of a peaceful bliss one day for me, died with her. Cancer is not easy on anyone, I'm sure, but to take someone that was full of faith and pure of heart, in that way. It just seemed heartless. It seemed godless even.

Surprisingly, with everything she endured, her belief remained. Even in her last moments, she tried to evangelize to me. It was comforting, something that I had always known. It was who she was, even until the end.

My mother had been in the hospital for weeks, unresponsive to treatments. Cancer had spread to her lungs and brain. She was dying slowly. I clung to her that last night, her frail hand holding me softly. It was heart-wrenching to see her like that, but I couldn't force myself to leave her side. Day and night, I sat with her. The nurses were kind but useless to ease her pain. It was crushing watching her filled with such discomfort, dying in front of me. I felt myself losing her with every passing moment.

Before her last breath, she pulled me close and hugged me tightly. I just knew she was going to say the words I had feared since I heard the dreaded word, *cancer.*

"Goodbye, my love."

Although the hospital staff tried to prepare me that her time was ending, her words hit me like a nuclear bomb had exploded in my chest. I gasped for oxygen and collapsed onto her, the tears flowed unwillingly.

"No. No. No," I cried into her softly.

Somehow, she lifted my body off of her own and took my face in her hands.

Smiling gently, my mother spoke quietly to me, "No, it is not what you think."

I sighed at her words, I knew what this was; it was her final send off. She was leaving me, and this was her last "I love you" to be spoken. I couldn't bear it; my heart throbbed with pain as the tears continued to stream down my cheeks.

"It is not the end for me and you." My mom held my head gently, "I am not dying. I'm being reborn. Death has lost its sting. You just have to find *Him*, find the *Light*. Then, we can always be together, my love." She placed her weak hand over my heart.

My skin shook under her cooled touch, "Find *Him*," she added.

She patted my chest lightly, smiling calmly, and then relaxed on the bed behind her.

"I will always love you," I spoke from dry lips, moistened only by salty tears.

I held her hand in mine against my chest.

"And I will always, always love you, my sweet, sweet girl," her hand dropped from mine as she spoke those last words.

And, then she was gone. My mother. My best friend. My life, gone with hers.

My eyes shimmered with the haunting memories, so fresh and filled with such pain. Sitting in the pews, I knew I was miles from her hospital room and light-years away from any form of redemption the song was alluding to.

What did my mother mean that death had lost its sting? She died, that was the end for her, right? What did she mean, Heaven? Did death did not hurt her because she is in Heaven? Is that it?

Her final words rang in my head, "Find the *Light*."

What is this Light? Can it be this simple? Can this Light be God? My mind was spinning in all directions, throwing me for an emotional roller coaster. I gripped the sides of the bench under me, trying to hold myself upright in my dizzying haze.

The last time I saw Evan, he spoke of his reflection of the *Light*. That I couldn't see the true source of the *Light* because all I saw was him. *Can he be simply talking about God?* That he reflected God's Light. *Could this be what I was searching for?*

God? It can't be that simple, can it?

He was right in front of me all those days sitting in church, singing the youthful songs like *This Little Light of Mine*.

Why didn't I see it before? The *Light* Evan and my mother spoke of was God all along.

"Hi, there!" A man's voice said, interrupting my thoughts.

I jumped, hitting my back on the wood bench behind me.

"Sorry to disturb you, but I…" The man stood over me, and I soon recognized he was the musician I had heard earlier. I hadn't even noticed he had stopped singing and the pianist had taken over for her own rehearsal.

"Are you okay?" he asked.

Frantically, I tried to compose myself. I ran my hands through my hair, wiped the tears from my face, and smiled nicely in his direction.

"Yeah," I managed to get out with a forced a smile.

He proceeded to sit next to me, and I awkwardly scooted farther away, fidgeting at his quiet stare. Neither one of us spoke. Through the stillness, I began to hear the words from his song replay in my head: *When mercy found me.*

What does that even mean?

Mercy was not a word in my common diction. But, if it contained anything that the song alluded to—peace, hope, a home—maybe that is what I needed. Mercy. Forgiveness. Grace.

"I'm Steven," he said calmly pulling me from my possible revelation. "I was playing…" he fumbled with his words and motioned to the front of the church.

There was an awkward, uncomfortable sense about him that set me somewhat at ease.

"I'm the music guy around here. I saw you sitting back here by yourself. And, well, you looked pretty upset," he said.

I smiled politely, noting his attentiveness.

"I just wanted to see if you were okay? If I could help you with anything?" he picked his fingernails nervously, looking up, and shyly smiled.

We locked eyes for a moment, and I could see this undeniable strength within him despite what his body language told me. Steven's eyes told a different story than the shy man that sat next to me. He emanated something familiar, something luminescent even.

"*Are* you okay?" he asked again.

"I'm okay," I said, surprising myself at the reality behind the simple words.

I knew now what I saw in Steven. It was familiar. It was safe. It was the same look that my mother had in her eyes. And, the same look that I saw in Evan's. It was a look of hope, faith, and life. It was a light that shown deep within them. This was the *Light* Evan and my mom talked about. And, if this *Light* was God, as I thought it might truly be, then maybe the *Light* or God was not merely an idea or insignia of a person even, but more a possession.

This *Light* that I saw in them was the one thing that separated us. It blocked me from my mom and from Evan. God is what separated us. But, not in the way I had initially thought. He didn't prevent me from getting to my mother. *He* was the path.

I didn't have Him and thus didn't have His *Light*. I knew instantly that I had to get it. I needed it.

"Can you tell me about the *Light*?" I asked.

I was desperate to find the answers, even if that meant asking a complete stranger.

"The *Light*," Steven repeated without question.

I nodded in agreement eagerly and straightened my posture turning slightly to hear all he was hopefully going to unveil.

"The *Light* is all around us. It is magnificently pure and peaceful, perfect and complete love. It is all consuming."

"God?" I questioned.

Steven nodded and continued, hopefully answering the question that screamed in my head. "But, for those who deny Him, push Him away. It will destroy them. You see, there is really only one question you have to ask yourself. Really, only one question that ultimately matters in the grand scheme of life," Steven paused. "Do you believe?"

Believe? I wanted to. I knew the Bible and the stories it housed. I knew that this *belief* Steven was talking about was the belief in God and believing that Jesus was the Son of God who came to Earth to save us from our sins. *But, do I believe?*

I knew I was a sinner. I suppose I believed in God. Maybe this is where *mercy* comes in.

"Believe?" I managed, as my mind continued to race.

"Believe in the Gospel, that God sent His Son, Jesus, to save the world from death… from sin. It is the only way we can get to the Father, the only way we can get to God, get to the *Light*. It is through the Son."

I sat in silence, soaking in the heavy words.

Believing in God didn't seem that difficult. I believed. But, what was belief? Was it just words, because I could do that, I could say I believed. Even in Jesus too. But was believing enough?

After a moment of hesitation, "I want to," I said honestly.

"Then, you will. Everything will be clear when your eyes are truly open to *His* magnificent grace and mercy."

There is that word again.

"Mercy?" I said.

"Forgiveness," he paused, "but, if I may be so bold. You have heard all this before, haven't you?" he shifted in his brashness, and continued, "I used to know your mother. You look like her, you know. She taught Sunday school when I was a little boy. She was my favorite," Steven smiled softly.

"Your mother told this to me. I'm sure she told you as well. It is so basic but so very true. *Jesus loves you.* And, that is where it all begins and where it all ends. See, it isn't in the words you say, or prayer you repeat. It is more than that. It is more than just acknowledging who Christ is and what he did for you. It's trusting in it. Belief is a full body emersion and acceptance that we are all sinners, you and me. We all need a savior. And, the sacrifice Jesus exhibited on the cross was for *you*, it was for me. It is a heart changing realization that you no longer want to be the one in control of your own life anymore. It is passing that weight over to the one that made you; handing the torch over to your Creator."

Steven spoke with such a passion and directness in his words, "Finding the *Light* is easy. Following it is a whole other journey."

CHAPTER 33

The rain had stopped outside the warm comfort of the church walls, and the moon had decided to come out behind a cloud dusted sky. I left the confines of the church after sitting and talking with Steven for a few hours. He had asked to drive me home, but I declined. I needed to think.

"Find the *Light*," were the words my mother had spoken right before she passed away.

"You need to see the *Light* for yourself," Evan had also said.

And now the musician had said, "The *Light* is all around us."

If discovering the *Light's* true nature, God, wasn't enough, then what else did I need to do to see Evan or my mother again?

Steven had talked about belief being more than a thought or acknowledgment of God, that it was much deeper.

As I walked past the safety of the streetlights toward my home and left the sleeping town behind, I felt the darkness began to press in around me. Soon, I began to feel the presence of the dark creatures lurking in the shadows. It was an evil that moved within the cloak of the night. I could feel their hunger for me, desperate to pillage and conquer me completely.

Being in the church was the first time I had not felt the creatures waiting for me. I felt safe there, secure within the holy walls of righteousness. But, I was no longer within the protection of God's house. Now, I was alone, on the darkened streets with the creatures hiding behind every turn.

My pace quickened. When I rounded the corner and headed

into our subdivision, I saw an all too familiar shadow standing under one of the antique bronze street lamps lining our street. His elongated frame leaned against the metal ornate post, arms folded and eyes intent on me.

It was Helel.

His sharp black eyes glared at me through the night. The overhead light bounced off his iridescent face making him more magnificent than I remembered—as if the moonlight added to his allure.

Helel's previous visitation was a whirlwind of emotions. With the greeting of a handshake, he had marked me. When he embedded me with an unseen emblem that would have alerted his minions to find and kill me. Thankfully, Evan had been there to save me; painfully cleansing the mark Helel had inflicted on my body.

Fear began to creep into every crevice of my being. *What does he want?*

Unable to stop or flee, I continued to walk toward him— pulled and willed to move closer, powerless to run from the terrifying creature I soon would be standing in front of.

Stepping from the streetlight into the shadows, Helel stood in my path.

"I told you we would see each other again," his words twisted in an enticing banter.

I smiled slightly, trying not to antagonize the *Beast* while I attempted to pass. Helel's statuesque frame blocked in my path. Moving to the right, he shifted as well. Quickly, I moved to the left. Unable to resist his eyes, I looked into them seeing the sinister delight he was having at my expense.

"It is still early, stay and play," Helel said.

He reached his hand out to me, and touched my shoulder slightly, trickling his fingers over my jacket and finding pleasure in its zippered closure. He stepped closer, only allowing me to see his chiseled chest, and feel his breath bearing down on me.

I was captivated—frozen in fear and attraction all at the same time. Magnetically pulled to him, I fought the polarity to not give into his appeal.

A chill radiated off of his intense perfection. He lowered his head to mine, whispered in my ear, "The night is young and so very alive. Come and play with me, Kara?"

Helel lingered, the cool of his breath licked my exposed skin. I heard him inhale deeply. His nose was only inches from my skin, sending a ripple of fear throughout my entire body. Helel was sniffing his prey. Then, with a quick jolt he pulled away quickly.

"Oh, I see Evan has removed the *Mark*. And so quickly too. I desperately wanted you to meet my friends," he pouted. "Hmm, pity."

I shook my head and stepped away from Helel's hypnotic presence. He reached for me, grabbing my wrist in his cold paw. Instantly, he recoiled, releasing my arm and shaking his hand in obvious discomfort.

Laughter violently filled the air, "Ha, and he has *Marked* you as well, has he?"

My hand instantly went to the charm around my neck.

"My necklace," I said.

Helel raised his eyebrows as a twisted smirk emerged across his face. Circling me like a wild animal honing in on his next meal, he moved hungrily around me.

I clutched the charm tightly, "You can't hurt me," I said in my weak attempt to sound strong.

"No?" he said. "Why do you think I want to hurt you? What did Evangel tell you?" Helel asked. "He is such a kidder, that guy. He is always playing games. You see, there is nothing you need to be afraid of. I do not wish to hurt you, sweet, innocent Kara."

"Then, what do you want?" I snapped with a strength I didn't know I had.

"I just want to be *friends*," Helel spoke with seductive words, "I think you are magnificent, even if Evangel didn't. I think you are special… unique even. See, you are the final puzzle piece to this whole thing," Helel said motioning to everything around him. "This whole game of life. It can end with you… or it can start."

"Stop!" I said.

He was a liar. Evan had said not to trust him.

"Stop? Stop what? We haven't even started yet," he said cunningly.

Seeing a way out, I quickly ran around him and into the darkness ahead.

Only minutes from my house, I knew Helel was behind me, hunting me. An eerie laughter filled the night. Helel was toying with his food before he ultimately consumed it completely, before he consumed me.

With each step, I felt his movement behind me, playing a twisted game of hide 'n seek. The air wisped by my nose and around my face, encircling me with the smell of rotting death—a smell I knew was Helel's dark creatures.

Soon, it wouldn't simply be noises behind me. There would be snapping at my feet as I ran for the house that was just too far out of reach. They would sink their teeth into my exposed legs, pulling me back into them and having me for their own. My capture was only an interlude to their sinister games; they thrived on fear, my fear. And Helel was the twisted puppeteer, pulling their strings.

The overhead streetlight shone brightly only yards from me. I sprinted toward it, finding refuge in its protection. As I reached the sanctity of the limited light I heard the breakers explode with a surge of electrical power all around me, sending the semi-lit homes into complete darkness. The streetlights overhead too began to flicker and lose their luminosity.

Fear ignited within me. The noises were no longer just behind me, but in every direction, intensifying with each passing second. Helel's dark whispers filled my ears as I stood in complete terror under the flickering streetlight. I wanted desperately to call for Evan, my protector, and savior, to come to me like he had before. But, I knew my words would be lost and only fuel the creature's relentless obsession.

Darkness was everywhere. Spinning around, I searched for an escape. The remaining streetlights began to extinguish before my eyes. Encircled by the dark creatures and their master, there was no escape. Ornate shadowed shapes jutted in and out of the wavering beam overhead. I didn't have long.

"Kara!" Helel called from the darkness, his voice coiling around the thickness of the night. "K-A-R-A," he wailed, drawing out each letter of my name in a sinister tone.

I reached for my necklace, desperate to hold it in my hands and feel its warming comfort. To my horror, it was gone. The protection encapsulated in its jewel was now somewhere on the pavement behind me.

No, no, no! It's gone. My mind raced. *Why is he so intent on me? Is this it? Is this my end—death by the hands of true evil?*

The questions didn't matter. Why Helel was here now was irrelevant. The creatures were still going to kill me, or worse—a thought that I had never wanted to think about, but knew was possible. The creatures might not want to kill me at all like Helel had said. But, they did want me for their own, to take me away with them to a never-ending torture.

I would be Helel's captive for all time, allowing him to continue his playtime here on earth, forever. It was never my *end* he was after. My death was never the creature's goal. I was the Akarah. The *Last One.* I was the one that held the key to the end of the world. And, if the key, me, didn't open the door to the *End,* then *this* world would continue. It was a world where pain was expectant and the sting of death, lethal—all would go on and on and on. An endless cycle set on repeat. That would be *true* Hell. Never able to seek any form redemption or amnesty from pain, no hope, no Heaven, just an endless cycle of anguish and fear.

I knew I had to fight this. I had to end this. This couldn't be the future of humanity. There had to be something more, something greater. There had to be an end to all this pain.

The only thing I knew repelled the darkness was the *Light*. Looking up, I knew it was only time until the streetlight overhead gave out too, sending me into complete darkness. The empty feeling of defeat crept in, and desperation settled deep within.

The musician's words from the church screamed in my head, shaking me to my core, begging me to give in and submit to the *One* that created us all.

I fell on my knees, looking high above the streetlight that

had already begun to fade.

"I need you!" I called out into the night. But, it wasn't for Evan or my mom. It was for something much greater, much higher. I called out to God with all my might.

"Please. Help me!" I pleaded. "I know I am nothing. I know that now. I am so sorry I didn't see it before. But, I need *You*! Please," I begged this time with a pure heart. "I see now that *You* are the only true *Light*. You and You alone. Please bring me your *Light*! Save me! Jesus, you are God, take away my sins, and rescue me! *You* are my Savior and *You* alone. Take me into your *Light*!" My words were choked and raspy.

The sense of the dark creatures and Helel's pursuit was below me, the only thing I focused on was the *Light*, God's Light. Just beyond the streetlight, a blue haze came down from the darkness and encircled my body. I didn't know if my mind was wishing it to happen or if it actually was, but regardless, I was safe and all darkness seemed a million miles away.

Why did I run from You for so long? Why was I so scared to call on Your name? You were right in front of me the whole time. You never let me go. All those times I thought that there was no God, no life, no Light. *I now see it all so clearly.* You were always there guiding me toward Your Light, guiding me for this moment.

It *was* more than just believing. It was a complete submission of one's soul, and I fully felt that surrender.

Soon, the cold ground became present under my body. As my knees and face lay on the wet, rocky pavement I felt the tender embrace of peace all around me. I was safe and secure, wrapped in the *Light*.

CHAPTER 34

My spirit came alive, breathing its first real breath. Or, maybe it was just waking the sleeping beauty within. Either way, my soul burst with joy, dancing in exhilaration. The feeling of exuberance centralized in my chest and spread to my stomach, stretching down my legs and through my arms. My whole body tingled as this strange thing inside of me grew and evolved with each breath I took. My head spun in its magnificent power. I closed my eyes to fully focus on the wonder that stirred inside of me. I felt like I was becoming one with myself, merging together. My old self; the insecure, self-loathing, fearful, fragile girl, was being absorbed by my own spirit. I was becoming one with who I always wanted to be, even though I never knew it.

Opening my eyes, the world seemed different around me. As if I was seeing it through my spirit's eyes for the first time—seeing life in a newness I had never known prior. The beauty was unmeasurable and shown with such magnificence, with strands of bright colors dancing around my head. The sweet smell of flowers filled my nose, enticing me to envision the placidity of a tranquil meadow.

It was like the lights in a dark room just turned on. The sad thing was that for so many years, I thought the darkness was my clarity. I was so wrong, and so very blind to the truth that was in front of me all along.

The strangeness of it all was the awareness I had of myself, that part inside of me—the thing that made me, well, me. The heart behind this bag of bones took its first, real beat.

A new feeling stirred within as if I had just gone home after a long vacation away. That feeling when you lay your head on your pillow after time away, anywhere from a day to ten, it didn't matter. Either way, it felt amazing. It was hard to put your finger on what was so wonderful about that lumpy bed, but it was yours. It smelled like home, felt like home. It was home. You were home.

That is what I felt in this exact moment. I felt like my spirit was home; comfortable, safe, connected, something it hadn't ever been before. I breathed deeply, trying to hold on to the feeling that I hoped would never fade.

I sensed the presence of someone standing beside me. I didn't open my eyes right away. There was no fear of the figure I could now hear breathing down on me.

Fully and completely at peace, I didn't want to separate myself from these feelings in any sort of way. I opened my eyes, slowly looking to the one standing beside me. My eyes met his chest first and then followed up his sculpted body. Gazing down at me, Evan's bright eyes and large smile filled his perfect face.

"You did it!" His deep voice spoke through the night.

I felt my newly awakened soul longing for the same thing my weak heart did—Evan.

CHAPTER 35

"Kara," Evan said.

He moved slowly toward me, cupping my cheeks in his hands and raising my body to stand with his.

"You are so very beautiful," he said, "wrapped in the *Light*."

Evan pulled me into his strong arms. My heart leapt from my chest in elation. My hands moved to his lower back and grabbed at his shirt, pulling him closer still.

I felt his jaw tighten against my flushed skin, and pull away slowly. Hanging on desperately, I begged for more. Evan held me for a moment longer, his forehead now resting on my shoulder allowed me to feel his breath on my skin, sending a warm exuberance to my core.

Evan's back stiffened, and he rose slowly. Letting me go, he stood quietly in front of me. His head was down and brow fixed, forcing small wrinkles to form where there was once none. My hand went to his face, touching the indentions that formed on his sun-kissed skin.

"I am so sorry I left, Kara," Evan said. "I know you were in pain, but I never meant to hurt you, I just…"

"Don't," I interrupted. "I know why you did it. I get it now. None of that matters anymore."

Evan grabbed my hands in his. "I will always…" his voice was raspy, "always…" He paused, still holding my hands in his as he held them against his chest. "My spirit will always love you," he concluded.

"I love you too, Evan," I said with baited breath.

I had found him again, or he had found me. Evan was here. He was back, and we were together. After accepting the *Light* and choosing to believe in something so much more than myself, I was amazed at the way the world looked. Even in those first few moments, life had changed so completely. And, now, Evan had returned.

My heart swelled with a completeness of joy and utter thankfulness that Evan had returned. Deep within, I knew God sent him; first to save me on the bridge, then to show me the Light. I had messed everything up. I had confused Evan's *Light* as the source and not a reflection. But, Evan showed me there was more to life than pain. He showed me how to love again.

"We will find each other again. This cannot be our end," Evan said with desperation, breaking my pleasant thoughts of our epic reunion.

What end? Didn't we just avoid that? And what does he mean, find each other? I am right here. What is he talking about?

Reading the confusion on my face, he continued, "The End is coming, I can feel it. You are going to have to leave here, and I cannot come with you. I have to stay here for now. There is a war that is to begin, and I am called to help."

He paused letting the weight of his words sink in. Instead, they spun around my fragile mind uncontrollably, sending disconcerting thoughts violently in all directions. My newly lightened spirit cried out for his. I had found him, truly found him, and now he was leaving, or I was?

"No," I pleaded. "No!" I shook my head uncontrollably. "I know who you really are. I get it now. I see the *Light,* and I understand. I'm not the same that I was before. I'm different now. I see God's *Light* that you were talking about. I understand, I do. I know I had everything backward before. That I saw you as the source of the *Light* and how messed up that was. I know now how wrong I was to think like that. I get why you had to leave. But, you don't have to go anywhere now."

Evan pulled me into him, holding me as my face rested on

his rising and falling chest.

"I know," Evan said softly. "I know you understand, but you still can't see all of it. You are not designed to. You have come so far. You have truly accepted who you really are, and that is so beautiful. But, there are some things that I can't even begin to explain. Some things you were not made to understand. You will be okay. You are safe now. You will be forever in the presence of the *true Light*."

"I don't understand. Why do you have to leave?" I searched for answers. When he didn't respond, I begged, "Tell me," I said, still holding tightly to his sturdy body.

"I cannot say any more than I have," he spoke cryptically. "It is time for me to go."

"Why do you have to go? I don't understand. Please, just tell me. Or, let me go with you. Wherever I am going I don't want to go without you…"

"Once you are there, once the *End* comes, you won't think like that anymore. We don't have much time. Soon none of this will matter to you. My only hope is that you will find me. That you will remember me," Evan said.

The tears filled my eyes and began to form within his as well.

Evan wiped away the salty drops streaming down my face. He leaned down and kissed my cheek gently. His lips were soft against my heated skin sending a pulse of vibrancy and peace through my whole being.

"*My beloved is mine, and I am hers*," quoting scripture, Evan spoke the same words he had once before.

"We will find each other again. This cannot be it for us. I will not believe that our love is insignificant in His eyes," Evan said.

"Stay with me then… until the *End* comes? Please, Evan."

"I will stay," Evan said, "Please, remember me."

"Of course, I will remember you," I said quietly into the night, clinging to the comforting warmth of his touch.

We both looked at the sky, watching and waiting.

CHAPTER 36 THIRTY-SIX

My spirit began to move inside of me. I could feel an unknown giddiness building in my gut and tickle my heart. I tried to hang onto Evan's words, but something else began to ignite inside of me, something that had nothing to do with Evan. This feeling churned and twisted, growing in intensity with each passing second.

I tried to cling to Evan and the pain I was feeling knowing he would soon have to leave, but I was unable to. The anticipation of something unknown swept in with the wind, increasing in power, churning around us.

What is going on? What is this feeling?

Joy began to fill my soul. My spirit danced inside of me. I could not hold back my eagerness for the unknown. I stood under the lone streetlight looking fervently to the sky, still holding Evan's hand tightly. My head was trying to make sense of the strange feelings of this newly found *self* inside of me, but I was unable to conceptualize it. Nothing seemed to matter—not the wind whipping around me, not Evan standing next to me. Everything left my mind, leaving it clear and serene. All else seemed to fade into a lull of peaceful stillness as Evan and I stood, hand in hand.

Soon, I no longer felt the warmth of Evan's hand on mine. His breathing too faded away. Strangely, I didn't miss it. I didn't even look over to see if Evan was still there. Nothing mattered but the sky, the stars, and something beyond, just out of sight, calling me.

I stepped out from under the low lit streetlight and waited for my eyes to adjust to the darkness. After a few seconds, I was able to see stars shining brightly overhead. The sky gleamed with life. I began to see the constellations bounce off the darkness like a holo-gram 3D puzzle. The Milky Way was noticeable amongst the stars that continued to come alive and illuminate the night's sky. It was absolutely spectacular. Even the moon, large and full hidden behind wispy clouds, was brighter and larger than I had ever seen before.

A smile graced my tear stained face as I waited, gazing ex-pectantly at the heavens above. The unknown sky gave no clue to why I suddenly felt so filled with wonder and pure elation.

My smile paled as I noticed the North Star, which I had just found amongst all the other glittering lights, beginning to fade. The star's dimmer switch was lowering for a dramatic event, continuing to decrease in power, until it went out completely. The North Star was gone, no longer amongst the other stars.

Maybe I didn't see that right. I scanned the sky for the miss-ing star, but it was no longer visible.

I rubbed my tired eyes, only to discover what seemed like more stars disappearing. The once lit sky, filled with stars and the beauty of the cosmos was now dwindling. The Milky Way, no lon-ger visible anymore, along with many of the constellations I had identified only seconds earlier.

What's going on?

My soul continued to reach beyond the fading lights above, begging me to follow them in their departure.

As the last lights faded, the moon was all that lit the dark sky. The once wispy clouds whimsically dancing in front of the moon had now grown into a full-blown cumulus, covering most of the brightness it once held.

The wind began to sweep around me and twist toward the empty night above. I stood in the darkness, gazing upward, watching the clouds roll in like waves. Everything else had slipped away. The house lights that were teeming with life from within were now quiet and dark. The streetlights all lowered their luminosity in unknown anticipation. Evan's presence was no longer with me, or maybe it was, and I simply didn't notice. The dark creatures and Helel were also gone, or maybe they too waited for the unknown as I did. The wind suddenly dropped; the night and I quietly sat in humble expectation of a great occurrence yet to come—a calm before the storm.

Through the quiet night, a trumpeting boom came screaming down from the air above me. I stood gazing at the blanketed emptiness of night sky, shocked at the volume pulsing in my ears. The wind followed the sound, rushing past my face and sending my hair in a whirlwind behind me. I felt like I was standing in the center of a tornado, churning around me, screaming in my ear as the noise roared with power.

The blast increased to a more tonal musical note that moved with an energy all its own. The sound became a part of the wind, one with each other, an entity completely alive, breathing and growing, gaining strength and power. Increasing with intensity, the sound took on a more rhythmic tone. The one note, playing loud for all to hear, now began to break into an instrumental arrangement of lyrical harmony. It was amazing how one noise became a multitude of musical symphonies encompassing me, twirling about in its warm gusts of harmonious movement.

The once dark sky above me gave way to a glowing dull light that came from the abyss of the night, growing from a deep charcoal to muted golden streams pushing through the thickness of the air above. The beams began to make their way through the atmosphere. The light quickly changed to an overpowering visual display of vivid luminescence beaming down on the earth. It was more exquisite than anything I had ever seen before, greater than any star or any manmade object—even the sun seemed dismal compared to this light that now filled the sky above me.

I fell to my knees, hiding my eyes from the penetrating sight of pure brilliance. The orchestra increased in amazing power. As it reached the earth, the light touched my exposed skin, fanning around me. The warmth of the light was extraordinarily unique and the intensity was unlike anything I had ever felt before. It reminded me of the warming energy that Evan emitted. But, his was dull compared to this power and warmth. It was a heat source all its own, which I felt throughout my whole being.

The light was safety and security. A feeling I had only begun to touch on before, existing with my mother's soft embrace or Evan's innocent touch. It was a feeling completely amplified beyond all reason. This feeling was love—complete, endless, all-consuming love.

Flashes filled my mind of my mother's sweet smile, her soft hand holding my face ever so gently, her arms cradling me into her embrace. Her love overflowed onto me. I felt her now. I felt her love, something I had not felt since the day she left this world. Then, I felt Evan, his eyes locking onto mine, his hand holding my own, our innocent, new love. My examples of love were minimal but quantitative. But this, *this* feeling of love I felt right now, was so much greater than anything else this world could have offered.

This feeling of love birthed inside of me, filling my soul in a way I had never felt before. The *Light* that now pulsed all around me in musical vibrations enfolded me in a massive hug, pulling me over the threshold into a home I had longed to find.

Tears fell from my eyes and down my face while my arms stretched toward the sky, reaching for the source of the protected refinement covering my body. Closing my eyes, I felt my soul submit to the *One* that I knew was calling me home and into the *Light*, to my Creator, to my God.

I heard a resounding voice echo in my mind. It was unmistakable in its power, "It's time my child."

My spirit answered, "Take me home!"

CHAPTER 37 THIRTY-SEVEN

A quiet, peaceful tranquility was all around me. I lifted myself and stood while my eyes remained closed in their own serenity. There was no ounce of fear within any trace of my bones. A feeling I had never felt before, a complete absence of anxiety or dread. Not only the absence of fear but all emotions were new and different, positively enhanced.

In addition to the new emotions, weight did not seem to hold me and the heaviness of each day was gone. The air was clean and fresh. I breathed deeply tasting the smoothness and softness of it, silky against the back of my throat. It was an unfathomable feeling with all my senses firing on full capacity, trying to grasp any bit of familiarity to my surroundings.

Opening my eyes, my mind spun by the clarity of the air and illumination of the space.

As a child, I often would hide under my covers and play for hours with my stuffed animals; creating my own world under a mess of sheets and pillows. It was dim, muted even, with my pink flashlight. When I would emerge from hours of adventures under my sheets, the room around me had changed. It was bright and new. The air was clean and fresh. The sunlight streaming through the window hurt my eyes, and the size of the room seemed vast compared to what it had looked like only an hour before my undercover excursion.

It was the closest thing I could relate to the feelings I was experiencing. It was as if the covers of my old life were torn away, exposing me to this new, fresh environment that was completely foreign to me.

It took my eyes a few seconds to adjust to the brightness. A smell of fresh, clean air filled my nose and rushed into my lungs. At first, I thought I was in a white room with an intense light overhead. As my eyes adjusted, I saw that I was not in a room at all, but a seemingly open space that went on and on forever. Spinning around, I searched for walls behind me, only to see an endless stream of white. The floor beneath me was not hard nor soft. It was present, but insignificant all the same.

I tried to focus on what could be past the brilliance of my location, yet looking out I only saw more of the same—whiteness, purity, and a peaceful stillness.

My feet carried me forward, and I noticed lightness to my muscle extensions that I had never experienced before. Ever since the bridge, when I walked, I felt an ache of pain in my knee. Even when I had begun to run again, the pain was still there, a dull persisting ache that had become my constant. As I moved now, there was no pain, no ache, no real feeling of my knee at all, no muscles stretching or bones reaching for the next step. It was only a fluid movement.

The whiteness continued as I followed a small path, leading me to what I could only assume was the source of the brightness that illuminated the space around me.

In front of me, I recognized a figure emerging from the path, a shadowy outline, not cloaked in darkness, but a light of its own. As a frame emerged, my eyes adjusted again to its kindled power.

Soon, a woman stood before me. Her hair was long and dark in stark contrast to the light still beaming around us and emanating from somewhere far beyond. Her face became clear, her green eyes popped against her iridescent face. She was absolutely beautiful, stunning even. Her scarlet lips parted with a smile, and her arms opened wide to embrace me. Pulling away gently, she placed her hand to my face and wiped away the tears I didn't know had begun to fall.

"Mom," my voice cracked, the tears continuing down my

cheeks.

"Oh, Sweetie," she gushed, smiling even brighter than the space around us.

We stood there; her hands holding my face, my hands holding hers. We didn't have to say anything; we both just stared into each other's eyes.

My mom dropped her hands from my face, nodded with a knowing smile, and led me down the narrow path. We held each other as we moved slowly together. In the distance, I could hear a soft tone of what sounded like a woman singing. As we continued walking, the sound increased to reveal not one woman's voice but thousands upon thousands, both male and female, singing an unknown song. Somehow, I felt that I knew the melody; there was an unknown familiarity to it. The words were unclear, but the notes rang loud in my ears and echoed in my head.

"What is that?" I asked softly.

My mother just smiled and led me closer to the sound ahead.

I began to see what looked like a structure off in the distance. As we came closer, the object formed into a massive gate with golden metalwork intricately twisting and turning with the utmost craftsmanship. Two large pillars stood beside the gate, made of marble, granite, or some other ornate stone. The gate was intimidating but inviting all the same. There was no sense of fear or anxiety regarding how we would get through the large barrier. A yearning filled my spirit to be past the gate to the waiting choir of voices singing from just out of sight. I was completely amazed at the beauty and awe of the structure. Its size overtook me.

I took my eyes off of the gated entrance and looked down at the diminutive path we stood on. It was easy to see myself in the cobbled humbleness of it. Each stone, dirty and warn, small and insignificant. I was the pebbles, so tiny in comparison to the entrance into this grand palace.

My hand dropped from my mother's and fell to my side, feeling the full weight of my iniquities. I was unworthy of standing here, my life so undeserving of even being in the presence of the gate to Heaven. That is what this place had to be, I was sure of it.

She was here. I knew my mother's heart, more than my own. She loved God and had lived her life serving His Kingdom. If anyone deserved to be here, it was her. Me, on the other hand, I didn't deserve to be standing here. I was a sinner, broken and bruised. I was nothing.

I felt myself retreating, trying to run and hide in my shame and disappointment—the gate's judgment looming down on me. Pivoting quickly, my feet entangled within one another, and I stumbled to the stone path below.

I tried to pick myself up, but felt the weight of the world on my shoulders, pressing me to the ground. As if a hand was pushing me toward the rocky floor, I felt every sinful thought and action of my past. The source of the pressure was unmistakable—guilt.

Amidst my despair, a hand reached out to me, and I found myself at the feet of someone other than my mother. His feet, wrapped in worn leather straps, were strong and glowed of metallic bronze. A white robe, crisp and clean, hung to the ankles. Hesitantly, I looked upon His face and instantly knew I was looking into the eyes of the Son of God. They were shining like the sun—blinding and all-encompassing. Still reaching His outstretched hand to me, I was able to see the wounds on his palms as if He had been crucified yesterday.

Shuddering in awe at the sight before me, I heard a voice boom with power and terrifying might, "You do not need to be afraid. *You* are my child!"

CHAPTER 38 THIRTY-F...

My eyes were open to the newness around me. Everything had changed. In a blink, an instant, everything was different. I was no longer in the celestial place of illuminating beauty with the songs of a heavenly choir. No longer was I humbled in the presence of the Almighty. I was somewhere new and different.

The wind kissed my cheek with a comforting smell of the familiarity of a summer's day. The grass beneath my bare feet was lush and comforting in an extremely visceral way. The sky was cerulean with white billowy clouds bouncing joyfully amidst the span of its openness. Rays of light streamed through the clouds and flowed to the earth in gentle ripples.

I felt the tight squeeze of a hand holding my own and saw my mother's loving face glowing next to me. She looked upwards, and I followed her gaze toward the place we had just left. On the clouds was a magnificent city of gold. A large gate, now open wide, parted the white pillows with a path leading up a hill where the city was aglow in ultimate golden glory. Words couldn't express its beauty.

We stood in awe for some unknown time. It didn't seem to matter like it had before. I knew we had all the time we would want and ever would need.

As difficult as it was, I pulled my eyes from the glowing city above to the beauty of our surroundings. The meadow we were standing in had the most delicate flowers growing in harmony with one another, dancing effortlessly in the wind. The elongated trees swayed gently with the breeze in lyrical tonality. Birds flew from the large oaks, maples, and evergreens just beyond the calmness of the field.

My mother's eyes were wide with wonder, taking in every last moment, as did I. She was absolutely beautiful. Her once sunken, diseased ridden face stricken with the burdens of cancer now gleamed with life. Her dark auburn locks danced on her shoulders and down her back in the intoxicating breeze.

"Mom," I said quietly trying not to disturb the artistry of creation displayed around us.

"Oh Kara," she said. "We are here. We are home! Can you believe how absolutely beautiful it is? Oh, my. It is just so amazing."

I shook my head in awed agreement.

"I know this must be hard for you. You being so new and all. But, Kara, this is *it*. We are here. We are finally where we were *made* to be. Don't you feel it?"

She turned and faced me, holding my shoulders in her gentle hands.

"I know this has been tough for you. You have to be so confused," she paused waiting for me to answer.

I couldn't find the words to speak, so I shook my head again.

Confusion had been the last thing on my mind while I moved from worlds so quickly; unable to react truly to what had happened to me. But, confusion was the one thing I wasn't feeling. I was in too much utter astonishment to have any questions or concerns.

"See, up there," she said, pointing to the city in the clouds.

I nodded yet again.

"That is the Celestial City," she paused, allowing me to find my voice.

"Heaven?" I asked.

She smiled widely, "Honey, this is all Heaven. All of this!" Motioning around as she spun in joy, her hands flying widely in excitement. "All of this is Heaven. All of it, forever ours," she danced singing praises.

I smiled in her bliss and allowed the happiness to erupt from my own body, a pure elation that had been budding inside of me since the moment we arrived. It was all over; all the darkness, all the pain and fear, all the sickness and death. We were here in this fantastically wonderful place, now and forever. We danced for hours together under the warm sun, spinning widely, singing jubilant praises to our Creator; it was the happiest my soul had ever been.

After some time, we crashed to the soft ground and lay together talking about everything and yet nothing of any true importance. Nothing from before mattered now. We were so extremely happy to be together again. I had missed her entirely. Her absence devastatingly consuming, but the pain of the past was a distant memory. My life before was a fog, a dream that was so distantly far away I questioned its reality. But, there was something my soul still clung to. It was a part of who I used to be before—a longing that stirred in the pit of my stomach. I tried to explain it to my mom, but could not find the words to express my feelings. She said it was only the newness of it all.

After some time I asked, "Why didn't we stay there?" I motioning to the city above us, still nestled in the sky amongst the clouds.

"You were the *Last One*; the *last one* to be saved, the *last one* written in the Book of Life. As soon as you believed, it all began," she said.

The phrase, *the last one*, hit a twinge of something from my past, from before, but I could not hold on to it, whatever it was.

"What began?" I asked.

"The End," my mother said as we sat under a large oak eating a ripe fruit from the flowering tree in the center of the meadow.

She continued, "It was the end of the world. Everyone that believed in the Creator came here, or there," she pointed to the clouds. "Just like you."

"But, why did we come back here to Earth? And why is it so, different?" I asked.

"It has been seven years since you left Earth, and the Believers were called *Home*. They called it the Rapture. But here, those seven years were only moments to us. Time is not the same as it used to be. It is very different now, and it doesn't matter like it did. We will never grow old, never age. We will be like this always. The earth is different too because it is back to how God intended it to be for us before the fall of man."

She paused, letting me soak in her words.

"And, we can go to the City whenever we want. We can see *Him* whenever we want," my mother spoke looking to the golden paradise in the clouds, her eyes sparkling with delight.

The way she looked toward the City with such desire and fervor, I knew she would be going back, and I wouldn't. She would sit at her Creator's feet for all time, in worship and adoration. Her spirit longed to be in ultimate devotion. It was who she was, who God created her to be. My spirit longed for something else. God had made me for something else, something different. Not that one was better or greater than the other, just that they were different. And, that was how it was. Each person was unique, from one to the next—beauty in diversity.

I wanted to ask her more questions, to probe her for the answers my mind raced with, but I knew they would come with time. Time was something we no longer had to worry about. Time was infinite and immortal, as were we.

"You go," I told her.

My mother longingly gazed upwards toward the heavenly city adorned in sparkling light.

"It's okay," I told her.

And it was. It wasn't like before. It would never be goodbye again. We would always see each other, we would always have each other. I was no longer alone. Loneliness from the past was gone. My isolation was gone. Both feelings evaporated to a time I could barely remember, barely even hold on to.

My mother held me in a warm embrace.

"I love you," she whispered.

"And, I will always love you," I said quietly back.

Her hands left mine, and she took a step back from me. Lifting her arms to the heavens and closing her eyes, she elevated her head to the clouds.

A white light began to grow around her. As it intensified, she looked to me through its shining power and smiled with the most joy and happiness I could have ever wished to see in her.

"Hallelujah," she sang in blissful chime.

And then she was gone.

I stood, watching the City, imagining her there: singing praises, beaming with worship, wrapped in light. She was at peace, and honestly, so was I.

I was by myself for the first time in this new world. My soul soared with excitement for the unknown journey ahead.

CHAPTER 39

The idea of leaving the sanctity of the meadow began to stir within me. After my mother went back to the City, I stayed for a while in the familiar area, but soon I knew I must venture beyond. The world was new again—alive. Creation's beauty as God intended it to be, and my spirit longed to see it, all of it, in its full glory.

Heading off into the wilderness meant a new beginning; it meant I may find what pulled me, what stirred my spirit. The excitement of the journey ahead had my muscles twitching in anticipated eagerness.

As I left the meadow and entered the woods, thick and lush with hints of sunlight gleaming through the open canopy, wonderment washed over me. Questions stirred as to where I was. *Is this South America or maybe South Africa? Do those places still exist or is it just one large garden now?* The questions didn't bring worry or anxiety only a desire to explore more.

To my astonishment, walking never made my feet tire or my legs ache with any bit of pain. I was at ease. Running, that was a completely different emotion. It was pure exhilaration. My breathing intensified, and I could feel the pull on my chest as I pushed myself deeper into each stride. But still, I felt no pain—no exasperation.

Flashes sparked in my mind as I pushed against the supple soil. The illusion of freedom I felt when the toxic air blew in my face, the twinge of pain pushing me harder with each new stride. How naive I was, how elementary that place felt. The flashes continued of days running in the world before when everything seemed so beautiful, but it was merely a prelude to the majesty that would soon be unveiled. This new world was spectacular. Amazing. Inspiring. Everything was so different, yet, the memories from the past only developed a greater appreciation for this new world. Every new encounter invoked an old memory, emerging from a clouded haze, bringing that much more adoration for the wonders currently around me.

Anything before that used to bring me any bit of happiness had been magnified beyond reason. From running to singing to eating and drinking, everything was a reason to celebrate.

This new world had negated everything sin had destroyed.

Even the most basic of human needs were insignificant now. Both hunger and thirst were obsolete. When I wanted to eat, I ate the delicious fruits that seemed to be around every turn. I drank only because the stream was so beautiful and the taste was magnificent and cool in my mouth. But, I did not yearn for it in any way. Hunger never came. Sure, the fruits sustained me, but the pain of hunger was no more. Pain itself had disappeared along with anxiety, fear, despair, and any other feeling that dragged humanity downward—had dragged me downward. All of it was gone from this new earth—humanity freed from all of it.

The sun moved slowly along with the skyline, never truly setting, only giving way to a coolness that provided relief from the warmth of the day. The warmth then gave rest to the coolness of twilight. It was harmonious how the two worked together in symmetry, complementing each other so beautifully. I rested and slept on the forest's blanketed carpet floor, wrapped in its splendor, but I was never truly tired. I never felt the need to sleep or the agony that used to come from not sleeping. I just felt like I wanted to lie down, and so I did. Other times, I walked for days without rest, and then I would stop and sit for a long while, enjoying the birds swooping and diving overhead. Their voices were musical in the air with the trees moving to their set beat. Everything was in perfect harmony with one another, and I was a part of the brilliant tapestry. I could feel the movement of the trees swaying under my soles, the wind filled my lungs, and the sun invigorated my skin. It was a dulcet masterpiece playing out all around me.

The animals I encountered were tranquil, and their company came with ease; even the deer drinking by the river's bend was undisturbed by my presence. Some of the more intimidating creatures came toward me without fear. I was no threat to them and them to me.

One night, I lay on the forest floor, awakened by movement high above me within the intricate limbs of the wide tree. The moss and vines covered its base and twisted to its top. The tree's leaves were wide with long blades and multiple tips. The deep green color only added to its beauty with the emerald moss covering the deep brown trunk and intertwining itself within the roots. The long branches spread in all directions above me in a fan of rich colors.

Amongst the tree's limbs, I saw the source of the rustling. A feline crouched and stealthily crept along a limb overhead. The cat had dark spots decorating its golden coat. The green eyes of the feline spotted me instantly as it moved slowly high above. I lay crippled in the tranquility of the magnificent animal. A panther or jaguar, I was not sure. The unknown cat swung its tail playfully until its eyes closed and rested. After lying beneath the peaceful animal for an unknown time, I rose and answered the pull to continue on my journey.

The forest soon was behind me, and the open plains were set before me. Although the landscape changed, nothing else was that different. I felt at ease with my new surroundings. My mind often wondered to before, a time when nothing was easy or simplistic. Although I could hardly see through my mind's haze, I yearned for a link to the past, something that could put the pieces together and lead me toward my spirit's longing. I tried to see into the dark dream of my before, but all was lost in the destruction of the world, along with my memories.

I rested under a petite tree filled with white blooming flowers; its petals were intoxicating and filled my nose with a sweet pungent smell. The early morning was as still as the tall grasses around me. Jarring my thoughts, an unusual sound came from behind me, and I twisted around the tree to see the muffled noises.

Through the brush, I could see two people walking in the distance. Their shapes were clear that one was a man and the other a woman. I crouched behind the budding tree while they walked closer to my location. The woman had long black hair that whirled past her shoulders and swayed effortlessly in the breeze. Her skin was dark and shadowed in the low setting sun. The man next to her was thin and lean, standing not much taller than his counterpart. His similarly dark hair danced at his chin in crisp curls. They walked and talked, smiling at each other as I watched from my undisclosed location.

I stood slowly, not to startle them, and raised my hand in greeting without uttering any words. They were the first people I had seen since departing from my mother, and I didn't want my enthusiasm to scare them away.

"Hi!" I said, my arm waving in the air.

Seeing me immediately, they turned to each other, exchanged a few knowing glances, and then proceeded toward me. I stepped out from behind the small tree, now equaling its size, and moved slowly to the two individuals.

A smile crossed both of their faces, as I smiled widely at them. Though both young, it was hard to say exactly how old they could be. Neither had any sign of aging, no wrinkling or baggy eyes; only young faces with knowing eyes and jovial spirits.

"Hi there," the woman said in a squeaky voice.

The man stood still, smiling slightly and nodding his head in agreement to the woman's introduction.

"Hi!" I answered back eagerly, stretching out my hand toward theirs.

The man instantly grabbed it firmly, smiling even wider than before. His grip was strong, though his hand small. The woman reached for mine next. Her hand was as dainty as I anticipated it to be.

"I'm Henry," the man said with a distinctive unidentifiable accent.

"I'm Tiffany, but everyone calls me Tiffy," the young woman

chimed in with the same unknown dialect.

"Kara," I said.

After a second, I continued, "Where did you two come from? I've been walking for, well…" I stopped trying to think of the time and realized that time was gone now. "I haven't seen anyone else since we first came here."

"Oh, are you here with someone else. Where are they?" Tiffy asked trying to scan the area behind me.

"No, it's just me, now," I said.

For the first time since my mother left, I thought of her and thought of going to her. But, that was not what pulled me, it was not my path—it was hers.

"My mother was with me when I first came here. But, she went to the City soon after," I paused as my thoughts fluttered back to my beautiful mother. "It's just me now," I added, smiling softly at the two of them.

Before they spoke, I knew they had come together.

"We were in the City for a while, too," Henry said.

"It was amazing!" Tiffy interjected, her eyes widening with her large smile revealing bright teeth.

"It was," Henry added with his own equally white smile.

"Why did you leave?"

"Oh, uh," Henry said unable to find the words.

"I don't really know, we just felt like we were supposed to do something else, be somewhere else. We loved being there. It was so fantastic, but… it just didn't feel like it was where we were supposed to be," Tiffy said.

"I know it sounds crazy. Why would you ever leave that place, but here we are," Henry added.

"No, I get it," I answered back.

They both looked for me to continue, so I did.

"When my mom left, I didn't even have the urge to follow her. I know that is where she should be. Me, I feel like *this* is where I am meant to be. Here in this new place. You know?"

"I do," Henry said.

"*We* do," Tiffy corrected with a large smile.

"Yeah, *we* do," Henry changed his original statement and playfully poked Tiffy as she squealed from his jab.

"I didn't really get to see the City," I said.

"No?" questioned Tiffy.

"No, I was there. I saw *Him*," I paused. "Then, I was here."

The two looked eagerly toward me to continue my story.

"My mother said I was the *last one*. The last one saved," I stopped, hanging onto the complex words.

Just speaking the words, *the last one*, sent a familiar feeling through my body. It was a phrase that I could not conceptualize. The words held an unknown weight to them. I recognized that weight to be from the past, hidden in possible pain that didn't allow me to see their true meaning.

"Everything moved so quickly," I said quietly.

"Tiffy and I were in the City for a little while. People said that it had begun, that *the End* was here, and soon Earth would be rebuilt," Henry said.

"There were so many *new* people. They just showed up. They called it the Rapture. God came to Earth for those that believed, and poof, they were gone, and *the End* began," Tiffy added with dramatic flair.

"The thought of seeing the earth again, renewed, was so captivating," Henry said.

"We knew we had to go," Tiffy chimed in again. "We had to see it."

"Then, we were here. Just like that," Henry said motioning all around him.

"Isn't it spectacular?" Tiff said with a wide smile as she spun around, happily grabbing Henry's hands in her own.

My smile turned to a small giggle as I watched them joyful play.

"Brother and sister, right?"

"Twins," Tiffy answered, as her brother pinned her playfully to the soft ground beneath them.

"I give, I give," she giggled.

Henry released his sister and turned his mischievous eyes to me.

"You two are crazy," I said stepping back slowly with a wide smile on my face. "Don't even think about it."

Henry perched above Tiffy, raising his eyebrows and pushing against the ground. Shifting his attention away from his sister allowed Tiffy enough room to wiggle from under her brother's grip and bound ahead, laughing wildly.

I followed Tiffy as Henry lunged at us; all amused in play. Their laughter was contagious.

"Come on, let's go," Tiffy yelled, running ahead when she had tired of the game.

No one had to say anything. We were together now. All of us. I was with the twins, and they were with me. We walked, ran, and played together until the scenery changed once again. The once open plains of sand and grasses changed to reveal large mountains reaching to the sky, then cascading down toward the ground.

"Wow!" Tiffy said as we all stood in amazement at the vast mountain range before us.

"Let's do this!" Henry said energetically.

CHAPTER 40 FORTY

The journey ahead of us was immeasurable, vast and distant. I felt tremendously minuscule closing the gap between the open spaces of the prairie and entering the forest that elegantly lay before the mountain range. It was a blanket of tufted trees—fluffed comfort across the scenic edge in magnificent harmony.

We rested in the cool of the night, tasting the sweet aroma of the evergreens and the anticipation of a summer rainfall on the back of our throats. When dawn came, we continued on our journey through the dense woods with large boulders jutting into the sky. The smooth rocks, speckled with glistening crystals, reached high in the air just under the crest of the trees, while others only rested feet from the thick underbrush.

Scaling one of the larger rocks, I heard a rushing noise that triggered a memory to flash within my mind. A movie began to play inside of my head, the details strewn out intricately developing into reams of images. First was the memory of a camping trip we took when I was only a young girl. We were canoeing, my mother and I, on a wide river. The water was dark and muddy, large rocks scattering its shore. We sat in the canoe and paddled gently. My skin reddened and blistered from the heat of the sun overhead. The water was cool as I ran my hand in its swift current. I heard my mother's voice behind me urging me to turn the boat to the left. Ahead, the water seemed to disappear out of sight.

My mind was able to activate the different elements within my memory.

Focusing, even more, I saw my mother's face clearer than my memory's haze. Her face was tired and weakened from our excursion. Barely making it to shore, my mother's eyes showed the worry I hadn't known existed at the time. I watched the water crash below never knowing my mother quietly thanked our Creator for our safety.

A smiled crossed my face at the memory and how her devotion to God was so strong. It saddened me, how I never took the time to thank Him before. Now, the majestic water before me, crested over rocks and splashed wildly below. Taking the time now, I too lifted my thoughts of thanks to the One that made this beautiful spectacle of watered marvel before me.

"It's a waterfall!" Henry called to Tiffy as she rounded the bend toward the rushing rumble of the water crashing onto the placid pool.

We all stood together on the rock and looked down to a cobalt pool below. The water rushed over the edge energetically. Several colorful salmon ran upwards to the clean ice-blue pools we stood over. Without hesitation, I felt my feet plant against the smooth rock and push with great intensity. The force sent my body into the air and over the cliff's edge. I screamed in exhilarating excitement.

My body plunged into the cool water below, spinning me under the silky pond. A large splash boomed beside me, and I soon saw Henry emerge under the clear water. Tiffy followed.

We all played in the inebriating waters for days. Like children, we dove deep under the surface to chase the many colorful fish and explored a dark cavern that housed an underground hot spring.

It was a truly magical place that sung to the deepest recesses of my soul.

Maybe this is where I am supposed to be? Is this my eternal city in the clouds? Is this my Heaven?

But, something told me it wasn't. A deep yearning within urged me to move forward, telling me that this tranquil place was also not my final destination I longed for.

Despite the connection I felt to this place, I knew that it was not my end. It was still out there, whatever it was.

Henry and Tiff were happy to follow me. I tried to tell them about this longing I felt inside, but they did not understand. And, why would they? They had each other.

Maybe companionship is what I am searching for? The same connection I saw in Henry and Tiffy—maybe that was what I longed for.

CHAPTER 41

Now under the canopy of the evergreens, the coolness was a bit sharper, but not unpleasant. It was a sweet relief, an inviting fragrance pulling me in. The ground was a mixture of mosses and fungi making a pillowed flooring of lighter and darker greens against our feet while we walked together quietly.

The once chatty Tiffy walked in silence. None of us spoke and only exchanged glances of wonder and amazement. This forest was nothing like the forest I had been in at the start of my journey. These were red barked marvels reaching to the tops of the clouds and beyond. The tree's girth was enormous. We wrapped our arms around in unison attempting to complete a circle with our connecting arms. We fell short, giggling together as we reached for each other's extended arms around the massive trunk.

We sat at the base of one of the largest of the trees, resting our heads on its sturdy base. My long limbs stretched over the roots jutting from the soft earth.

Henry leaned gently into the tree with Tiffy's head on his lap.

Tiffy looked to the sky, smiling slightly at the wonder of the massive hardwoods above.

"Let's climb it," she said.

I shook my head and stepped back from her. Henry stood and stretched his arms over his head in excitement.

"You too?" I questioned.

"You bet!" Henry said.

"Come on," Tiffy called, already attempting to find her footing.

They both began to climb, finding grooves and notches in the base of the enormous tree. Laughing quietly to myself, I knew in that moment that they would not be continuing with me in my journey. They were home; this was their place, their final heaven.

My home was not here, as much as I would have loved to stay with them in this magnificent place. Something inside of me stirred, pushing me forward, with more urgency than I had ever felt, leading me somewhere that I still did not know existed.

With a simple embrace, we left each other. No one felt any sadness. Instead, I felt a sort of completeness for them. Henry would spend his days chasing the frogs and lizards, jumping and climbing from tree to tree. I was sure that if I would ever find him again, it would be amongst the trees and the things that crept within them. Tiffy would choreograph her movement with the forest's, climbing to its highest points and crawling on the ground with its roots.

Both Henry and Tiffy would move together, never apart. Two souls relationally and eternally joined as one, throughout time. They were each other's perfect pair, the ones that made each other complete: soulmates in the literal sense.

The phrase danced in my mind. *Soulmate. Did everyone have a soul partner—one soul matched to another? If so, do I have one?* I longed to think of the time before, if in my old life there was anyone I loved so deeply. My mother was a person I would have thought was my *soulmate*, but here, things were different. The connection I felt to her before wasn't there like it used to be. I searched for anyone else that may have meant something to me, but I met resistance. Maybe it was to avoid pain if they were not here with me on this new earth, or maybe something else. *Maybe my soul connection is still out there? Maybe that's what pulled me forward?*

With the protection of the Sequoias behind me, I knew I was leaving a piece of me with them. But, maybe that was the point. Maybe that bond was what would always hold us together. It would allow us to find each other wherever we were.

I pushed on, filled with a sense of peace and joy, knowing they would always be with me, and I with them.

CHAPTER 42

A sweet aroma filled my nose, as I stood in the midst of a sea of petals, every color imaginable painted before me in fantastic arrangements. Yellows danced in the rays of the sun while purples shifted to darker shades as the tree cast its wispy shadows on them.

I sat amidst the sea of colors, miles from Henry and Tiffy. I felt that same longing to keep moving forward that had stirred me to leave my friends. I knew they were happy, at peace in the beauty of the redwoods. I had not yet found my peace. My ending was still out there, somewhere.

This unknown urgency seemed to intensify as I left the sanctity of the meadow and stood in front the enormous mountain, tall and grand. It's gray base peaked to the clouds with white caps hiding just out of sight. A desire welled in the pit of my stomach, moving my feet to find their footing and hands to find notches on the rocky surface of the mountain. The base was an easy ascent with a path winding upwards toward a more ridged cliff-face. After I could no longer walk, I began to climb.

High above the trees, I scaled the face of the rough wall; exhilaration filled my soul. My heart pounded within my chest as I reached one hand above the other. The ground below began to pull away, the trees became a patchwork, beautifully knit together. My muscles flexed with the enjoyment of their movements. With each grip and grab, I moved my body upwards. The air became a bit cooler, thinner with each breath. My lungs strained to adjust to the altitude, motivating each new extension. I settled against a ledge only a foot wide, allowing my lungs additional time to adjust to the thin air. My feet dangled over its edge, swinging slightly in the breeze, letting me feel the cool wind curl around each toe. Goosebumps soon rippled the surface of my exposed legs. Quick snips, flashes of my life before, flickered in my mind reminding me of a time when I was fearful of even the most minuscule heights. I smiled widely and almost laughed aloud at the thought of that girl. It was like she was a different person. I was so different now, so free from all the things that defined my life before. Fear was gone, along with so many other things. Now, I was able to experience moments like this; feet dangling miles above the earth, head literally in the clouds. All fear removed. Free.

Thankful worship filled my thoughts, looking over the beauty of the world, seeing miles of magnificent creation crafted before me.

After an unknown time of quiet devotion, I continued toward the top of the cloud-kissed mountain. I felt like I was on top of the world. Yelling in exhilaration, I raised my arms above my head and spun wildly in delight. Soon, I collapsed onto the coolness of the fresh snow under my warm body. I breathed in deeply, trying to hold onto the feeling of pure elation as I watched the clouds flowing over me only feet from my body. My hand reached toward the wispy clouds that poured between my fingers, feeling like silky linen and smelling of a sweet rainstorm just over the horizon.

Maybe this was my peace, my heaven. It felt like heaven. With white billowing clouds beneath me and wispy remnants above, the visual wasn't far from the classic illustrations. Just beyond the clouds, I could spend my days basking in the beauty of the world, able to see miles and miles in all directions. Maybe if I strained my eyes, I could see Henry and Tiffy on the tops of the massive trees below or my mother in the City above. I would be close enough to both of them for my spirit to reach out and touch them whenever I missed their presence.

As I rested on the idea of staying amongst the clouds a voice whispered from the stillness, "The way of the righteous is like the first gleam of dawn, which shines ever brighter until the full light of day."

I knew this was a verse from the Bible, Proverbs 4:18; I had heard a sermon about God's redeeming light. Another opportunity missed before, but, now, the meaning and fullness of His words were rich and satisfying. I knew I had to follow the light like I had done all along. Since the day I arrived on this new earth that is what I did. When setting out, after my mother left for the City, I had headed toward the sun, shining brightly before me in the meadow. I then found Henry and Tiffy, and we too followed the sun from the plains to the trees. And right before this mountain, I had watched the sun's light disappear behind it.

My thoughts had never gone to what I was going toward or why I was going there. I just went, following a feeling or longing to something unknown. *Maybe I was chasing the sun all along.*

If that was true, I knew what I had to do, and where I had to go. I had to follow the light.

On the other side of the mountain, I started my decent. Once past the cloak of the clouds, I could see what looked like a collection of trees in a row or column-like arrangement. Miles and miles away, I thought there seemed to be some kind of order to them. Beyond the rows, I saw a lush valley teeming with life. I pushed my eyes further, longing to see more.

Surprised at what I could see from my vantage point, I looked closer to see the rows connected to another line of trees, which connected to another. I strained my eyes, commanding them to see further, and saw manicured hedges reaching as high as the trees scattered around the exterior of a foreign coulee.

My soul burst inside of me, literally, I almost jumped out of my skin. *Are there people down there?* And, not just one person or two but many people, all around the perimeter. I tried to focus my eyes to see further, but the distance was just too great.

There are people down there!

Before that moment, I didn't know how much I missed being around people. Thoughts returned of Henry and Tiffy: how we had such wonderful times exploring the world as we found it. Looking behind me, I thought of how they would have loved climbing the face of this commanding mountain. Henry would have raced to the top, cheering Tiffy and me on while he pushed ahead of us. Tiffy would have taken her time, enjoying the beauty around her, her little legs dangling off the side of a ridge on the mountain, humming playfully. She would have stopped for hours to marvel at a meek vine growing out of a seemly impossible nook in the rock.

I longed for the gentle giggle of Tiffy's high pitched voice and Henry's playful jolts and jabs. But, the prospect of the group of people miles below and the sun's light filling the valley urged me to continue my journey.

When I reached the base of the mountain, I took a moment to marvel at the creation I had just repelled. *He* created this wonderful mountain for us—for me. Thankfulness filled my heart as I lifted my eyes to the City shining as the sun in all its glory.

I thought of my mother there, in the City, walking the golden streets with a glow of glorified light all around her. She would be skipping and singing as she hurried to sit at her Creator's feet. Looking toward the sky, thoughts of her allowed me to truly see her there. Not in my mind, but actually, visually see her. My eyes moved past the wide gates once closed and daunting, now open wide and inviting. My mother had a haloed glow around her dark hair and radiant skin. Hearing her voice as she sang a song of pure joy brought a smile to my face. She was so very happy, so at peace walking the streets of gold, singing praises with a group of worshipers.

My large smile faded when I heard a small giggle from behind a bush, pulling me back to the solid new earth I stood on.

"Who's there?" I questioned, moving closer to the rustling branches still giggling with a youthful sound.

"Come out, come out, wherever you are," I played, now standing in front of the still plant.

"Boo!" yelled a small boy lightheartedly. He instantly erupted in laughter as I jumped back, pretending to be frightened. "That was fun!"

I knelt down in front of him, and patted his head of red quaffed locks, his eyes beamed behind his adorably freckled nose.

"It was fun," I smiled back at him.

He was only the fourth person I had seen, and my mind raced with excitement. My mom was the first; she looked more beautiful than I had ever known, elegant and youthful, free of any flaws. Then, I met Henry and Tiffy, both were youthful as well, but somehow their souls seemed much younger than my mother's. This boy was the first child I had seen. His joy for the world was contagious with his large smile and rosy cheeks; it was hard not to partake in his infectious giggling.

"What's your name?" I asked, looking into his bright blue eyes.

"I'm Will," he said, looking back into my eyes just as deeply, "You're *new* here, aren't you?"

I hesitated at his question.

"Yes," It was the best answer that really fit all the possibilities he may have been referring to.

"Come on," Will said, grabbing my hand and pulling me forward.

"Where are we going?" I asked.

Will stopped and turned to me quickly, "It's what you were looking for. It's where you were supposed to be, right?"

Shocked by the insightful response from the youthful boy, I was frozen in my own reserved anticipation.

"Come on," he said again, smiling and pulling me with more eagerness than before.

Will and I walked hand in hand down a path of pressed sand that moved slightly under the weight of my stride. Beside the path were small bushes and plants with mixed wildflowers strewn randomly amidst the landscape. Taller trees obstructed any view I might have had of our future destination.

"Hurry!" Will said energetically starting to run, yanking on my hand to keep up. "We are almost there," he said, dropping my hand and increasing his speed, putting a bit of distance between the two of us.

"Wait!" I yelled after him, trying to keep up with the surprisingly quick boy.

Rounding the bend in the path, I almost ran right into Will

standing motionless at the edge of the path, opening to a sun filled valley.

"There," he said pointing with an outstretched arm.

I took a few steps forward, left the shaded tranquility of the trail, and saw what Will was motioning toward. Two large pillars of ornate bushes twisted to the bright sky, their girth almost as large as the redwoods I had encountered earlier on my journey. On both sides of the pillars was a wall of green ivy stretching in both directions.

Around the base of the structure, there were people, hundreds, maybe more, in the open valley. Some talked in groups while others sat quietly. Children ran around, ducking behind legs and popping out behind the colorful fruit trees. A woman even held a baby in her arms while a young man helped a slightly older man reach fruit from the top of a tree. There were just so many people. My heart filled with joy as I watched them talk and play and sing, all wrapped in light.

"Told you," Will said from the stillness beside me.

I frowned and shot a confused look in his direction.

"This was what you were looking for right?" he said.

"It's, it's…" I stammered for words. "It's amazing!"

Will smiled at my little understanding of what was ahead, "You haven't seen anything yet. Come on, I'll show you," he said walking to the towering entrance.

We walked quietly among the people. Will held my hand in his small grasp, gently guiding me forward toward the botanical labyrinth.

Amidst the people, I noticed other unique individuals. They were standing beside the tall, walled garden. I couldn't help but stare at the extraordinary creatures. They looked human, but different somehow. They were all male, with strong arms and a wide frame. Their faces chiseled from fine granite, smooth, without any imperfections reminded me of someone, but I couldn't think who it may be. My eyes followed their tanned skin, kissed by the sun's gentle rays. Their stature amazed me, standing feet above all the people around them. There were four; two stood silently guarding the garden's entrance while the other two crouched next to a child younger than Will. The child had her eyes hidden behind delicate hands, and when she moved them away, her face lit in excitement. One of the unique men held a yellow finch while the other picked berries, feeding it to the small bird. Both smiled at the joy of the child. Their eyes emanated a familiar light.

Passing by them and entering the enchanted garden, an image of intense light flashed in my mind; a memory from before. I saw the same frame of a statuesque figure with the same sapphire eyes, surrounded in an intense brilliance. *Who was it?* He was magnificent, even in my limited memory, his beauty was astonishing. My mind searched for answers behind a clouded haze of what I was sure was painful memories.

"You coming?" Will called, pulling me from my thoughts.

CHAPTER 43 FORTY-THREE

Inside the garden, it was breathtaking. Bright, depictive colors beyond imagination shown through every intricate inch and decorated every bush and plant with the most ornate flowers and petals. Floral fragrances tickled my nose and ran down the back of my throat with a rich aroma. I could taste the sweetness in the air, the coolness of the canopied oasis, and the nectarous light beams encircling me. My senses felt invigorated, dancing in joy under my skin at the perfect ornate arboretum that moved in unification with the flowering bouquets.

Birds swooped in and out of the trees, singing as they flew gently in the sweet air. Two squirrels chased each other playfully around a mature maple. Blue flowering trees decorated the border of the garden with lilies littered around their base in warm yellows and calm whites. An unknown type of ivy-covered the hedged walls that enclosed the garden into its own private sanctuary.

I could feel the energy flowing and moving inside of this place; the swaying of the trees as the finches hopped on their branches, the flower petals lifting toward the sun's rays pushing through the trees above, and the grass cushioning my exposed feet holding the weight of my body with ease. I felt utterly connected, one with myself and nature.

A buzzing bee at the edge of the garden perked my ears in its direction, only spin me around again by the flickering of a monarch's wings.

"You feel that," I said looking down at Will, full of the same wonder.

Looking up at me he said, "Told you," with a half smirk gracing his mischievous freckled face.

I nodded in agreement and took in the rest of the spectacularly amazing utopia around us.

"What is this place?" I asked moments later.

"It's Eden," Will said quietly, not breaking his eyes from a playful fox chasing its tail in and around a flowering hibiscus.

"Eden?" I said, following his eyes to the creature and giggling at its playful demeanor.

"The Garden of Eden," he said, leading me to sit under a tree in the center of the garden.

Motioning for me to sit, Will continued. "It's where we all started. Adam and Eve," he stated so precisely.

"Yeah," I replied, as the memories of Sunday school stories danced within my head.

A memory filled my mind of a younger me sitting beside my mother in a room with a handful of other children. I was back in that moment with the ability to see and feel everything around me. The room had white book shelves filled with Bible study workbooks and colorful picture books. Toys cluttered the corner of the room and spilled over onto the carpeted rug. Sitting quietly with legs crossed, the class eagerly awaited the story to come. My mother, elevated in a wicker rocking chair, read from an oversized picture book outstretched over her lap. Her hair braided loosely against her capped sleeve, her bright blue dress embroidered with patterned flowers. I sat on the rug at her feet, heels bobbing with each spoken word. The sweet perfume of lavender and vanilla filled the air around us.

"In the beginning, God created the heavens and the earth," she said turning the large book around so the class could see its illustrations. A black sky and newly formed planet decorated the pages spread before us.

"And on the sixth day, God said, 'Let us make man in our image.' God made Adam and then made Eve out of Adam, both man and woman, God made them."

She turned the book to the awaiting class and showed us a

picture of two people sitting with all different kinds of animals.

She continued, "Then Adam and Eve disobeyed God, listening to the serpent, they ate of the tree of *Good and Evil*."

She showed us all a picture of a tree with a snake twisted around its trunk. The next page had Adam and Eve eating a red apple together.

"Adam and Eve noticed they were naked and hid from God. Because of their sin, God sent them from the Garden of Eden. Sin separated Adam and Eve from God," my mother's soft voice spoke tenderly.

My young mind reiterated the story in its juvenile nature, but I was able to pull myself beyond that moment and feel the love my mother had for all of us. The yearning in her eyes for all of our souls to one day be reunited with God in His perfect garden.

Now in the garden, the power of the situation overtook me, and I breathed deeply, resting my back on the smooth bark behind us.

"So this is it? This is the real *Garden of Eden*," I finally said, looking all around us.

"Oh no, this isn't it," Will said leaning his tiny frame next to mine.

"What?" I said quickly, "I thought you said…"

"Oh, this is Eden, but you haven't seen anything yet. Eden goes on and on. People say there is no end. But, I'm gonna try to find it. I've been to the east side and down the back wall. I'm gonna try going west right out of the gate next time. But, the east has all these funny squirrels and foxes that run around and around. They always want me to play with them," Will snickered. "Wanna come?"

Giggling softly, I nudged his shoulder, and he nudged me back playfully.

"It'll be fun! Come on, let's go!" Will said.

"Right now?"

"Yeah, why not?" Will said, rising in excitement and dancing around me eagerly pulling me to my feet.

"It does sound fun," I answered, "but, I'm going to explore around here a bit."

"Okay, that's cool," he said, bounding off skipping and humming to himself. "See ya!" Will shouted, darting between trees and hopping over bushes until he was out of sight.

I was alone with myself in the fantastical natural space. The wind blew gently in my hair, tickling my check. I felt the soft grass on my feet, a blanket of velvet cushioning my movements. My toes gripped into the ground, attempting to pull the comfort closer. I closed my eyes and lifted my head toward the canopy above, a few gleaming shimmers of the illuminating rays reached down on me.

"Hello there," a man's voice spoke from behind me.

CHAPTER 44 FORTY-FOUR

The strong voice sparked something inside of me. A memory, a fleeting thought from before, a thought from when the world was not this peaceful and serene. The image floated in my mind, only an arm's length away from fully remembering; I was unable to grasp onto the memory that I knew existed somewhere in the depths of my mind.

I turned to face the familiar voice. Instantly, new emotions filled my entire body. A sense of companionship was at the surface. It was a oneness with my soul, a match to who I was and who I had become.

"Evangel!" I yelled, seeing Evan's face shining in the light of the Garden.

I ran to his open arms as the memories of our time before filled my awakening mind: his cobalt eyes wrapped in light as water was forced from my lungs, his warming touch eliminating an evil mark, his strong hands holding my own, overlooking the cresting waves.

I pulled him closer, feeling the strength of his arms wrapping around me tighter and his face finding its place next to mine. I felt his breath on my shoulder and his lips gently grazing my exposed skin sending a familiar warmth through my entire body. My pinked cheeks nestled into his chest as it rose and fell; his strength showing with each movement of air entering and leaving his lungs.

The memories continued to flood like crashing waves,

sweeping in swiftly and dragging me willingly out to sea. Memories from the first time I saw his true nature, his reflected glory shining in my darkened room, chasing away all traces of evil. Detailed thoughts continued with Evan sitting next to me on the cliff overlooking the waves below. I felt the wind in my hair, the saltiness of the water below, the hardness of the rocks against my back. It was all there, in the memory of us.

Now in his arms, I pulled away gently and looked into his eyes, not knowing what I would see. Would I see a reflection of what I knew had grown within me, a resurrection from my old self? *Will Evan see that? Will he see the Light I now have inside of me?*

Evan's hands held mine tightly emanating a familiarity of warmth. His eyes fixed on me, looking deep into my soul, and I looked back at him. I saw something magnificent in his eyes, something deep within him. For the first time, I truly saw Evan for who he was. Not just the beautifully angelic creature he became or the man before me, but I saw him, who he was beneath it all. I saw past the physical form he took. I saw his soul, his spirit—who he was and all God had created him to be. I saw the movement behind his eyes, whirling deep sapphire and violets filled with golden light dancing within the beauty of who he was. Behind those eyes, I saw a reflection of myself. I was able to see myself as Evan saw me, not the lifeless creature I had been before, but the radiant, illuminant soul I had now become—wrapped in light.

My mirrored spirit stood with Evan's, spirit and soul, in a warming embrace. My reflection was the same hue as Evan's, both golden light. We were similar in design, crafted from the same hands. The same brush used to paint me, painted Evan as well.

A hum passed between us both, sharing the same tune; a song my soul sang in unison with his. Still holding each other's physical form tightly, I felt a current pass between us lifting our spirits beyond our bodies. I was floating, leaving my physical body below and joining with Evan's spirit. Our souls pulled beyond our physical bodies, past the beauty of the Garden and all the wonders this new earth housed, we were becoming one. Going willingly, my inner being bonded with his as an intoxicating incense sending its smoke toward the heavens. Our souls braided together, interlinking with one another, binding together in warmth and light, song and beauty. Our spirits rose above our bodies still twisting into one another, wrapping, twirling and intertwining; two of the same, unifying us together as one.

My eyes fluttered, bringing me back to the plane we were on, back to the new earth and our physical bodies. Evan's eyes fluttered as mine did and shut softly. His hands held mine tightly, his tall frame leaning over me. Gazing at him, I desperately wanted his eyes to open. Hoping this was not an illusion I had created and that he too had felt the completeness I now felt with him; our souls now tied together. I reached my hand to his face. Evan gave into my touch, collapsing into my hand. A glimmer appeared from the corner of his closed eye, streaking down his cheek hitting my hand with its wetness. Still not opening his eyes, I pulled his face close to mine, resting my forehead on his. His breaths were short pants, attempting hold back the emotions that he had bottled up for what felt like an eternity.

Without fear or hesitation, I reached my lips toward his. Pressing my body into his as I pulled him closer with each passionate kiss we exchanged. I felt his hands now on my waist lifting me into his arms and off the floor kissing me deeper. His soft lips against mine filled with warmth, comfort, and deep love.

Evan placed me down on the lush ground and smiled lovingly. Leaning into me he kissed me tenderly, holding my face as I just held his.

His lips parted, speaking so close I could taste his sweet breath on my lips, "I *have* missed you."

I pulled away from him slowly and hesitated in my response to him. "I didn't know to miss you," I said confused by my own words.

"I know," Evan said with a kind softness to his words. "It's alright. You weren't meant to miss me."

I shook my head, "I don't understand. Why didn't I remember you? I would have looked for you. I would have found you sooner."

"You weren't supposed to remember me because it might have caused you pain. There is no pain here," smiling Evan continued. "If you were supposed to find me, you would have. And you did." Evan paused, "I wasn't sure if you would. It has been years since we came to the new earth. I desperately wanted to look for you, but I couldn't. You had to find me if it was meant to be. And, I am so thankful you did."

He pulled me closer, holding my hands in his, he continued, "Our spirits are designed for each other. Our souls created one for the other. *Echad Ne'phesh.* It means *One Sprit.*"

"*Echad Ne'phesh,*" I said clearly.

Evan nodded his head slightly in approval.

"Every human has one, someone their soul was designed for. For some, it is a love from before, a husband or wife, a parent, a sibling, even a child. Others, it is a friendship from before that blooms and blossoms here. And, some would have never met and only find each other in this new world. It is a *true* spiritual connection—a unification between two people," Evan said.

"Two souls etched in the same mold, created for each other, for all eternity," I added.

Evan smiled and nodded, "It originated with the first humans, Adam and Eve. God created them to live in complete accordance with one another. When sin entered the world, this bond was broken. But, still seen before, just twisted."

"Marriage?" I asked.

Evan only smiled.

After a long pause, he continued, "For some it was. Others called it *soulmates.*"

I smiled with Evan at my limited understanding of how we were created to share this world with another, not how man perverted marriage to be or how I may have fantasized love to be before. Now, it wasn't a physical relationship—it was souls connecting.

"It is just so much more than that now," Evan added.

Thoughts of Henry and Tiffy filled my mind. Their love for one another was different than what was between Evan and me, but it was similar as well, a deep true love, full of care and kindness for one another. They would do anything for each other. When Tiffy moved, Henry moved. Linked together, welded to one another, a bond never to be broken—they were one of the same; two souls, together as one soul. *Echad Ne'phesh.*

Evan spoke quieter with a more concerning tone in his voice, "It's a *human* connection. Something designed to bring companionship to this new world. From the first two *people*, their bond formed. I have never heard of *this* connection between a human and an angel. There have been… but nothing like this." Evan said, "Not like this."

Evan stepped away from me, dropping my hands and turning to hide his face from mine. I could feel his anxiety, the stress and weight of his thoughts. Evan's brow was fixed as his face looked at the earth, hands pulling at his strong neck in frustration. He began to pace slowly, his thoughts screaming through the quiet space between us.

Confused at his emotions, I could no longer relate to his pain, sadness, or fear. I was unable to comfort him and unable to understand his struggles. It was evident that although I was without these emotions here, Evan was not.

"Hey," I said grabbing his shoulder and turning him toward me.

"I thought there was no pain here, no sadness," I said, sternly trying to turn his troubling thoughts.

"There isn't for *you. Humans* will no longer feel those things. They are gone. But, we are not like you. *I* am not like you," Evan said.

"We are," I interjected. "You are an angel, and I am a human. But, we are the same inside. We are both spirit beings, under all this," I gestured at my body, and then his.

I grabbed his hand with authority, "God made us with souls that are one, linked somehow. Just because you haven't seen it before doesn't mean it isn't good. This…" I pushed my hand and his against his chest, holding both our hands over his heart, "This… us. This is good. This is right. We *are* the same. We *are* one."

Touching his face gently, I felt him fade into my embrace.

"I never thought I could have this with you," Evan said. "I

wanted it desperately. But, when you weren't here. When you didn't come. I thought… I thought I lost you forever. That maybe, you were destined to be somewhere else. With *someone* else," Evan's voice was weak despite the strength he outwardly possessed.

"I am here. I found you. *He* brought me to you. God, the Creator of everything. The One who made you, He made me too. He made us to be here on this new beautiful planet, together," I said, looking into his eyes deeply.

"I don't know much of anything about this new place. I trekked through the forests, swam through rivers, and climbed a mountain, all to come here to this wonderful Garden. This is why I felt I needed to come here. This place called out to me. You called out to me. I have so many questions. And everything is new and unknown. But you… you are me. That is something that doesn't have any merit for questioning. We are one, true *Echad Ne'shesh*. I believe it," I said passionately.

Evan stood immobilized in thought, my words unable to calm his ailing mind.

We sat in silence under the tree in the center of the Garden. We didn't speak as the light rose and fell, leading into the cool of night, followed by the warmth of the day. I watched the beauty around me, birds of all sizes and colors singing and dancing in the wind, flying from tree to tree as the flowers bloomed in the morning light and glowed at dusk.

Evan's thoughts rang out at first, making it hard for me to quiet them with a loving touch or kind words. Troubling concerns about what the future would bring for the two of us and if it was truly what God wanted ,or if it was an illusion he created to justify his unnatural mortal feelings.

I knew Evan was wrong. Everything inside of me told me this was the way it should be.

Evan hadn't seen the world without evil and destruction, both caused by the sin of man and by the plots of Helel, the once archangel who rebelled and turned from God. This new earth was as new to Evan as it was to me. The tricks once played to deceive humanity into falling away from their Creator were gone, wiped clean from the earth when God brought it back to its original design. This included the deceit that caused the Fall of Evan's angelic brothers. Sin was gone, along with Helel and his manipulation. Images of Helel flashed in my mind—distant and blurred, but still there. I smiled at their inability to evoke any ounce of fear.

There was no evil here. I knew now why the two angels were standing guard by the Garden. They were not protecting it, as I had originally thought. They were free, as were Evan and me, but they felt a need to protect it. Fear caused them to stand watch so no one would fall again. But, there were no more tricks. They didn't understand that we didn't need their protection. All evil was gone. Sin forced into the distant fabric of our clouded memories, only allowing us to remember a shadow of the darkness. Keeping it at a distance brought forth a greater devotion to the purity of the light.

With sin gone, so was Evan's duty to protect humans from sin and our own destruction. Now, his spirit was free, as mine was, to fully enjoy what God had originally created for all of us, both humans and angels, to enjoy *His Glory*.

Yet, unlike me, Evan still had his memories in full because he had never fallen away from God like mankind had. Sin never cursed him. He did, however, have the memories of our sin still playing in his mind; memories of death and pain, misery and sadness, deception and disobedience. Evan had witnessed it from the beginning of time. He had watched over mankind for thousands and thousands of years. He had watched man rise and fall, watched us wage war against each other and watched us scorn and curse God in the process. He witnessed his angelic brothers' fall when they chose to turn their backs from God and follow Helel. Evan had seen the consequence of their disloyalty to their Creator and felt the pain of their betrayal.

His thoughts rang loud in my own head if he too was betraying the way God intended it be. He yearned so desperately to follow *his Father's* will and not his own.

I tried to comfort him, but his own desire to please the Creator made him ignore the truth, I already knew. It was something Evan had to uncover by himself, something that I could not help him with.

Evan went off into the light when the morning warmth came into the Garden. We didn't speak or say goodbye. I knew he would return. It was something he had to do on his own. He had to speak with God, something that he had not done in a very long time. I didn't know why. Evan's thoughts were fragmented and jumbled with pictures I could not make clear, about things unknown to me. But, our connection was still there, still strong; we were still one, and I knew this was something he had to do.

Sitting under the protection of the flowering willow branches, knowing he would return, I waited still until he did.

CHAPTER 45 FORTY-FIVE

Awakened by a gentle touch I opened my eyes to see Evan standing in front of me, his long legs bending down to my level while I lay perched against the tree in the center of the whimsical Eden. The evening had come and the warmth of the day had passed away. His face was soft in the subtle light, and the cool breeze rustled Evan's hair slightly.

I smiled softly up at him and he returned my smile. He extended his hand for mine and pulled me to my feet. We both leaned back on the wide tree that held us upright. Its bark was a distinctive maze, a labyrinth of twists and turns, bending and moving with each ripple. I felt it against my back, rough and sturdy.

Looking up at its branches bending in arched movement around us, they stirred slightly in the wind. I could see the intricate design of the wonderful leaves. They were magnificent in color, a dark green exterior with veins of lighter green emanating from the spine, like nothing I had ever see before. The flowering bloom within the darkened leaves was a white, wispy fluff of peddles. It was as if the tree was a collaboration of all the world's trees, scattered with different leaves and patterns, colors and styles.

An image filled my mind when Evan and I had sat under a tree with similarly encasing branches. Sitting on the bench outside of the hospital, under the spindled willow tree, sadness clouded the air. I couldn't see much beyond the dangling limbs casting shadows around the two of us.

The memory made me appreciate the beauty of this tree. Its

branches, full of life and vibrancy, seemed to sway with each breath I took. There was no trace of fear in the shadows cast by the long branches, only whimsical delight. I felt a lone root under the soles of my feet surrounded by lush moss. This tree invited me into its base. Touching the trunk, I shifted my thoughts from the past to current praise for the beauty of creation's intricate design.

"Come with me," Evan's strong voice broke my mind's focus on the beautiful tree.

Evan led me out of the Garden. I quickened my pace and tried to match his stride, moving with ease past the valley once filled with people. Now, it was quiet in the low light and cool of the evening. The light from the City above was a soft glow shining through thick billowing clouds.

"Wait up," I called, racing to reach him.

Evan paused and walked back toward me, allowing me to catch up to him.

"What happened?" I asked.

Evan smiled slightly without speaking.

Continuing my questioning, I asked again, "Is everything okay?"

I knew the answer but still wanted to hear Evan's words, to hear his voice and the excitement I could sense inside of him.

"Did you see *Him*? Talk with *Him*?" asking energetically, I stepped closer to Evan with wide inquisitive eyes.

Evan shook his head, yes, still smiling and staring intently at me.

"Everything is good," Evan said. "We are good. Together."

"I know," I quickly chirped with a large smile strewn across my face.

Evan laughed with a deep masculine rumble.

"I know you did. But, I didn't," he said holding my hands tightly in his.

"I desperately want to make *Him* pleased with me. To abide by all the laws, to follow *His* way, and I didn't want to fail Him by…" Evan paused.

"By loving me," I said. "It's okay," I continued. "The God

that made me, to then save me—this broken, misled infant that I was—that God also made you too. He made you, to show me the *Light*; *His* ultimate *Light*. He made you for me. So, that is how I knew. I knew He wouldn't keep us from each other here. Once I saw you, I knew that to be true."

"I'm sorry I didn't see it," Evan said with concern in his eyes.

"We are different," I said. "But, not that different. The same hands that made me, made you too."

Evan smiled widely, "I see that now."

"Good," I said, returning his smile.

"You know, you are very insightful, now," Evan said with a crooked smile.

I playfully poked his side making him jump and tease me back joyfully.

All jokes aside, I knew he was right. I *was* different now. I was fully me.

"What was the Creator like?" I asked skipping to catch up to Evan who walked slowly away, not answering my question and motioning for me to join him.

"Come on. Tell me," I begged.

Evan just smiled at me and put his arm around my shoulder, squeezing my neck slightly, "Come on, I want to show you something. These are the fields. Here is where all kinds of different fruits and vegetables are grown," Evan said.

Ducking from under his arm allowed me to linger behind, I noticed a woman to our left. She was petite with curly brown hair just above her shoulders. She moved slowly amidst the low bushes as her lips hummed a familiar tune. It was one I heard when I first arrived, but I had known it before, somehow, somewhere. But, I couldn't remember its origins.

"Hi there," the woman said.

"Hello," I responded.

"Aren't they just beautiful?" she said, gesturing to the plants around her.

"They are fantastic!" I said, energetically looking around at the rows and rows of every kind of fruit or vegetable I could have ever imagined.

"They are!" The woman beamed.

"What is that song you were…?" I began to ask the woman.

"Kara!" Evan yelled from ahead of us.

Smiling at the woman, I waved goodbye as she continued to tend to the plants, humming the same familiar tune. I wanted to stay and talk to her about the familiar song I was unable to place but felt tied to Evan, so I ran to catch him.

"Nice to meet you," I yelled, running after him.

I raced down the path lined with colorful fruits; from large round melons to small berries.

"Wait! Strawberries!" I called, pointing excitedly at the sight of something familiar, "It's a strawberry! They were my favorite."

Evan turned back to me, stepped over the soft mound of dirt, and picked a red berry that was nestled in a bush next to me.

"Taste it," he said, putting the fruit to my lips.

Hesitating only slightly to look into Evan's eyes, I leaned into him and allowed Evan to feed me the familiar food.

"Good?" he questioned.

My eyes widened as the flavor hit my tongue and slid down my throat. I tried to savor every last ounce of the absolutely spectacular food.

"This is fantastic!" I raved. "It tastes like a strawberry, but different, better. It is hard to even compare the two. It's amazing!" I said, licking the remaining juice from the berry off of my lips.

Evan took the remaining berry, half eaten from my rather large bite, and popped the remaining fruit into his mouth, stem and all.

"It *is* good," he said smiling. "Come on, I want to show you something."

Evan grabbed my hand in his and guided me through the rows until we came to the arbors. Handcrafted wooden marvels held the massive vines of red, purple, white, and green grapes. On top of a foothill, I could see them scattering the hills with their splendor for what looked like miles and miles.

We approached the base of mountain and Evan directed, "This way."

I followed him without hesitation as Evan nimbly climbed the rock face disappearing over its edge. We ascended higher. The ground began to fade away in a blurred haze. Reaching the summit, Evan pulled me over the ridge, and we settled on a small ledge that only held the two of us. The mountain continued toward the sky, stabbing the wispy clouds with its sharp rocks.

Our position allowed me to see the other mountain I had previously hiked days, weeks, or maybe months prior. I didn't know, and it didn't matter. Regardless of the time, the mountain was intensely grand as we stood in its shadow. The memories from my journey made these moments extraordinarily special. *I found Evan. We were together; my soul complete.*

Evan remained close to me, with his hand on my hip. We scooted across a thin ledge to the backside of the mountain. There was an opening, a private patch of green grass, growing on a ledge that emerged from the steep edge of the cliff.

Evan pulled me to sit under a petite tree that grew isolated, serenely out of touch from anyone or anything else. We sat quietly, breathing deeply as our lungs recovered from our rigorous adventure and slightly thinner atmosphere.

CHAPTER 46

Perched high on the escarpment edge, I was fully able to bask in the beauty of this space. It was absolutely breathtaking. The soft mossy grass cushioned the rocks beneath us as we sat under a flowering tree, no more than five-feet tall. It's almost bare branches were dusted with miniature pink flowers in stark contrast against the dark wooden extensions of the tree's base. I felt the sweet blustering of the wind rushing past my face. My ears alerted me to the crashing of water below and I pushed myself from my resting place and leaned over the edge of the large cliffs to discover an ocean of water below. Even from our distance, I could smell the saltiness from the water's spray crashing against the exposed rocks.

Evan came behind me and wrapped his masculine arms around my delicate frame, pulling me tightly into his body. He leaned in and rested his chin on my shoulder, gently nestling into the nape of my neck, breathing me in deeply and holding me tighter with each breath.

"It's beautiful," I said quietly, not taking my eyes off the view we were experiencing.

"Just wait," Evan whispered.

Collapsing into him I allowed his body to hold my weight. I tried to spin and face him, but met his resistance.

"Just wait," he said again in a whispered voice.

"There," he said, releasing me from his hold and pointing beyond the two of us toward the horizon.

My mind brought me to the moment Evan and I had shared

together on the edge of a cliff, oddly similar to this one. Then, we sat as the sun set in front of us. The memories of Evan filled with so much pain, so much sadness housed within his eyes. I could feel his pain; see why his heart broke for me that night. It was because of his love for me and the pain I was destined for. If I had continued to deny the *Light*, to deny the *truth*, we would never have seen each other again, never shared in this new and exciting earth together. My ignorance and blindness were obvious. *Why hadn't I seen it then?* The beauty of the Creator was right in front of me, shining forth in His glory before me, but I just couldn't see it. I was so very blind.

Now, in this new world, I saw all the beauty as I wish I saw before. The creation I was destined to marvel at, pointing to *His* ultimate glory, was right in front of me all along.

Evan pointed into the dimness. "Listen," he said quietly.

I strained to hear, urging my ears to push past the petals moving in the tree behind us, and the waves crashing below us. Beyond that, I could hear a subtle interlude of something in the distance. The lone tone increased, harmonizing into a familiar song.

It was the melody I had heard when I arrived: the choir at the gates, my mother's voice in the city as she walked in worship, and the sound of the woman tending the crops. I knew now, why it sounded so familiar all those times. I had also heard it before when the world was noisy, and hearing anything beyond myself was difficult. But, it was still there. My soul had heard it, even if my ears couldn't.

It was in the wind on a warm summer day or the pitter-patter of rain droplets on a tranquil pond. It was there when the sun set at night, and the lightning bugs lit up the fields like candlelight. It was in the leaves falling or the stillness of fresh snow. It was birds singing, bees buzzing, and grass growing. It was *Creation's Song*, as Evan had called it. I could hear it now, in all its beauty and glory singing an enchanting song.

I heard the wind whipping past my ear, the branches creaking with movement behind us, Evan's breath on my neck, and my heartbeat thumping in unison with his: all added to the spectacularly wondrous sounds of His creation—*Creation's Song*. Everything came together to form this magnificent hum of excitement, an electrifying beginning of something magical to come.

As the song intensified, a light emerged from behind tufted clouds hanging near the sky and water's infinity. At first, it was a soft pink. Then, the pastels moved to a more vivid tapestry of oranges and yellows. As the wheel of colors concentrated, it moved past the clouds, illuminating the water below and stretching across the ocean. Within the center of the array, a single ball of light became evident as the source of the glorious colors. Another harmonious strum, played louder for all to hear. But, this one was different from the other notes, set apart from the rest of creation's voice. It was as if the conductor of this beautiful symphony began to sing amongst the instruments. As the single note increased, so did the light. It moved past the sea, extending its rays toward us. The light, brighter than any light I had ever seen—brighter than the sun, brighter than Evan—climbed up the walls of the cliff with distinct, intricate movement. The musical orchestra continued growing with instrumental strength as the light moved closer.

I excitedly leaned forward, desperate to be closer to this beautiful light that gleamed as clear crystals and purest gold. The song continued to play in a magnificent harmony while the luminosity encircled Evan and me, twisting and churning around us. Wrapped in the light, a spectacular warmth filled me, encircling me in a familiar warming comfort. Evan extended my arms wide with his, allowing the light to fill all around us in dancing and singing brilliance.

In that instant, my eyes shot open, and I truly felt what this light really was. It was like another veil lifted; a curtain over my eyes opened to reveal the wonderful, beaming glory that shown all around me and through me.

"It's Him!" I said softly, a tear falling from my eyes unwillingly. My soul moved within my body, and emotion overtook me.

Every feeling filled my being; great joy, peace, grace, mercy, love—so much love.

Encapsulated, I knew I was in the Light of my Creator, His Spirit holding mine, gently in His merciful touch. My soul cradled in a graceful embrace. Love. So much magnificent love.

Love filled my thoughts and mind as the Light of the Lord wrapped around me one last time. I could not hold back the joy, and jubilant laughter erupted from my soul.

The Light curled around my face, in a final embrace, and passed by us continuing down the mountain to the Garden below. Illuminated under His presence the Garden was aglow, as was the valley, and the new earth; everything bathed in His magnificent Light. There was never any need for the sun, not now. His Light was all we would need, all we really ever needed—all I really ever needed.

Evan spun me around, and I saw the same wonder I had felt, written on his face as well. His large hand wiped away the tears that unknowingly ran down my face.

"There is no need for those here," Evan smiled and kissed my cheek gently.

"It was Him," I said, amazed at the presence that was just around us.

"It was," Evan said, holding me tightly in his arms.

I regained my composure and stood in awe with Evan, looking down on the illuminated Garden below.

"It was Him," I whispered.

"It will always be Him. He will always be here," Evan added, "for all time."

After a few moments of wonder and amazement, I asked, "Now what?"

I giggled at my damp cheeks.

Evan smirked, "Now..." he paused, "now we live!" His smirk turned into a full, wide smile. "But first, I race you to the bottom," he called from over his shoulder already bounding ahead.

I stood there on the edge of the cliff for a moment longer, paused in the awestruck power and energy I felt coursing through my veins.

This was everything that I always longed for, but never knew was possible, or even knew existed. I smiled watching the last wave crash against the rocks below before a peaceful calm came over the water.

This is my heaven. My eternal happiness with exciting new adventures and experiences, all shared with the One I loved more than words could explain. Thoughts of that true love flashed in my mind, memories of the moments that would sustain me for eternity; thoughts not of Evan, but of His resounding love, His warm embrace, God's unending *Light*.

As much as my heart, my soul, loved Evan, he was just a gift from God, something to help my soul navigate this new world. New thoughts filled my mind of my journey on this new earth and even before. I was never chasing Evan. My soul was never reaching out to his. It was reaching out for the *Light*—for God.

Bending over, I felt the hard stone under my feet and hands. I pushed against the cliff and extended every muscle in my body. I followed Evan down the mountain and toward the lit valley below. I earnestly ran, not to Evan, but to the *Light*.

-The End-

BECCA JUERGENS

Coming Soon
Book 2: In the Devil's Hands
Take a sneak peak of what's to come. Hope you enjoy.

Coming Soon

IN THE DEVIL'S HANDS
book two

BECCA JUERGENS

CHAPTER 1 ONE

"Teagan… Tea, can you hear me?" Kale frantically said into his cell phone, hands trembling.

"Kale! Oh my goodness, Kale. I… I… can't believe it is you. I have been trying to call all night. No one picked up. Not you, or Jen, or Kara. Have you talked to them? Are they okay?" Teagan rambled, trying to hold back her tears.

"Teagan," Kale said after a moment, "Teagan, she's gone."

"What?"

"She's gone. Jen's gone. She…" Kale's voice struggled and then trailed off unable to speak the words.

There was silence on the other line. Neither one of them spoke.

"She's gone?" Teagan finally said behind sobs.

They cried together until Kale could speak. "I'm sorry I didn't call earlier. The University was on a lock down. They just released us to phone home. I called my parents and then, I saw you had called."

"Did you reach your parents?" Teagan asked, her voice still shaking.

"Yeah, they are okay. Yours?"

"Mine are fine. They're at home. My brother is okay too," Teagan paused, "Kale."

"Yeah," he answered slowly.

"I can't get a hold of Kara. I tried her cell and her home number. But," her voice cut off. "Kale, George called me."

"Kara's dad called you?" Kale questioned.

"He hasn't heard from her either. George said he was at some business meeting thing… in Baltimore, I think. Anyways he wasn't that far from home, so he got back pretty quickly after it happened. And, she wasn't home. She wasn't anywhere. Then, he called me. Kale, he was panicked. I've never heard him like that before. I just don't understand. Where are they?" Teagan broke down in tears again.

"Teagan, listen. You need to listen to me. Where are you right now?" Kale said with a strength he didn't even know he had.

"I… I am… I'm at home. My parents are trying to get Sam home, he was at school in New York. They are afraid something else is going to happen."

"Teagan, you need to focus and listen to me. Stay right where you are. Don't go anywhere. I will be there in three or four hours. The roads are crazy, but I should be able to get back," Kale said.

"How? You don't have a car at school. I would come, but my mom and dad are freaking out."

"No, it's okay. I'm gonna take Jen's car. I tried to call her parents and her sister. But, they didn't answer." Kale paused, swallowing the lump forming in his throat at the thought of Jen's family being gone as well. "So… I think it'll be fine. I will be there soon okay. Just stay put. Don't go outside?" Kale pleaded.

"Why?" Teagan's voice was full of concern.

"They are saying here that it might have something to do with the air or a solar anomaly. I dunno… just be safe, okay."

"I will. And, Kale?"

"Yeah, Tea."

"Whatever is happening… wherever they went…" Teagan struggled to finish.

"We are going to find them. I will be there soon," Kale said hanging up and rushing out of bustling dorm into a world of panic.

For more information on Becca Juergens and her books
check out BeccaJauthor.com.